RYDER

STEELE SHADOWS INVESTIGATIONS

AMANDA MCKINNEY

HH TISEVICH

Paperback ISBN 978-1-7358681-0-3
eBook ISBN 978-1-7358681–0-53

Editor:
Pam Berehulke, Bulletproof Editing
Cover Design:
Steamy Reads Designs

AUTHOR OF SEXY MURDER MYSTERIES

https://www.amandamckinneyauthor.com

DEDICATION

For Mama

A note from the author:

Welcome to the small, southern town of Berry Springs! If you're looking for sizzling-hot alpha males, smart, independent females, and page-turning mystery, you've come to the right place. As you might have guessed, STEELE SHADOWS is a spin-off series from the Berry

Springs Series. But don't worry, you don't need to read Berry Springs first. Think of Steele Shadows as Berry Springs' darker, grittier, bad boy brother. That said, grab a tall glass of sweet tea (or vodka if you're feeling saucy), and settle in for a fun adventure that—I hope—gives you a little escape from the day to day... (and maybe a new book boyfriend).

Enjoy!

ALSO BY AMANDA MCKINNEY

Lethal Legacy

The Woods (A Berry Springs Novel)

The Lake (A Berry Springs Novel)

The Storm (A Berry Springs Novel)

The Fog (A Berry Springs Novel)

The Creek (A Berry Springs Novel)

The Shadow (A Berry Springs Novel)

The Cave (A Berry Springs Novel)

Devil's Gold (A Black Rose Mystery, Book 1)

Hatchet Hollow (A Black Rose Mystery, Book 2)

Tomb's Tale (A Black Rose Mystery Book 3)

Evil Eye (A Black Rose Mystery Book 4)

Sinister Secrets (A Black Rose Mystery Book 5)

#1 BESTSELLING SERIES:

Cabin 1 (Steele Shadows Security)

Cabin 2 (Steele Shadows Security)

Cabin 3 (Steele Shadows Security)

Phoenix (Steele Shadows Rising)

Jagger (Steele Shadows Investigations)

Ryder (Steele Shadows Investigations)

★*Rattlesnake Road, coming Spring 2021* ★
★*Redemption Road, coming Summer 2021* ★

And many more to come...

AWARDS AND RECOGNITION

THE STORM

Winner of the 2018 Golden Leaf for Romantic Suspense
2018 Maggie Award for Excellence Finalist
2018 Silver Falchion Finalist
2018 Beverley Finalist
2018 Passionate Plume Honorable Mention Recipient

THE FOG

Winner of the 2019 Golden Quill for Romantic Suspense
Winner of the 2019 I Heart Indie Award for Romantic Suspense
2019 Maggie Award of Excellence Finalist
2019 Stiletto Award Finalist

CABIN 1 (STEELE SHADOWS SECURITY)

2020 National Readers Choice Award Finalist
2020 HOLT Medallion Finalist

THE CAVE

2020 Book Buyers Best Finalist
2020 Carla Crown Jewel Finalist

DIRTY BLONDE

2017 2nd Place Winner for It's a Mystery Contest

~

"**The Woods** is a sexy, small-town murder mystery that's guaranteed to resonate with fans of Nora Roberts and Karin Slaughter." -Best Thrillers

"Danger, mystery, and sizzling-hot romance right down to the last page." -Amazon Review, **The Creek**

"A dark, ominous thrilling tale spiked with a dash of romance and mystery that captivated me from start to finish..." -The Coffeeholic Bookworm, **The Lake**

"**The Storm** is a beautifully written whodunnit, packed with suspense, danger, and hot romance. Kept me guessing who the murderer was. I couldn't put it down!" -Amazon Review

"I devoured **The Cave** in one sitting. Best one yet." -Amazon Review

"**The Shadow** is a suspense-filled, sexy as hell book." -Bookbub Review

Fair Warning: Ryder contains adult language, content, and steamy love scenes. Just FYI.

LET'S CONNECT!

Text **AMANDABOOKS to 66866** to sign up
for Amanda's Newsletter and get the latest
on new releases, promos, and freebies! (Don't worry, I have
no access to your phone number after you sign up.)
Or, you can sign up below.

Amanda
MCKINNEY
AUTHOR OF SEXY MURDER MYSTERIES

https://www.amandamckinneyauthor.com

RYDER

I killed a man.
Paid ten years of my life for it.
Then she blew through my front door, all train wreck and
temptation.
A broken soul . . .
an invitation to danger.

Photographer by day, Ben and Jerry's enthusiast by night, Louise Sloane isn't known for her organizational skills or attention to detail. But when someone from her past goes missing, she makes it her mission to solve the case—especially when the mystery becomes linked to the notorious serial killer, the String Strangler. During one of the worst snowstorms on record, Louise sets off to the small Southern town of Berry Springs, bulldozing her way not only into the investigation, but also into the home of a reclusive former inmate with eyes as cold as ice.

Ryder's one goal in life is to be left alone—a desire unacknowledged by the five-foot-two-inch train wreck who breaks into his house in the middle of the night. He wants nothing to do with her and all her curves, until she uncovers his secrets and unearths a link to the past that changes his life forever.

As boundaries are shattered and relationships are questioned, a body is found on Ryder's land, and it becomes apparent that the killer is closer than anyone realized. With his freedom on the line, Ryder must risk going back to prison or losing Louise forever.

1

I knew I was dying.

I knew it when my arms and legs went numb. When I was too weak to suck the blood from my mouth in a feeble attempt to quench my thirst. When I stopped feeling pain, my body no longer mine, instead a plaything of the devil himself.

I knew it when I stopped caring.

As I lay there like a gutted fish, my body rocking back and forth under his weight, I stared at the ceiling, merely rotted planks stained with mold. Feeling nothing, I focused on a hole in the roof. At the stars beyond it, gleaming against a night sky as black as coal and as cold as ice.

My thoughts drifted, perhaps as a survival mechanism to cope with the physical and mental trauma. I thought about weird things you wouldn't think someone who'd endured hours of torture would think about.

I thought about the universe above me, about evolution and creation, two things I didn't know much about but felt like I should at that moment. I thought of the bitches who'd bullied me in school, wondering if they were home with their perfect parents in their perfect houses. I thought about my first kiss with the boy I was sure I was going to marry.

I also thought of the first time I saw my dad hit my mom, dislocating her jaw. The horror in her eyes as she turned to me, her mouth hanging open, distorted to the side like a ghost in midscream. I thought of the first time I saw her shoot up. And of the time she told me it didn't matter if I went to school or not, because I was born trash and would always be trash.

I thought of hope, and the fact that I didn't have any. Never did have—not in my whole life, and definitely not in the moment I knew my end was coming.

My parents didn't teach me right from wrong, good from bad. My mother didn't teach me to recognize that warning bell, that dip in your gut, that sixth sense telling you something wasn't right. Telling you to leave, to run.

I knew that warning bell now. Much too late. *What a shame.*

I wondered what it would be like to have parents who were proud of their offspring. Who would move mountains to make their son or daughter happy.

As he finished on my face, I wondered if my parents were looking for me now.

Would they look for me after I was dead?

Would anyone care that I died?

That thought—that *single* thought—had more power than my will to survive. The realization that no one would miss me or care that I was gone was more devastating than what the monster was doing to me. My name would be whispered for a few days, if that, then gone in the wind, along with the single shred of dignity I'd clung so desperately to.

I was nothing, an eighteen-year-old fuckup who'd made

one bad decision too many. And for that, I was paying the price. A fitting end to the wasteful life I'd lived.

That's when I started to cry. The desperation and panic bubbled up again as it had when he'd first hit me, at the moment I realized I was going to die a nobody.

In my final moments, a face appeared behind my swollen eyes like an apparition. The one person—the only person in my life—who'd made an effort to put me on the right path. The one person who'd offered me her home when I needed it, and food and shelter. The one person who believed in me. She wasn't family, or even a friend. She was a total stranger.

An angel.

As his hands wrapped around my neck, I closed my eyes and accepted my fate with her name on my lips.

Louise.

Find me, Lou.

LOUISE

a crow called out from his perch atop a rusted pole, its long black wings flapping, illuminated by the headlights at my back. An eerie blue glow had settled on the trees, soon to fade into a moonless night. The crisp scent of snow was on the air, although not a flake had fallen.

Yet.

I yanked at the brown plaid scarf around my neck, suddenly suffocating. My breath came out in puffs, lingering a moment before evaporating in the icy wind. Frigid had nothing on that night. It was the kind of brutal cold that cut through to your bones, stiffening your muscles no matter how many layers you wore.

Three rusted old gas pumps stood in front of an abandoned gas station. Brown streaks marred its formerly white brick facade, and dead vines snaked up the sides. Trees, bare and dormant in the winter, crowded the rusted metal roof. The windows had been busted out, and broken glass and stacks of old tires littered the gravel lot.

It was perfect.

My hair whipped around my face, tickling cheeks that

had gone numb. I adjusted my camera's focus, crouched, and—*click*. Shifting my weight, I quickly took another picture and another, frustrated that I was losing the light.

As I shuffled to the side, my flip-flops caught on a gnarled root, sending me stumbling forward, one foot catching on the other like in a slow-motion rom-com. My two-thousand-dollar camera flew into the air as I face-planted onto the frozen ground.

"Good grief, Lou!" Miles, my old friend and partner on this unexpected journey, jumped out of the vehicle. "You okay?"

Camera, camera, camera. My thoughts crystallized on the single word.

Frantic, I scrambled forward, dragging myself through the dirt to pluck the camera from the ground, turning it over in my hands. She was still in one piece. *Thank God for small blessings.*

Miles grabbed my arm and yanked me up with the grace of a silverback gorilla. "What the hell have you got on your feet? Are you wearing flip-flops? Your toes are going to fall off. Who the hell wears flip-flops in the dead of winter?"

"I do," I muttered, rubbing my lower back as I straightened.

"You're crazy, Lou."

"Not the first time I've heard that." *And won't be the last.*

I dusted off my coveralls, the left knee now sporting a two-inch rip. *Just as well. Now both knees match.*

"Don't you have other shoes?"

"My boots are in the car."

"Why aren't you wearing them?"

"I don't like to drive with cement blocks on my feet. Flip-flops are more comfortable."

"I'm pretty sure flip-flops are a driving hazard."

"I'm pretty sure sitting next to you for three hours is a driving hazard."

"Good one." Miles nodded to the camera I was wiping down. "You gonna try to sell those pictures?"

"I'm not freezing my toes off for nothing. Might as well make myself useful while we wait."

"I still can't believe you own your own business."

"Now, that's just insulting."

"No, I'm proud of you, Lou."

Our gazes shifted in the direction of the distant sound of tires on gravel.

"Come on," he said. "Let's get back in the car. I don't want to be the victim of a drive-by shooting tonight."

"We're more likely to get shot by tobacco spit out here."

"Even worse. Come on, Gumby."

I hobbled back to the car. The left thong of my flop—no *flip* anymore—had popped, but I wasn't going to tell Miles that. God forbid the guy have a coronary.

After setting my camera in the back seat, I settled behind the cracked wooden steering wheel of the driver's seat. My car—Ansel, as I'd so lovingly named him—was a fifteen-year-old burnt orange and brown 4Runner that had been my travel buddy for as many years.

He was a classic, despite the names hurled at him during his last oil change. The tank might be a piece of shit to most people, but Ansel was a battle-ax that refused to quit. I admired that. Took pride in it. No luxuries like power seats or power windows, but he got me from point A to point B, and that was what mattered. Ansel was temperamental and unpredictable. I loved the guy.

"Jesus. Turn the heater up." Miles shut the passenger door and focused on the headlights approaching in the distance. "You think that's them?"

"Zip up your coat. And I don't know."

"It is zipped." He flashed his palms. "I also have gloves, a scarf, and three pairs of underwear on."

"Thanks for the visual."

"Hard to contain something that big."

"Pervert."

"It's one of my best qualities. You seriously don't even know what the people we're supposed to be meeting drive?"

"Brace yourself, my friend. I don't even know their last names."

Miles gaped at me a moment, then shook his head. "Of course you don't."

"What's that supposed to mean?"

"It means you haven't changed much."

"And?"

"And . . . you're not exactly known for dotting your t's and crossing your i's."

"Switch that. And you're not exactly the best road-tripper."

"This trip isn't supposed to be fun."

"Exactly. So quit your bitching."

Swirls of dirt spun up from the tires as the truck drove past, its taillights fading into the trees behind us. It was the third vehicle to pass by the abandoned gas station in over an hour—each truck rustier and its tires bigger than the last.

Miles ran his fingers through his perfectly layered brown hair, leaving him with a nineties boy-band look and causing wafts of spicy cologne to circulate through the vents. He was wearing a pair of spotless khaki pants—pressed, based on the line down the middle, an obnoxious blue all-weather coat, and brown hiking boots with bright orange laces, not a scuff on them.

Not much had changed with Miles either. The guy liked his cologne like he liked his clothes. Expensive and loud.

I glanced at myself in the rearview mirror, resisting the urge to cringe. My long brown hair was a tangled, matted mess, thanks to the synthetic bubbles the motel I'd stayed at last night considered shampoo. Not that I was much of a product whore, but I knew the difference between shampoo and dish soap. The bangs I'd decided to give myself during a particularly boring night at my apartment a few weeks earlier had turned into frizzed waves resembling the coat of an unkempt Yorkie.

Here's your friendly tip of the day. Wine, PMS, and a pair of scissors do *not* mix.

This clusterfuck was half-concealed under a brown beanie I'd purchased at the local farm and feed store the day before. No makeup because, one, I didn't really care, considering the circumstances. And two, no amount of paint would cover the circles under my eyes or the smattering of zits that had popped up overnight as if I'd been thrown back into puberty. I blamed the motel sheets. I was wearing my warmest pair of insulated coveralls over white long johns. Over that, a red puffer jacket. All in all, I was New York fashion week's worst nightmare, and Miles's too, apparently.

I grabbed my socks and boots from the back seat and quickly pulled them on while Miles was styling his hair for the third time. If he didn't approve of flip-flops, he certainly wouldn't approve of the duct tape I'd wrapped around the toe of one of my boots where the sole was beginning to peel away.

Pleased with his reflection, Miles sat back and sighed. "God, Lou, this place is creepy."

I looked up at the black sky. No moon. No stars. "Sorry it's not up to your usual search-party standards."

"I'm just saying, couldn't you have chosen a meeting place in town? You know, around civilization and not in the middle of freaking *Deliverance*."

"Thought you'd want to see your mom," I said with a wink.

"You'd have to go way farther south than that, sweetheart."

He winked back, and I chuckled.

Although it had been years since I'd last seen Miles, there were two things the guy couldn't let go of: his football championship ring—from *high school*—and taking jabs at his mom who'd dated half the town while he was growing up. Back-seat Betty, she was dubbed by the time Miles was eight.

The woman was a local legend. As was his dad, the town doctor, who'd turned a blind eye to his wife's many indiscretions for years. Miles loathed his mother and rebelled by spending his father's money on frivolous things like hair gel and nice cars. And most recently, on a medical degree that I assumed he was studying for just to pass the time. If the past was any indication of the future, Miles would graduate with straight As, just like his dad, whose book smarts he'd inherited. His common sense, on the other hand? From his mother.

"I've told you ten times," I reminded him. "We're meeting here because this is the midway point between Berry Springs and the meeting point for the search. It made sense to meet here."

"It makes sense to meet somewhere with electricity, a heater, and a working bathroom. Hot coffee would be nice too. And I really don't want to be out here when the snow hits."

As if on cue, pellets of sleet began to ping the windshield.

He thrust out his hand. "Shit. See? Winter Storm Barron is upon us. Side note, I don't think your heater is working."

"It only works when I accelerate."

This comment was so disturbing to Miles, he couldn't even look at me.

I grinned. I'd forgotten how fun it was getting under his thin skin.

I clicked on my phone, checking for a missed call or text. Another minute ticked by as we stared at the dirt road ahead of us, growing darker by the minute.

"Let's go," he said. "They're going to start the search without us."

"Let's give it five more minutes."

I clicked on the radio to drown out Miles's groan.

"*. . . storm has already produced two inches of ice under eight inches of snow in Oklahoma and is moving slowly into our area. The first snowfall is expected around midnight tonight and will pick up over the next twenty-four hours, accompanying freezing temps. Remember, folks, this is only the first round of two strong systems over the next week. Get your groceries and any medical supplies you might need now, and please have a plan in place as electricity outages are expected. We're monitoring these storms closely. Stay tuned for further . . .*"

While Miles groaned again, inconvenienced by the weather, my gut clenched. It was a bad time to go missing.

I grabbed my slushie from the console and took a sip.

Miles looked over. "What is that?"

"Fruit punch."

"You still drink fruit punch?"

"Nectar of the gods."

"Yeah, if you're in pre-K."

"That hurts, Miles." I chugged the rest to prove my point.

A moment passed as he looked out the window. "I'm hungry."

"You just had a bag of Doritos."

"You ate half."

True.

Miles twisted in his seat and rummaged through the bags in the back. "Holy crap, Lou. You feeding an alpaca back here?"

"Hey." I turned around and slapped his hand. "Stay out of my stuff. And watch out for my camera—"

Three flashes of light bounced around the inside of the car.

I blinked, bright dots blinding my vision. *"Jesus,* Miles."

"Sorry. Guess I hit the button." He turned back around. "Can I *please* have one of those fifty packs of peanut butter crackers you've got back there?"

"Yes, you can have *one.*"

"Thank you."

"For the record, I buy in bulk. It's cheaper."

I stress eat. Sue me.

"Yeah, like you're a pillar of health," I muttered as I turned off the engine to conserve gas.

"I won't be if we sit here much longer. My fingertips are already numb, and don't get me started on my balls."

"Don't worry."

Headlights twinkled in the distance.

"What do you think?" he asked as he ripped into the crackers like a starving POW.

Why is it that a man can eat whatever they want and not gain an ounce, while I have one Slurpee and my ass sags for a week?

"Care to make it interesting?"

"Oh, honey." Miles gave me a wicked grin. "If there's anything I'm good at, it's gambling."

"I don't doubt that. Okay. I say it's another rusted truck, but this one is going to have two flags in the back. One American, and one rebel—no, *wait*—one American, and one don't tread on me flag."

"Real SEAL or wannabe SEAL?"

"Oh, wannabe. No question about it."

"All right." He cleared his throat. "I'm going to go with a truck, no flags, spray painted camo, with a rack of rifles in the back window."

"You're on."

Headlights bounced off the windshield. Moments later, an old extended-cab red Chevy with a dent in the hood the size of a body came into view. Considering our current situation, the latter was a bit unsettling.

"It can't be . . ." Miles shook his head. "No way that piece of shit could make it three hours in these mountains."

"Mine did."

"Sheer luck." Miles flicked the visor, broken at the hinge for I don't remember how long. It swung back and forth, squeaking with each slap.

The Chevy slowed as it pulled into a small gravel lot on the opposite side of the road.

"Why are they stopping over there?" Miles shivered, rubbing his palms together. "Take a picture."

"Of the truck?"

"Yeah."

"Why?"

"In case it's the String Strangler, looking for his next victim."

"Not funny, Miles. Not funny."

"I'm not laughing," he deadpanned.

LOUISE

*W*e turned our attention back to the mystery truck.

"Flash your lights or something," Miles said. "Those work, right?"

"One does."

He rolled his eyes.

"What if it's not them?" I asked.

"Then maybe I can convince whoever it is into letting me wait in a car with a working heater."

"I don't think good ol' Southern hospitality stretches this far into the woods."

"If this isn't them, let's go. They'll figure out where they're supposed to be. I'm not exactly loving being here."

The truck crossed the road, the headlights flashing across the cab, and I blinked. Miles dramatically shielded his eyes like an idiot. The truck rolled to a stop next to us. Our windows rolled down simultaneously, mine a bit slower due to the hand crank and all.

"Louise Sloane?"

I nodded. "Austin Kemp?"

He nodded.

Austin was the total opposite of what I expected. Although we'd only chatted briefly on the phone, I'd expected a forty-something redneck with an anchor tattooed on one arm and a pin-up girl on the other. Maybe a pack of Marlboros rolled up in one sleeve.

What I got was a thirty-something, brown-haired, blue-eyed country boy with a solid Southern accent and a smile like in a Colgate commercial. A John Deere baseball cap topped his head, and brown gloves were on his hands. I wondered if his truck had heater issues too. Like Miles, Austin wore a thick all-weather coat. Unlike Miles, I guessed the bulk underneath said coat was from muscle rather than layers.

"Sorry we're a bit late," Austin said. "It's already snowing down in Ponco."

Ponco was our hometown, three hours east of Berry Springs.

"No worries. This is Miles Baker."

They nodded in greeting.

Austin leaned back. "And this is Margie Cruz."

A blinding marshmallow leaned forward. White ski coat, white beanie, bleached hair, pink scarf—a look-at-me electric pink, not a sweet-newborn-baby pink.

Margie smiled, blinding white too, as she wiggled her fingers in a delicate wave, flashing glittering rings and pink nail polish to match her scarf. In her early to mid-twenties, she was nearly a decade younger than the rest of us, and barely older than Ansel. Her hair was down and curled with little braids on the sides. Trendy, and totally inappropriate for the occasion.

I'd bet my one working headlight the girl didn't stress eat.

I wondered if she and Austin were a couple. Ken and Barbie, lending their precious time and energy to search for a missing girl.

Miles and me? We were more like Larry and Floyd. I'd be Floyd.

My gaze drifted to the reflection of my uneven bangs in the rearview. *Definitely Floyd.*

Although we were all from the same teeny town, neither Miles nor I knew Austin and Margie. Perhaps that was because I rarely left my apartment. When I did, it was either to work, go to the grocery store, or go to the gas station and liquor store. The last two, one and the same.

Rumor had it Austin was in some sort of special forces unit in the Army, gone half the year. One failed marriage under his belt, no kids. Margie, on the other hand, was single, never married. She was the daughter of the youth pastor at the local church, and a part-time employee at her mother's hair salon.

"Well, hop in," I said, eager to get this show on the road.

Windows rolled up.

"She's hot," Miles said as we watched them climb out of the truck.

"She's your type." I reached back and began cleaning off the back seats.

"Yeah. Hot."

"No. Blonde and barely legal."

"Damn straight. I wonder what she's got on under that ski coat . . ." His lustful gaze tilted up and he frowned. "Hey. You know your roof is coming down?"

I stuffed a handful of wrappers in an empty grocery sack and glanced at the fabric beginning to drop away from the ceiling of my SUV.

"Have I told you how happy I am that you came with me

on this blessed adventure?" I yanked three windbreakers off the seats and shoved them on the floorboard between Miles's feet. *Since when do I have three windbreakers?*

The back door opened, sending a blast of icy air scented with discount perfume into the cab. Vanilla. Always vanilla with that type. Margie climbed inside, picking a few specks of something off the seat before she sat.

I cleared my throat. "Hey, Austin, just put our bags in the back behind your seat."

Austin did as I asked and then slid in beside her, putting his tool-laden backpack between his feet.

I couldn't help but notice how small Margie was compared to him. I also noticed her bright pink boots with white trim, and wondered if her flip-flops were bedazzled.

Austin closed the door. "Damn, it's cold."

No one said anything as I turned the ignition. Ansel stuttered, stalling, and I tried again. No luck. My cheeks burned as I tried one more time.

"Ha-ha." I smiled freakishly wide as the engine fired up. "Sorry. He's a bit moody in the cold."

"Not the only one," Miles muttered.

Margie looked out the window, clutching her backpack in her lap.

Miles suggested we all exchange numbers, so we did, then pulled onto the dirt road. The woods had dimmed, with barely enough light to see past the tree line. It would be completely dark in ten minutes.

There'd been an instant shift in energy the moment we started driving. Anticipation. Anxiety. Fear. In Miles's case, pure disdain for being there.

We drove for a few minutes, looking out the windows, avoiding small talk.

Few things really bothered me. One, the discontinuation

of Chiclets; two, mean girls; and three, awkward silences. I'd been known to have a conversation with a brick wall for an hour.

Fine. Thirty minutes sober, an hour after some red wine. Red, always.

"So," I said as I glanced in the rearview mirror. "Thanks again for coming. We need all the help we can get."

Margie smiled at my reflection. "Thanks for organizing the effort to get people from Ponco to help search."

"Organizing is a bit of a stretch."

"Well, it's the effort that counts. When I saw there was a signup sheet, there was no question I was going," she said.

"The signup sheet had stickers on it." Miles rolled his eyes.

"Hey, I wanted to catch people's attention," I said, defending myself.

"Where are you guys staying?" Margie asked.

"Towering Pines Inn. Miles and I came up yesterday."

"We're staying there too. Just checked in," she said. "Did you participate in the search yesterday too?"

"I did. Miles watched Netflix in his room."

He turned around, wagging a finger. "Never eat fish tacos from a gas station."

Margie wrinkled her nose.

I laughed, glancing in the rearview mirror. Austin was staring out the window with a blank expression on his face. A man of few words, apparently.

"It was the first search for her, right?" Margie asked, returning to the subject.

"Right." Five damn days *after* Kara was reported missing. "Nothing turned up."

Margie leaned forward. "Where did you search?"

"We searched a field beyond some campgrounds that led to the river."

I braked at the T in the road and glanced at Miles.

Staring at the map on his phone, he said, "Take a right."

The road narrowed, trees and bushes crowding the rutted dirt. Dark woods closed in around us, and I had a feeling we were about to learn where the real "sticks" were. The sleet had stopped and was replaced with flurries dancing in the headlights.

"Why are they doing the search so late?" Margie's voice had turned small and loaded with concern.

"They've been searching all day. We're coming up on the tail end of it. I'm sure this will be the last one of the day."

"Better be, with this weather," Miles muttered.

"And no sign of her whatsoever?" Margie asked.

"Not that I'm aware of."

"When was the last time you two had talked?"

"Six months ago. I reached out to her recently but never heard back."

Margie shook her head. "So, so sad. I heard you two were close."

My jaw twitched. No one knew how close we were.

Another moment of silence passed.

"So, how do you two know each other?" Miles asked Austin and Margie.

"Well, we don't, really." Margie glanced at Austin, and I got the impression she was going to be the speaker of the two. "Austin's a volunteer officer when he's in town. When my dad mentioned someone was organizing a search for Kara, I asked Austin if he wanted to go too. We had five other people from church signed up to come, but because of the weather, they backed out. Can't blame them. Austin offered to drive me."

"How long have you been volunteering with the department?" Miles asked Austin.

"A few years. Passes the time when I'm not deployed."

"What branch?"

"Army."

"Good for you. And thank you for your service."

Miles's appreciation landed like a dead weight. I got the vibe that perhaps Austin's experience in the military wasn't a great one.

"What about you guys?" Margie returned the question. "How long have you known each other?"

"We volunteered together at the Sunshine Club," Miles said. "Then Lou here went and got all businesswoman on me, and I never saw her again."

I snorted. If being a businesswoman meant living barely above the poverty level, then yep, I was the most successful businesswoman on the planet.

"Not until she called me up asking me to come on this search, anyway," he said.

"The Sunshine Club. Is that where you met Kara?"

I nodded. "I was her assigned buddy in the program. We became close."

"I heard her mom was abusive."

I hesitated before responding. Abusive was an understatement, but Kara had shared the details in confidence. And I kept secrets. "I don't think she had a good home life."

"It's been two weeks since anyone has seen or heard from her, right?"

"Thirteen days, to be exact. Her friend began to worry after Kara didn't respond to her calls or texts for a week. The next day, she called me, remembering I'd been her friend in the program. The day after, I called the cops. Five days later,

BSPD finally got off their asses and decided to organize a search."

"Why didn't she call the cops herself?"

"Shauna isn't exactly a model citizen. The less interaction with the cops, the better. Her words, not mine."

"Has her mom been interviewed?" Austin asked.

I glanced in the rearview mirror. "According to the officer I spoke with at the police department, yes. Kara hadn't been home since her eighteenth birthday, four months ago."

"Her mom hasn't seen her since then?" Margie asked, horrified by this.

I nodded.

"How awful." A heavy moment ticked by. Finally, Margie addressed the elephant in the room. "Do you guys think it could be the String Strangler?"

Miles glanced at me, and my fingers tightened around the steering wheel.

"Why are you so sure she's dead?" Austin asked.

My stomach twisting, I nodded. "Good point."

"No one has seen or heard from her in two weeks," Margie said. "She travels to Berry Springs to visit a haunted house, and *bam,* she's gone. Seems suspicious to me."

"That's incorrect," I said, shaking my head. "According to Kara's friend Shauna, her main reason for coming to Berry Springs was to go camping with someone she'd recently met. No one knows who that person is."

"But I heard she'd planned to visit that famous haunted house while she was here. Hollow Hill Estate, I think it's called."

I glanced in the rearview mirror. "She'd mentioned she was going to check it out, but no one really knows."

Margie shivered. "I looked the place up on the internet. It's so creepy."

That's an understatement. Hollow Hill was an abandoned plantation-style house built in the 1940s, rumored to be haunted by a family of four who were brutally murdered while sleeping—a man, his wife, and twin girls. Over the years, the estate became a popular spot for local teens to smoke pot and play Ouija, and for tourists to visit while passing through town. Kara hung out with the pot-smoking Ouija crowd, so it made sense.

"Isn't that where we're searching? Next to the estate?"

I nodded. "There's a campground a few miles west of Hollow Hill. It's the only other campground in town, besides the one we searched last night. The cops have already searched the estate. Tonight, I believe we're searching the area in between."

Silence settled over the cab.

Margie stared out the window. "The String Strangler supposedly lives in this area," she whispered, almost to herself.

"That's hearsay," Austin said.

Miles shook his head. "No. He has to. All six of the victims lived within a sixty-mile radius of Berry Springs."

"Five," I said, correcting him.

"I heard six."

"Five victims."

"Hopefully not six now," Margie muttered.

I rolled my eyes, but we'd all been thinking the same thing.

Ever since the news broke that Kara had gone missing, the gossip mill had been in high gear with the String Strangler on everyone's lips. Her profile—I learned the definition of that word during my personal investigating—fit the other victims.

According to the multiple articles I'd dug up on the vicious psychopath, the String Strangler preyed on young at-risk teens. His youngest victim was fifteen, the oldest twenty-one. The five girls were raped, beaten mercilessly, then strangled to death with a thin ligature. It was his signature, hence the name. Each woman was disposed of in a wooded area—naked, battered, and bruised.

The String Strangler had become sensationalized, some even suggesting he was a ghost, neither dead nor alive. The devil himself, lurking in the mountains of Berry Springs. Five women dead, and the FBI had no leads on the guy, according to what I'd read. No DNA left on any of the women, no trace evidence, nothing in their cell phones or computers that linked back to the killer.

Nothing.

And what made him even more elusive was the fact that his first victim was over a decade ago. According to my research, this went against most serial killer's MOs. Modus operandi, another word I'd become familiar with over the last few days. This is a killer's habits of working, or his signature.

I learned that most killing sprees are triggered by something—an emotional event or milestone—and last only a short period of time, usually before the killer is either caught or kills himself. The notorious Ted Bundy killed over a span of only four years. There are a few famous exceptions, like Dennis Rader, the BTK Strangler, who killed ten people between 1974 and 1991; Jeffrey Dahmer, who murdered seventeen males between 1978 and 1991; and Terry Blair, who raped and murdered an estimated seven women in Kansas City over a span of two decades. All three of these men lived "normal" lives, only killing when the mood struck them.

It was assumed that the String Strangler also lived a normal, mundane life and likely walked among us, hunting for his next victim. But no one knew for sure because the guy never left a trace. A phantom, indeed.

A phantom who'd haunted my dreams since I learned of Kara's disappearance.

"You know, my dad didn't want me to come today," Margie said. "But I feel like someone from the church should be a part of the search." She laughed, although there wasn't much humor in it. "I wore the cross necklace my mom gave me."

"Because that will keep the Strangler away," Miles said, joking.

"How much longer?" Austin asked.

"According to my map here, we've still got twenty more minutes."

"Are they expecting us?"

I nodded. "I've been in communication with the detective on the case, Tommy Darby. I've also chatted with the chief a few times. Prickly fella."

"I know Kara would appreciate everything you've done."

My stomach clenched. *I only hope it's not too late.*

"This must be it."

My headlights bounced off a line of trucks, a squad car, and a search-and-rescue van parked along a narrow dirt road. Although you couldn't call it a road; it was more like a rutted path made by hunters. There were no roads this far into the mountains.

Thick tree cover blocked the night sky, not that there was a moon to lead us, anyway. To this day, I don't remember a night so black.

Slowly, I pulled in behind the last truck, a tree branch squeaking down the side of Ansel. I parked and shut off the engine, but no one in my vehicle moved.

I glanced into the back seat. "You guys ready?"

Miles let out a sigh and pushed open his door. Austin and Margie followed suit.

Lights twinkled in the distance through the trees, muffled voices carrying on the wind. The meeting point, I assumed.

I slipped on my backpack and checked my phone one

more time, praying for a missed call or text from Kara saying, "I'm okay."

That's all I wanted. Those two little words. *I'm okay.*

People say the not knowing is the worst. *Incorrect.* At least with not knowing, you have hope. You can force your-self to be optimistic, look at the bright side and all that bull-shit. In some cases, the knowing, the seeing, or perhaps not being able to *unsee* was far worse than the not knowing.

I know that now.

I clicked off my phone and slid it into my pocket.

"God, it's cold." Miles's teeth chattered as he pulled on a beanie.

Margie was busy slipping on her designer backpack, which I assumed contained one manicure kit, twelve almonds, sparkling water, and a makeup bag. Maybe a bottle of fruity hand sanitizer. Oh, and a matching wallet, of course.

Austin towered over us, bristling with impatience. I guessed he was a few inches over six feet tall. A pack with dangling cords and clamps was strapped onto his back, which I was sure included every survival kit known to man. He was alert and ready, with a steely look in his eyes reflecting his experience. I found myself intrigued by the guy, but I wasn't sure if it was in a good way or a bad way.

I glanced at my watch. "We're five minutes late, crew. Come on."

Four flashlights clicked on, illuminating the woods. The path carved from foot traffic was so narrow that we had to walk in single file. I led, followed by Miles, then Margie and Austin. Our lights bounced around the trees as no one said anything, tension thick around us. The air felt even colder in those woods, burning my lungs as flurries whipped around us.

Nerves tickled my stomach. I readjusted my backpack and focused on the sound of my boots crunching on dead pine needles.

When the trail curved, darkness was replaced by a lighted area glowing from behind a dozen trees. The meeting point.

Here we go.

I picked my way through the brush, stepping through the trees and into the clearing, with Miles, Austin, and Margie at my side.

Multiple klieg lights had been set up around what was being called "base camp," where a handful of people huddled around folding tables, sipping coffee spiked with honey whiskey. Not regular honey, to be clear. I'd learned that the hard way the day before, after accepting a mug from a gap-toothed man they called the Huckster, who was in charge of supplying the food and drinks for the search party.

Sure added a boost to the search, though, and I earned an entirely new respect for whiskey.

A pair of brown horses were tied to a tree in the distance, bowing their heads in silence as if they carried the weight of the world on their shoulders. Their glum expressions mirrored those of their handlers.

Steam rolled from Styrofoam cups as a smattering of volunteers waited for the official send-off, their once anxious, alert expressions now grim frowns as if it pained them to be there. The energy around the base wasn't nearly as electric as the night before. Day two of boots-on-the-ground searches had a way of losing that exciting luster, especially when the night was the coldest of the year. The team had dwindled too, I noticed, busy cowboys and bored housewives no longer eager to put on their do-gooder caps and be the one to find a missing girl.

I'd learned a lot in the last forty-eight hours.

One, don't expect to be taken seriously when you file a missing person's report on an eighteen-year-old runaway alcoholic with one DUI and two indecent exposures under her belt. Coupling that with the fact that Kara Meyers wasn't born and raised in Berry Springs, her case was only slightly more important than finding Mrs. Berkovich's chicken thief. It also made my nagging as popular as mad cow disease—a current hot topic in town, according to the regulars at the local diner.

Two, if you're a friend or family member of the missing person, expect to be interviewed as if you're a suspect, because most missing persons are kidnapped by someone they know. Also, expect *not* to be included in the investigation.

This leads me to point three. It's frowned upon to seek out witnesses on your own, visit them at three in the morning, and attempt to interview them. At least I could check off "riding in the back of a cop car" from my bucket list.

Four, the first forty-eight hours were the most important, a mark we'd passed over a week ago. Ninety percent of missing persons were found within the first twenty-four hours. The odds of finding that person after the forty-eight-hour mark dropped by seventy-five percent, and that number continued to drop until the case eventually was downgraded to a body-recovery mission.

And finally, the most efficient way to be taken seriously was to perch yourself on the police station steps, asking anyone and everyone who entered or exited the building if there had been any advancements on the case.

Did I mention I was unpopular?

"I figured there'd be more people," Miles whispered as he stepped next to me.

"There were only a few more than this last night. I'm telling you, no one around here cares that an out-of-towner with a rap sheet is missing."

"Well, at least they're searching, right?"

I snorted.

The search effort was made up of three segments, best I could tell.

One, an "official" search-and-rescue team headed by a man named Aaron Knapp who sported a long braided ponytail and a hard look in his eyes. I'd only seen him twice, and both times he was covered in dirt from head to toe, wearing the grime as comfortably as one might an old pair of running shoes. But he seemed competent, and that's all I cared about. Answering to him were two other rugged-looking guys who rarely spoke, one with sleeves of tattoos, the other with a wad of dip permanently secured in his bottom lip.

Then there was the local PD, understaffed and under-paid, from what I could tell. This team was led by Police Chief David McCord and a few beat cops who switched out multiple times throughout the day.

Lastly, the local volunteers, untrained and raging alco-holics, apparently. God bless them. And that pretty much summed up the dream team I was counting on to find Kara Meyers.

Heads turned in our direction as we crossed the clear-ing. I swear I heard someone groan.

We were waylaid by a woman requesting our names on the sign-in log. I spotted McCord's balding head and paunchy stomach bent over the first folding table. A few others gathered around him.

I signed in, then tossed the pen to Miles. "Chief McCord . . ."

The moment the sixty-something chief of police heard my voice, he swallowed the chuckle he was in the middle of. The guy despised me, and I wasn't sure why.

McCord turned away from a sparkling blonde in full makeup who was wearing a fur-trimmed jacket that barely concealed the watermelons on her chest, and matching ski pants. A sales tag hung from her left elbow.

"Miss Sloane, glad you could make it," he said, although his tone suggested otherwise.

I squared my shoulders. "This is Miles, Austin, and Margie, volunteers from Ponco, Kara's hometown."

The chief dipped his chin, his gaze lingering on Margie. "Pleasure to meet y'all."

Austin broke off, meeting Aaron Knapp in the middle of the clearing and shaking hands. The two appeared to know each other.

"Hi there." The Pamela Anderson lookalike stepped forward, stretching out freshly manicured fingers. She grabbed my hand, dry and rough as a trucker's ass, I was sure. "I'm Tabitha Raines with NAR News. We finally meet. Have you received my voice mails? I was hoping to chat with someone who knew Kara personally. I'd love to get some coffee together, and maybe we can—"

"Maybe later." I pulled my hand from her limp grip and shifted my focus to the chief. "I thought we were supposed to have tracking dogs for this search. Where are they?"

"It's detection dogs, and they'll be here within the hour. They're finishing up searching the other site now. Sunny Harper, their handler, found some caves on the west end of Devils Cove. It's taking more time than expected."

My stomach dropped to my feet. *Caves.* I hadn't even considered searching caves.

"There's thousands of caves in these mountains," Chief McCord said with no regard to my paling cheeks. "Half of which take a trained eye to find, and none of which have cell-phone reception. Have you heard from Kara?"

"No."

Margie whispered something to Miles, and the two stepped aside.

"Well . . ." I shrugged out of my backpack and unzipped the top, the zipper catching on the frayed fabric.

My cheeks burned as I wrestled with the faded red JanSport I'd gotten on the discount shelf at Walmart years earlier. *Get. New. Backpack,* I inwardly demanded of myself as Ass-hat and Pamela stared at me. Finally, with a swift jerk that almost sent me off balance, the zipper released. I pulled a folder from the pocket, ripping the edges as I did so.

I cleared my throat.

"I printed flyers with Kara's picture today and posted them around town." When the chief didn't take them from my hands, I shoved the folder at him. "Maybe your team can put some up first thing in the morning?" Something I'd realized they should have done already, among a million other things that only took five seconds of googling "how to find a missing person."

I'd never felt so useless in my life. I was a fish out of water, doing anything and everything I could to help in a situation that was as foreign to me as designer ski coats and fake eyelashes.

"What are we waiting for?" I asked.

McCord glanced at his watch. "Supposed to have a few more folks for this search."

"Why can't everyone else get started?"

"We're pairing up. Rough terrain, and on account of the weather."

The sharp scent of mothballs carried on the wind as a cross-wearing elderly woman stepped up, eyeing me like someone might an injured wolf. A pitying smile crossed her face. I could handle the repeated questions, the whispers, and the doubt, but not the looks of pity. Pity meant hope was gone.

"Louise, I'd like you to meet Mrs. Hammonds. Clara was born and raised in these mountains, knows the area, and is eager to help."

I guessed the area had changed a lot since the fifties, as had her memory, but I bit my tongue. I also guessed the woman had the speed and agility of a CBD-laced gummy bear, so I declined the chief's thinly veiled suggestion that I search alongside Mrs. Hammonds. The man was trying to distance me as much as possible from the investigation.

"Thank you. It's nice to meet you, Mrs. Hammonds, but I'm going to search alone this evening." As I had the night before. As I would continue to do.

McCord nodded in a way that a parent might to a misbehaving toddler. "Suit yourself."

A chorus of claps pulled our attention to folding table number two.

"All right, folks," Aaron, the search-and-rescue leader hollered. "Everyone, come here. We're about to get going."

The team gathered around the folding table. I squeezed between two cowboys double my size. Something about this town made me feel even smaller than my five-foot-two frame. I stretched on tiptoe and peered at the table. Next to a carafe of coffee and bags of doughnuts lay stacks of paper and printed maps, lined and marked with color-coordinated quadrants.

"Everyone got their pairs?"

Murmurs rippled through the crowd as people shuffled into pairs.

"Austin and Aaron are going to search together. Guess they're buds," Miles whispered. "Margie asked if I'd go with her. Do you have someone from last night you can pair up with?"

"Yep," I lied.

Aaron clapped again. "Okay, gang, let's get started. This area is pretty different from yesterday's. It's much denser and rockier. Walk carefully. There's also dips and valleys in the terrain you'll need to watch out for."

He nodded to his tattooed buddy, who began passing out the maps to the groups as Aaron explained.

"Each map is specific to your group. Search your quadrant only, staying on the marked path. Remember, we're looking for any trace of our missing person, or any sign that someone traveled through this area recently. We're looking for footprints, clothing, a blood trail, broken twigs or limbs that indicate someone pushed their way through the brush—"

"What about deer?" a woman in the back asked.

"That's a good point. A deer path is going to be carved out of the brush, the branches pushed aside, not typically broken. That said, people tend to take the path of least resistance, so always check a deer path if you see one. Now, special circumstances. You obviously see the snow."

Aaron motioned to the flurries and then continued.

"But I'm not too worried about that because it's not supposed to pick up until tomorrow. What I am worried about is the temperature. We're already barely hovering above freezing, which is why we're calling this thing off in exactly two hours. It's imperative that you stay focused, on course, and keep track of time. Keep moving. If you stop, your body temperature drops and you'll freeze. I'm not in the mood to save any of your asses tonight. And, Huckster, if you have one more drop of whiskey, I'm pulling you from the search."

A throaty giggle sounded from the back, and I grinned.

"We're using GPS for this search." Aaron nodded to a tattooed guy who began passing out GPS devices. "According to the roster, we've got six pairs for tonight's search. I've already programmed your search quadrant into your device. It's specific to your group, so don't mix them up. Again, stay on course. We're lucky enough to have solid cell reception right now, so I'm not worried about any of you getting lost and not being able to call for help."

Aaron stopped for a moment, cueing everyone to stop checking out their GPS devices and return their attention to him.

"If for some reason your GPS stops working or you get off course, text or call me and I'll come get you. My number's on the top of the paper. If for some reason you lose cell reception *and* your GPS—I'm looking at you, Huckster—use a compass and follow it southeast. You can't fuck that up. That will take you to the river. As soon as you reach the river, stop and wait. Someone will be coming for you once we realize you're lost. I repeat, southeast. Everyone got that?"

Nods came from around the group.

"So, follow GPS. If that fails, cell phone. If that fails, compass to the river. If that fails, you probably shouldn't be here."

I chewed my lower lip.

"We typically don't do searches at night, but we made an exception to extend today's efforts because the chief and I agree that this will be the *last* boots-on-the-ground search for Kara Meyers due to Winter Storm Barron coming our way. It's not worth the risk to lose one of our own."

"That's bullshit," I blurted.

Miles and Margie whipped their heads toward me. Austin grinned.

"That's how it goes, Miss Sloane," Aaron said. "We're supposed to get two inches of ice and a foot of snow over the next week. This area will be shut down."

The chief nodded. "These mountains will definitely be shut down. When roads become impassable, we'll have to close them."

"But what about Kara? What if she's out there?"

"Then I hope she hangs on."

I bit the inside of my cheek. There was no doubt in my mind they'd continue the search if Kara were one of their own.

"All right, guys. Bruce, Johnny, you take the horses. Everyone else, let's head out. *Vamonos*." *Let's go.*

"It is bullshit," Margie whispered as if expecting demons to rise and discipline her for cursing.

"I won't stop looking for her," I said adamantly. "She's out there. I can feel it."

Margie nodded, but pity shone from her eyes.

That damn pity. I'm so damn sick of it.

"We'll find her." Miles buckled the front strap of his backpack, then turned and checked Margie's pack. Search parties sure brought out the chivalry in the guy.

I hung back while Mrs. Hammonds was handed her equipment. I didn't feel right taking it if supplies were limited.

"Hey."

I spun around, coming nose to nose with Aaron. "Jeez, you—"

"Got your head on straight?"

Is it possible to have your head on straight after forty-eight hours of no sleep?

"Yep."

"Good. McCord told me you're searching alone. I don't like it, especially with you not being from around here. I want to make that clear. But I'm also not your dad, and I'm not going to tell you that you can't help. So here's a GPS." He shoved a black device at me. "But I will tell you that when we call this thing off, you're going home, or to your hotel, or wherever you're staying. It's too cold, and this area is too remote to stay out here alone."

"Or what?"

"Or you'll be the second missing person tonight. Do you understand that?"

"I'm not stopping until I find her."

"You will if you're dead." With that final warning, Aaron walked away.

My gaze skimmed the crowd. Everyone was busy fiddling with their GPS devices. I quickly slipped into the shadows behind the trees. There, I took out the headlamp I'd gotten on sale with my coveralls and secured it to my head. I took one more glance over my shoulder before clicking it on.

I snorted, looking at a map that resembled something a toddler might draw in preschool. I had no idea how to read one, so I folded it up and stuffed it into my pocket.

Next, I tapped the screen of the GPS thingy. When it didn't light up, I realized it wasn't a touch screen and started pressing all the buttons. A few angry beeps sounded, followed by a flashing screen, then blackness.

I shrugged. Just as well, as the device was slightly less useful to me than the map.

After checking my cell phone and verifying reception, I pulled off my backpack and fumbled with the zipper. Broken, definitely broken.

Dammit.

I shoved my phone in the side pocket and shrugged my backpack on again. I slipped behind a tree and watched the others as they set off on their designated courses. Considering none were walking in my direction, I assumed I must be on the right course. After repositioning my headlamp, I took a deep breath and set off.

The chatter behind me faded as I journeyed deeper into the woods. Ahead of me, a thin pool of yellow light from my headlamp illuminated the ground. Beyond that was inky darkness.

I walked, and walked, and walked for what felt like hours, searching the ground and the trees above, heading deeper and deeper into the mountains. My feet felt heavy as fatigue started to take its toll. I cursed myself for canceling my gym membership six months earlier. Figured it wasn't worth the weekly hot tub visits.

As time passed, my thoughts wandered.

I thought of Margie and the newscaster, both beautiful women who seemed to have it all together. Perfect hair, perfect makeup, perfect skinny little toned bodies. Trendy matching outfits that made my JanSport look like it belonged in the freebie box at the thrift store.

Bargain-hunting was fun. There was something about finding hidden gems buried under full-price items that gave me a high, second only to red wine. I appreciated finding the beauty in things that people discarded or overlooked, and had made a career out of capturing beauty in unexpected places.

I imagined Margie and the newscaster spent a lot of time admiring their own beauty. *Can't blame them.*

Scowling, I reached back and pulled a PayDay from my pack. Always kept those within arm's reach. I ripped into it and devoured the sugary, caramel stick, as had become routine when I was stressed.

I liked to eat. Liked good food. *Real* food.

I was carrying fifteen extra pounds on my small, curvy frame, pounds that seemed hell-bent on staying, no matter how many times I tried to lose them. Diets, the gym, Zumba, whatever, nothing worked. On my thirtieth birthday, I'd decided that I was what I was, and I made peace with it. I accepted my quirky, curvy, unfashionable self. Didn't love my body, but I accepted it.

I have good lips, though. Damn good lips.

Kara had been "cool" like Margie and the newscaster, but in a different way. Kara had an energy around her that seemed to draw people in. I admired that.

A knot tightened my throat as I thought of her, picturing her in my house, teaching me to cook. Attempting to, anyway. Hidden behind all her sharp edges, Kara was a sweet girl. Just out of practice.

I stuffed the empty PayDay wrapper in my pocket.

Silence engulfed me, with only the whisper of the wind through the trees. It wasn't until that moment that I realized how truly alone I was. Suddenly, old Gummy Bear didn't seem like such a burden.

Despite the chill, my scalp was hot and sweaty, a reflection of the nerves that had crept up on me. I kept checking my phone, verifying I had reception.

As Aaron had warned, the terrain became rockier and

steeper. Harder to navigate. In a short time, the landscape had changed from only trees and frozen vegetation to fewer trees and more cold gray rocks.

My pace quickened, and my eyes watered from the wind. I swiped them with the back of my gloves, the Velcro scratching my cheek. I pressed on, forging into uncharted territory, somehow knowing I was going in the right direction.

My heart pounded harder, and my head filled with an insistent voice telling me to turn around. But I didn't listen.

I could *feel* her.

The beam from my headlamp bounced with each step, a strobe light against the oaks and pines I was maneuvering through. Ahead, I spotted a larger opening in the trees, a cluster of boulders centered among soaring pines. Massive, jagged rocks speared up from the earth.

I stopped, staring at the rocks. The energy, the vibe around me shifted as if I'd stepped into another world. Fear trickled up my spine. Instinct, I know that now.

My adrenaline picked up and I pressed on, as if my body were being pulled by a magnet.

Go back. Go back, that voice in my head whispered. But my legs didn't listen.

The wind died down and an eerie stillness settled around me. I could *feel* evil. And that's when I smelled it.

Rot.

Death.

My hands started to tremble.

I remember the moment like it was yesterday. Like a photograph burned into my brain that I know will never go away.

I climbed onto a boulder that was ice-cold to the touch,

my entire body shaking as my gaze followed the light from my headlamp.

That's when I saw her.

Her naked body looked like a rag doll, her arms and legs bent at odd angles around the peaks of the rocks she'd been thrown onto. Her head was twisted awkwardly, her neck apparently broken. Her blond hair was fanned out like a spiderweb spun from her head, slashed across gray skin. Her mouth was gaping open. The skin and muscle had been chewed from her limbs, and one foot was completely gone, bone and all. It was the left foot.

Her once sparkling blue eyes were now simply two empty holes, pecked out by the birds. Empty. Dead.

I'd found her.

I'd found Kara Meyers.

*a*fter finding Kara's body, I went back to base camp. Scratch that—I threw up peanuts and caramel first, then stumbled my way back to base camp.

After that, everything was a blur. Within ten minutes, the place was swarming with half the town. I gave my statement, and after that, we were asked to leave while the authorities searched the scene, and the medical examiner, a red-headed spitfire named Jessica Heathrow, did her thing.

I overheard Chief McCord telling another officer that the body was likely too decomposed to find anything useful to determine if something nefarious took place. Someone suggested that maybe she'd overdosed, and perhaps her "friends" had dumped the body to avoid being implicated.

McCord instructed an officer to track down Kara's mother to inform her that her daughter was dead. Her mother wouldn't care, and that would be that. I didn't get the vibe that much more time was going to be spent on the case of a missing wayward teen with a record.

It made me sick. Almost as sick as the vision of her body permanently tattooed on my memory. I'd never seen a dead body before, but I knew the image would haunt me for the rest of my life.

After a few beers and conspiracy theories, Miles, Margie, and Austin retired to their rooms sometime after one in the morning. Sometime between three in the morning and my second bottle of wine, I decided I wasn't going to accept it.

Kara deserved justice, and I was going to make sure that happened.

6

LOUISE

I'd never been known for my judgment, or good sense, as my mom had once told me. I was, however, known for my inability to let things go, among other charming characteristics. I was bullheaded. Annoying. A gnat that wouldn't go away.

Steadfast, I'd convinced myself.

And that was exactly what had me driving to a private investigation firm in the middle of a snowstorm after having exactly one hour of sleep the night before. I'd overheard two cowboys discussing the firm over a plate of flapjacks at the diner earlier that morning. After breakfast, I'd told Miles and the crew that I had a few things to follow up on, and we parted ways.

The weatherman hadn't lied. Winter Storm Barron had hit hard. According to the weather report I'd caught while checking out of the motel, it was only going to get worse. The sleet had started again after midnight, followed by ice and two inches of snow on top of that. A steady snowfall was expected over the next twenty-four hours, along with more ice.

I'd only reserved three nights at the Towering Pines Motel, so my time there was up. Miles, Austin, and Margie had the foresight to extend their stay due to the weather. No way in hell was anyone going anywhere for a few days.

After spending an hour calling around to area hotels, I booked the last room at the only hotel with a vacancy, a five-star resort just out of town and way out of my budget. I'd figure out the rest later, including how to pay off the bill.

I clicked the windshield wipers on high, metal from my ratty windshield wipers scraping against the frozen windshield with a piercing screech. I slowed to twenty miles an hour. I'd never been in a blizzard, but I assumed this was close.

Glancing at the map on my phone, I confirmed I was still on the right track.

I'd expected the private investigation firm to be in the middle of town, perhaps the bookend to a modest brick shopping center.

Nope. According to the address on the website, the place was smack dab in the middle of nowhere.

Should have been my first clue.

Ansel handled the roads surprisingly well until we hit the "sticks." No one had traveled the dirt roads that seemed to be getting slicker by the minute, along with my forehead and palms.

According to the maps app on my phone, I had five more minutes until my destination. I peeled my fingers from the steering wheel and chugged the rest of the hot chocolate I'd gotten at a gas station/feed store an hour earlier. The foam and sprinkles had melted into a thick, cold whip that stuck to my upper lip. I licked it off, then checked the map again.

"Make the next right in point two miles," the woman with an Australian accent told me. Always loved that accent.

I squinted as I turned onto the dirt road, thinking there was no way this was the right direction. How would an Australian know these back roads anyway?

"Destination is five hundred feet on your left . . ."

A large structure came into view, an inky blackness against swirling snow. It was a long steel building resembling a large workshop, nestled in a thicket of trees. Hard to see, unless you were looking for it. No windows, no landscaping, no sign out front. Private, indeed.

Hmph.

I braked, considering my options. Deciding I didn't have any, I pressed on.

I parked next to a blacked-out Chevy with no tags. Next to it was a black Ford Superduty with massive tires. Next to that, a black SUV that reminded me of a presidential detail. And nestled under a massive oak tree was a charcoal-gray Maserati that I was sure wouldn't make it past the last mountain I'd climbed.

Double-hmph.

I checked the address one more time—*yep, right place.* So I tossed my keys into my backpack, yanked up my hood, and stepped out.

A gust of wind blew past me, spinning snow around my face. I dipped my head and darted across the gravel parking lot, slipping on a rock and catching myself against the trunk of a tree. After a quick breath, I walked to the front door, barely noticeable if not for the silver handle. A buzzing sound had me looking up where a camera was slowly spinning toward me.

I tried the knob. *Locked.*

Looked for a doorbell. *None.*

I took a step back, squinting at the door that in tiny letters across the middle that read:

Astor Stone, Inc.

This was definitely the place. I looked over my shoulder at the vehicles and noted that two were clear of snow, meaning someone had to be in that building.

I pounded on the door. *Nothing.*

I pounded again, this time harder. *Still nothing.*

As I raised my fist to knock again, the door flung open. Behind it was the biggest man I'd ever seen in my life. Instinctively, I stumbled back a step.

He was wearing one of those obnoxious bare-chest T-shirts that make you look like you're not wearing a shirt at all. On his was an American flag bikini top over an aggressively large pair of breasts. This look was completely in contrast to the rough skin of his face and arms, a sharp jaw covered in scruff, and a pair of narrowed eyes that suggested he questioned my right to be on the front stoop.

He tilted his head to the side, working the toothpick hanging out of the corner of his mouth. "You got somethin' on your lip," the man drawled coolly in a thick Southern accent.

I licked my lip. *Chocolate sprinkles. Damn them.*

I cleared my throat. "Thanks. And you've got boobs on your shirt."

"It's funny-shirt day at work."

I glanced over his shoulder. "This is Astor Stone, Inc., right? The private investigation firm?"

He paused a moment, sweeping me with a look filled with curiosity tinged with amusement. I get that a lot.

"Yep. You found us."

"Great." I exhaled. "Can I come in?"

He continued to stare at me like he was trying to figure me out. Or eat me, I wasn't sure which. He studied my red puffer jacket, my faded and baggy boyfriend jeans, and boots repaired with duct tape.

I shifted my weight.

"You got an appointment?"

The camera above me spun again, and I got the idea I was a laughingstock to whoever was watching me from the other side.

"No. I tried to call, and I emailed, but I never got a response."

His brow arched in a way that asked, *Then why are you here?*

"Listen. Sir. My name is Louise Sloane. My friend Kara Meyers was found dead not ten miles from here. I get the vibe the cops have dropped the case like a bad habit, and I'm not willing to accept that. So, here I am. I want to hire a private investigator because my friend deserves justice."

He spun the toothpick between his lips, assessing. Finally, he stepped back and held open the door. "Bad weather comin'."

I stepped inside. It smelled like technology. "Pretty sure it's already here."

"No, ma'am. Supposed to get more ice, then another foot of snow on top."

The door shut behind me, followed by a series of locks automatically clicking into place. Unease settled in my stomach as I followed Toothpick Guy across a small waiting room with a few chairs and nothing else. He keyed in a ridiculously long password and opened another door that led to a long, dark hallway.

In the distance, a door opened. Three loud cracks blasted through the air before the door closed again.

"Were those gunshots?"

"Target training."

What the hell kind of PI firm is this?

I looked at the ceiling. A million multicolored wires ran across it between thick steel beams and some sort of insulation padding.

Toothpick Guy ushered me into a small room that resembled the interview room at the Berry Springs police department. But instead of stained tiles and dingy walls, this one was spotless and blinding white, with only a table, two chairs, and a window looking out to the hallway.

"Make yourself comfortable." He gestured to the chair. "Be right back."

The door was shut, and I was left standing in the middle of the room. A distant ticking sound came from somewhere, but I couldn't find a clock. The ticking was followed by a buzz, pulling my attention to yet another camera repositioning itself toward me.

I wrapped my arms around myself.

Tick, tock, tick, tock . . .

The door swung open and Toothpick Guy returned, followed by two more massive men. The fact that I didn't hear their footsteps made me realize the room I was in must be soundproof, as well as whatever room they were doing "target training." This realization didn't make me feel warm and fuzzy inside.

"Miss Sloane, this here is Justin Montgomery." Toothpick Guy gestured to the bigger guy. "And behind him is Roman Thieves, new to the job."

My gaze shifted between the men, Justin eyeing me like

ribeye steak, and Roman like a poisonous species yet to be named.

Justin had shaggy dirty-blond hair that looked like it could use a cut and shampoo. He was the shortest of the three, maybe over six feet but built like a superhero and had a face like a cornfed cowboy.

Roman, on the other hand, was totally different. He was the biggest of the three, with tattoos covering a beefy body, and a look in his eyes that made me mentally scan my purse for any kind of weapon. He had jet-black hair matching the tattoo licking up his neck. Something about him made me uneasy. He was the kind of guy that if you saw him on the sidewalk, you crossed the street.

Justin's T-shirt had a goofy yellow smiley face that read i pooped today. Roman's T-shirt was black.

Refocusing on Toothpick Guy, I asked, "What's your name?"

"Oh, sorry. Mack McCoy, PI. Been here over a decade."

"You're all private investigators?"

"Yep. We're the whole team, aside from the boss," his gaze flicked to Justin, "and one we're trying to get back."

"Well, perfect." I wanted to get this show on the road. "How do we do this?"

Mack crossed his arms over his chest, and the others followed suit. No one sat. I clutched my backpack in my hand with nothing but a table between me and the army of intimidating men staring back at me.

"Let's talk about finances first," Mack said.

"I've got the money," I lied.

"Tell me about your friend."

I wasn't sure what to do with my hands, so I slung my backpack over my shoulder and stuffed them into my pockets. "Kara Meyers, age eighteen, born and raised in Ponco, was found last night, her body left to rot in the woods. I was the one who found her."

"You were part of the search party?"

I nodded. Mack knew more than he let on.

"She was last seen here in Berry Springs fourteen days ago, at a gas station in town. Alone. The cops have made no arrests, brought in no additional resources, and have no leads."

"How do you know this? About the leads?"

"Spoke with the front desk receptionist an hour ago. Ellen is her name." I heaved out a breath. "Truth is, Kara wasn't exactly a model citizen, and she has a rap sheet. I'm worried she's not getting as much effort as someone from here who doesn't have a record. So, here I am, hoping you guys can do a better job than the Berry Springs PD at finding who killed her."

"How do you know someone killed her?"

I hesitated because I had no proof other than the certainty swirling in my gut. "Well, that's what you should find out."

"Are you a relative?"

"Kind of."

"What's *kind of* mean?"

"I was her mentor at a local afterschool program. Like a buddy program for at-risk youth."

"How was she at risk?"

I shifted my weight. "Along with her previous indiscretions, her dad is in federal prison and her mom is a drug addict. She's pretty much been on her own her entire life."

The room fell silent, and I got pissed. Why was it that someone who was at risk seemed less important than the straight-A captain of the cheerleading squad?

"Listen. Kara deserves justice, and I'm not leaving Berry Springs until she gets it."

"Where was her last known location, exactly?"

"Not sure. Her friend Shauna, who I believe the cops also spoke with, said Kara told her she was going camping somewhere along Shadow River. She said that Kara mentioned checking out that old haunted house, Hollow Hill."

The men exchanged glances.

"Who was she camping with?" Mack asked.

"No one knows. But I think whoever that was is who killed her."

My attention was pulled to a shadow in the hallway. A figure that seemed to appear out of nowhere stood outside the room, looking in through the window. My stomach did a little dip the moment I saw him.

The man looked chiseled out of stone. A really, really cold stone.

His jet-black hair was combed perfectly to the side above a face like granite, with a demeanor to match. I didn't know much about expensive suits, but his had to be because it draped over his wide shoulders like butter. His skin was flawless, and he looked young to be wearing such expensive clothing. Maybe mid-thirties. He even had one of those pocket squares.

He wasn't rough like the other men. This man was well-kept. Something about his demeanor sent a chill up my back.

Mack followed my gaze.

"Who's that?" I asked.

"That's the boss. Astor."

"Astor Stone?"

"Yep. Owns the place."

And just like that, the man disappeared into the shadows.

"Anyway," Mack said, easily returning to the subject as if accustomed to Astor Stone's random and brief appearances. "That house, the Hollow Hill Estate, is one gust of wind away from being dust. No one goes there. Anymore, anyway."

"I did."

"When?"

"Yesterday."

"Why?"

"To see if I could find something the cops missed."

"Not smart."

"Never claimed to be."

"Stay away from it." This deep voice came from Roman with a hint of an Irish accent.

"What was her official cause of death?" Mack asked.

"She . . ." The image of Kara's rotting body flashed through my head. "She was in bad shape."

"Dead a while?"

"A week, maybe more. That's what I overheard the medical examiner say."

"What other information do you have on her?" Mack asked.

"Kara was homeless. She was living out of her car." I glanced down, guilt twisting in my gut. I didn't know she'd been homeless since her eighteenth birthday. This was according to her friend Shauna.

"They find her car?"

"I don't think so."

"Did she have anything on her when you found her? A cell phone? Purse?"

I shook my head. "She was naked."

"Do you know if she had a computer or a laptop?"

"I don't know."

A moment passed as all three beasts stared at me.

"We'll see what we can do." Mack motioned to the door. "This way, Miss—"

"That's it? Don't you need her picture?" I set my backpack on the table and began searching through the mess of crinkled papers and candy wrappers. "Or her old address, her mom's house, or maybe the last number I know she had, or—"

"We'll handle all that. I'll have our office manager email you the particulars, the contract, the financials." He looked at my duct-taped boot. "Once you review that, you'll sign on the dotted line, and we'll get moving."

"But I want you to get moving now."

"We don't make a move without a signature and retainer. Boss's orders."

"Fine. Anything else?" I remained glued to the floor, thinking there was no way this meeting was done. I'd expected copious notes, additional information requested, an emptied carafe of coffee, a few cigarette breaks.

"Nope."

Roman opened the door. Mack motioned me ahead.

I was led down the hallway by Mack, with the two other beasts at my back.

"You said you're missing a man."

Mack frowned as he looked down at me. "What?"

"Back there, in the room, you said 'one we're trying to get back' when you were talking about the team. Who?"

Mack's expression pulled tight. "Honey, I don't even know anymore."

7

LOUISE

*A*fter the fruitless meeting at Astor Stone's, I'd gone back to the police station to see if they'd started the autopsy on Kara's body. Ellen from dispatch, my new BFF, told me she'd heard that the chief had requested a rush on it, but that was it.

Then I went back to the gas station where Kara was last seen on camera and chatted with the salesclerk for the third time. After that, lunch with the crew, then back to the campground for additional snooping. And that had been my entire day. Due to the weather, destinations that should have taken twenty minutes to reach took triple that.

After visiting the last campground and getting a warning from a drunk hippie that I'd better "git on home on account of the weather," I decided to call it a day.

I plugged the address to the fancy-schmancy Shadow Creek Resort into my maps app on my phone, popped open a fruit punch, and hit the gas. I started out a cool twenty miles an hour on the two-lane asphalt. Once I hit the steep mountains, twenty dropped to ten miles an hour and white knuckles.

Not long after that, I lost phone reception—along with the directions. A drive that should have taken forty-five minutes was well into two hours when shit hit the fan.

I'd just passed a sign that read county road 2355 with a horse xing sign beneath it, featuring a horse with five legs. I'd been staring in the rearview mirror, contemplating that fifth leg, when Ansel hit a patch of frozen horse shit and slid off the road into a tree.

I got out and assessed the damage. The hood was dented from the tree, but considering there was no smoke or liquid leaking out, I assumed the engine was in good shape.

The tire was another story. Flat as a pancake. That didn't bother me as much as the fact that my only working headlight had been busted out.

My options were none, so I decided to give changing a tire a whirl. Figured I could strap my headlamp onto the hood until I got a new headlight.

It took me less than three minutes to realize that I didn't even know where the spare tire was, or the tools to change it. I climbed back into the car and went over my options.

1. I couldn't call Miles, Austin, Margie, or 911 because I didn't have reception.

2. I couldn't drive because my tire was destroyed.

3. I didn't have a snowmobile.

4. Or a knight in shining armor.

5. Basically, I was fucked.

Thirty minutes of brooding later, I resorted to opening the bottle of wine I'd packed for the trip. I'd also packed a box, but this particular situation called for the good stuff. I unscrewed the cap and took a swig. Then another.

A half bottle later, fear started to get the best of me. I imagined freezing to death, getting kidnapped or killed. Or worse, eaten by a mountain lion that knew how to unlock car doors.

None of these options appealed to me, and I knew I couldn't be far from the resort, so I packed up what I could and abandoned my ride. I figured if someone was desperate enough to steal Ansel and all his broken-visor glory, I'd probably get two thousand dollars from insurance, double what he was worth.

Wine in hand, backpack strapped on, and duffel bag and purse dangling from my shoulders, I set off down the narrow dirt road. The snow was already past my ankles.

The hours blended together in a dizzying haze. The sun had set, although I wasn't sure when. Twilight had taken over, blanketing the snow-covered trees in a muted blue glow. Night was soon to follow.

Gusts of brutal wind stung my cheeks, a million diamonds reflecting in the headlamp that I'd had the good sense—*there you go, Mom*—to put on. Except for the wind and my feet clomping in the snow, it was eerily silent. Every now and then, a crack sounded somewhere in the distance, probably a limb breaking.

My toes had gone numb, that no-feeling, looking-down-to-see-if-they're-still-there numb. So had my nose and ears, but considering I could still smell and hear, I figured they hadn't succumbed to the elements. *Yet*. My ankles and knees felt like rusted gears on an old machine that had been abandoned long ago in a run-down shed.

As I was contemplating how long it took for internal organs to freeze, I stumbled on a tree root and my body was thrown forward into four erratic leaps, my arms flailing about like a twenties-style flapper girl.

Finally, gravity got the best of me, and I hit the ground with a hard thud.

Snow exploded around my body, catching in the icy wind and swirling into the black sky above. Pain shot like lightning in my knee. The sound of my cursing echoed through the woods.

With a guttural groan, I rolled to my side like a beached whale and spat out the snow from my mouth. For a moment, I considered not getting up. I was so tired. Exhausted. But then I remembered that sneaky mountain lion that walked on its hind legs.

Pushing to a seating position, I winced at the pain in my knee.

I lifted the bottle in my hand that I'd somehow managed not to drop. *Gold-medal worthy, right there*. I might not have been able to feel half my body, but dammit, I had my wine. If this was going to be my last hurrah, I was going to make damn sure I wouldn't remember the last half.

My stonewashed denim duffel was three feet away, miraculously dangling from a wilted pine tree that had caught its fall. *Small blessings. They don't make stonewashed denim anymore.*

My purse, on the other hand, lay at my feet, half its contents scattered over the snow. A new tear slashed through the red pleather, matching the one on the bottom that I'd sewn up days earlier. Pleather purses were aplenty, so I wasn't too worried about that one. One glove had blown off during the fall. My cell phone had slipped from my pocket but was still in one piece.

I clicked it on and checked the reception. Still no bars.

I shrugged, confirming my JanSport was still strapped in place. I shook my head like a dog, ice and snow flinging around me.

Blowing out a breath, I began plucking my things from the snow. A broken watch with half of the band missing, seven hair clips, a handful of bobby pins—*damn the bangs*—a tube of bubbles, used dental floss, a pair of scissors . . . the missing watch band suddenly making sense . . . a foldable tripod, wash cloth, a hammer, a flashlight, a tube of super-glue, two tampons, a condom labeled orgasm donor that I'd gotten from a bachelorette party years earlier, and finally, two used tissues.

Once everything was back in its rightful place, I pushed to my feet, my back and knee screaming with each move-ment. A fresh sheen of sweat broke out over my body, underneath the five layers I'd stuffed myself into. *Thank God for Gore-Tex.*

I wobbled a bit, from the wine or exhaustion, I wasn't sure. At that point, I debated on turning around and sliding my way back to Ansel, but I knew I was close to that damn resort. Besides, I was too far in at that point.

I couldn't find my other glove, so I used my scarf to wrap my bare hand. My left arm looked like one of Loch Ness monster's fins. My body, the Michelin Man.

My breath came out in short, quick puffs as I pressed on, me against the elements.

Desolate: A place deserted of people and in a state of bleak and dismal emptiness.

My definition? Being stranded in the mountains of Berry Springs while Winter Storm Barron unleashed hell upon you. It was me against the elements and I was starting to question my resolve.

Minutes passed into another hour, and my wine bottle was empty. The trek had turned into a tree-to-tree stumble when *finally*, my hands wrapped around a mailbox.

Mailbox?

I'd made it. The Shadow Creek Resort.

People.

Shelter.

Food. Bed.

Not. Alone.

Praise the Lord.

Renewed energy spurted through my frozen veins as the light from my headlamp bounced off an ornate black iron gate. *Locked.* That seemed weird, which was about as far as that thought went.

I humbly admit now that there were many things I'd failed to notice at that point, like the lack of a welcome to shadow creek resort sign, or the lack of cars or lights. I also didn't notice the herd of cows to my right, or the hay bales to my left.

I heaved my bags over the fence, pulled myself over, and dropped like a stone on the other side. After dusting off my ass and coat, I picked up everything and made my way up the long winding driveway, flanked by endless snow-covered fields in the fading light. I could barely make out the dark silhouette of a sprawling structure on the hill, and behind it, soaring mountains.

A castle on a hill.

I made it.

Shadow Creek Resort to save the day.

Tears of exhilaration filled my eyes as I jogged the rest of the way, my bags and headlamp bouncing with each step like a drunk firefly in the night.

My chest heaving, I topped the hill, where my lamp reflected off rows of sweeping windows. Rock walls and weathered wood beams stretched to an A-frame entryway of a building that seemed to stretch for miles on each side. Massive and long, like a mega ranch house.

I pulled off my headlamp as I stepped onto a front porch that was completely bare. It didn't have a stick of furniture on it, no pots or plants.

That was the first moment a little alarm bell rang in my head. I hadn't been to many five-star resorts in my life, but this wasn't what I imagined. I imagined lush lounge areas, furniture, lights, people. A bar.

I took a step back, considering that perhaps I wasn't at my intended destination. *Shit.*

Chewing on my lower lip, I turned around and looked back down the path I'd come from. No way *in hell* was I going back. The woods would be completely black in ten minutes. I turned back to the sprawling ranch house. No cars, no lights, no sign of human existence whatsoever.

I stepped to the window, cupped my hands, and peeked in. *Darkness.* Not even a digital clock, a night-light, or little red dots glowing from an entertainment center.

Lifting my headlamp to the window, I swept the narrow beam of light to illuminate a massive room with slate flooring that stretched to a wall of sweeping windows. *No furniture.*

I didn't recall seeing a for sale sign, but then again, I wasn't looking for one. Regardless, the house appeared to be vacant, which meant it was my lucky freaking day. The castle on the hill was my savior, my own little oasis in the middle of cursed mountains, I'd convinced myself.

For good measure, I knocked. *Nothing.*

I tried the doorknob. *Locked, of course.*

I dropped my bags and grabbed a rock from an area that I imagined would be a glorious flowerbed one day. I propped my headlamp onto the rock, positioning the beam on the door. I pulled out my trusty credit card, marked with scrapes from each time I'd used it on my own lock after leaving my keys inside my apartment. After popping my neck from side to side, I knelt down. Locks had nothing on this gal.

One try, two, three, and—*pop*.

I allowed myself a little jig before sliding the card back into my wallet and gathering my bags. The huge wood door was thick and heavy as I pushed it open with my toe and stepped over the threshold. The air inside was ice cold, scented with fresh lumber, as if the place was being renovated to sell.

Using my headlamp as a flashlight, I swept the beam from right to left.

Long hallways stretched in either direction, wide enough for a truck to drive through. It appeared that someone had knocked down the walls, leaving a bunch of open rooms. Kinda weird, but what did I know about modern homes? My apartment still had wallpaper.

I took the handful of steps that led down to an enormous living room, leaving a trail of bags in my wake. The focal point of the room was a massive stone fireplace, flanked by the floor-to-ceiling windows I'd noticed when peering inside from the front porch. To the right was a kitchen bigger than my apartment, with a breakfast nook, and copper cookware hanging above a center island. Perhaps staged for sale. To the left was an arched doorway with intricate woodwork around the trim.

Intrigued, I crossed the living room and stepped through the arched doorway.

My jaw dropped.

You know the scene in *Beauty and the Beast* where the Beast gifts Belle a library of epic proportions? This was *that* room. The walls were lined with shelves, each overflowing with books. Thousands and thousands of books. And in the corner were two brown leather chairs next to a floor lamp.

That was it. A billion books, two chairs, and a lamp.

I ran my fingers along the shelves. Not a speck of dust. My finger stopped on a thick leatherbound book. *To Kill a Mockingbird.*

The real estate agent must be staging the house for old people. Made sense, considering the home was probably worth close to a million dollars. If the surrounding land came with it, likely much more than that.

I took a step back, gazing up at the log beams running across the ceiling. *What would it be like to live in this house? To have that kind of life?*

Bottomless bank account. No problems. Not a care in the world.

A life I knew nothing about.

Never had.

I slowly walked along the shelves, running my fingertip along the cold wood until my nail bumped over a crack. I stopped, frowned, fingering the slit in the wood. I raised my light, peering at the thin line running vertically from the shelf to the floor. Looking from left to right, I didn't see any other cracks.

A secret door?

Frowning, I took a step back, but was halted by an ice-cold barrel pressing into the back of my neck.

8

LOUISE

*T*he headlamp slipped from my fingers, splashing light across the bookshelves as it tumbled to the floor. The squeal that came out of me echoed off the walls, reminding me of how totally alone I was—excluding the person holding a gun to the back of my head.

How did he, or she, get the drop on me?

The room had been dead silent. I should have heard footfalls, or hell, even breathing. But I'd heard nothing, not even as I stood there frozen in place, my heart hammering hard.

"Name."

I startled at the deep timbre of the voice. Man. Definitely man. Big. And not young, I guessed.

Shit.

"Louise." The blurted word sounded more like a sheep's bleat than an answer.

"Louise," he slowly repeated, questioningly.

Yeah, I knew I had the worst name on the planet. He didn't need to drill that one home.

"Louise what?"

I examined the tone of the question, trying to gauge the mood of my captor. Was he mad? Was I about to take my last breath?

Was he the String Strangler himself?

"Sloane." Terrified, I breathed out the word. "Louise Sloane."

"What are you doing in my house, Louise Sloane?"

My house.

Holy. Double. Shit. The house wasn't vacant. And I was a total, complete idiot. I'd just broken into someone's house.

Idiot, idiot, idiot.

The gun pressed harder into the back of my neck.

"My car broke down. Down the road. I didn't know anyone lived here. I'm sorry."

An endless moment passed, and I swear I had a mini heart attack. Right then and there, in the *Beauty and the Beast* library.

My heartbeat roared in my ears as I waited for him to pull the trigger. No one would hear it. No one would find me. I'd be another Berry Springs cold case, my body in a freezer that I guessed had double doors.

I closed my eyes and began counting in my head.

Three . . .

Two . . .

One . . .

The metal lifted off my neck, leaving a circle of tingles on my skin.

I released my breath but didn't dare move.

"Turn around," the voice demanded.

I didn't move. I don't know why. Maybe because I didn't want to see the monster who had just held a gun to my head. I glanced at the windows across the room and considered jumping out. But the run across the room would take me a solid five seconds at my fastest sprint.

How fast does a bullet travel?

"Turn around," he said again, less a demand and more of a growl.

My knees wobbled as I slowly turned.

A tall shadow loomed over me, silhouetted in the dark by the headlamp that I'd dropped.

He was *huge*. Massive. Not only tall, but as wide as an ox. The top of my head came to his chest.

I didn't want to look at his face, but I also didn't want to appear weak. So I focused on his chest—at eye level for me —and jerked my shoulders back.

The man didn't move. Not a single muscle. But I could *feel* his stare on my face. I'd never felt so small in my entire life.

"You smell like a liquor cabinet."

My chin jerked back, my eyes popping out of their sockets. *Uh, what?* I looked up at the face I couldn't see, but could feel the disapproval rolling off of him.

I took a step back, having no idea how to respond to that. *Jerk* came to mind, but then I remembered the whole gun thing.

Without another word, he turned and strode out of the room like nothing had happened. Like he had some important appointment to get to, or maybe the babies he kept chained in his basement needed their nightly whipping.

What. The. Hell?

I blinked a few times, frozen in place, watching the silhouette pass under the arched doorway, gun in hand, and fade into the shadows.

Then I snapped to action, spun on my heel, and darted for the windows. Desperately, I patted the icy glass, searching for a lock or a way to open them. There was nothing.

Frantic, I whirled around, scanning the room. *Now what?*

I ran back to the scene of my almost-death and plucked my headlamp off the floor, spun around, and aimed the light at the doorway.

The man was gone.

Brandishing the light like a weapon, I slowly crossed the library. Ice pelted the windows from outside, the only sound in the house.

Where did he go?

My hands started to tremble as I crossed under the doorway and stepped into the living room.

My bags were no longer in the haphazard line that I'd left them in when I'd crossed the room. Instead, they were tucked neatly in a row against the wall by the front door. My purse, my backpack, my duffel bag. Smallest to largest.

The faintest smell of disinfectant hung in the air, but I didn't have time to dissect that weirdness at the moment.

I jogged across the living room, grabbed the bags, and yanked open the door. Biting wind whipped around me as I pulled it shut behind me, lunged across the porch, and fell flat on my ass.

Third time in two days. Millionth time in my life.

My bags flew into the air, spiraling above me, and landed at my feet. My purse bounced off my head.

Embarrassment was my immediate reaction, as it usually was. Then anger. Pissed-off, wine-induced rage. I was mad at the weather, mad at myself for being such an idiot, mad at the tree Ansel had slammed into, and mad at *him*.

On top of everything else, I was mad at the asshole

who'd scared the beans out of me. Did he really have to pull a gun on me?

"You smell like a liquor cabinet."

What an *asshole*. I was stranded on the side of the goddamn road in the middle of the night with hell raining down around me. If there was any time for a drink, it was then. What the hell was I supposed to do?

Maybe not drink an entire bottle of wine, Lou.

I clenched my teeth and pushed to my feet, gathering my things with the last shred of dignity I had in me.

Night had fallen and the conditions had gotten worse. The temperature had dropped. I figured it would take me double the time to walk back to Ansel, which meant more than two hours. And that was assuming that I could pry open the frozen door once I got there.

I stared down the winding driveway, a blur behind the snowfall.

Well, I have no choice, do I?

I was crossing—make that *limping* across—the porch, when the front door opened behind me. Curious, I looked over my shoulder but kept moving. The fall had given me a pair of balls. Honestly, I didn't care if the guy shot me at the moment, I was so pissed.

The man's silhouette disappeared back into the house, leaving the door standing open.

Confused, I stopped and stared at the door.

I looked back at the journey ahead of me that could quite possibly end in loss of life. Then I turned back and stared at the open door for a good five seconds, trying to decipher his actions.

Is he inviting me back in? Airing out his house? Warming it, perhaps?

Now I had a choice. Die in the elements, or die by gunshot to the head.

Gunshot to the head would be quicker, I mused, then made a decision.

Gunshot to the head for the win.

I turned and crossed the porch, carefully this time, and poked my head into the open doorway like a baby bird peeking out from the nest. Still not a single light on. I didn't see him, so I stepped inside. The silence was jarring, the cold air now thick with tension.

The door creaked as I slowly closed it behind me. The click of the knob turning back into place echoed off the walls. A shadow moved past the kitchen. I kept my light low and peeled open my eyelids.

A minute passed.

I wasn't good with awkward silences, never had been. But the truth was, I didn't know what to say at that moment.

Ask him if he meant for me to come back inside? Ask his name? Ask if he meant to kill me? Make me his sex slave for the evening? Perhaps put my orgasm donor condom to good use?

But of all the things I could have asked him, I, Louise Sloane, went with, "Are there no lights in this place?"

A few seconds passed before there was a faint click, followed by a dim light in the kitchen. That was what I was granted—a freaking stove light in a house the size of an airport.

At least I could see his outline again. The Man, as I'd named him, was leaning against the counter with his arms crossed over his chest, staring directly at me. Watching my every move.

Dear God, please forgive me for my sins . . .

Next to the front door, I dropped my bags with a loud clunk onto the tile. *My hammer.*

I have a weapon!

Casually, I slowly knelt down as if I weren't plotting his death. Keeping my eyes on him, I searched blindly in my purse until my fingertips traced a long metal object.

I had no clue when, why, or how a hammer had ended up in my purse, but I assumed it had nothing to do with maiming another human being at the time. Regardless, I was now no longer helpless, and this gave me just enough confidence to accept my current situation.

Keeping the silhouette in view, I lowered myself to the cold slate floor. I leaned my back against the wall, the lip of the windowsill poking into my shoulder blades. Silence wrapped around me like a straitjacket as I stared at him, staring back at me.

Although I couldn't see his face, I memorized every line of his body in case I needed to meet with a sketch artist later. The man was definitely north of six feet tall, and heavy. Based on the way his broad shoulders slimmed to a *V* at the waist, I assumed his size was from muscle, and that he was shirtless.

All the easier to hammer him to death.

Seconds became minutes without a single word spoken between us.

He didn't move. Simply stood in the shadows, watching me as I huddled next to the exit with my bags at my side.

What the heck does he think I'm going to do? He has to realize I have zero options.

Minutes became an hour.

Exhaustion gripped me, but I didn't dare close my eyes.

I'd always wondered what it would be like to have a man watching you while you slept. In my fantasy, though, the guy had done it with little hearts dancing in his eyes, not a pistol in his hand.

My fingers tightened around the hammer.

I leaned my head against the window. Frozen glass against heated skin.

Why the hell is this house so cold?

I pretended to close my eyes while watching him through the slits.

I didn't know who this man was, where I was, or if I'd even make it through the night. But I knew one thing for certain.

I was totally, completely, one hundred percent unwelcome in this house of ice.

9

LOUISE

I jerked awake to a beam of sunlight burning my retinas.

Where the hell am I? Sitting on the sun?

I blinked rapidly, the *whomp, whomp, whomp* of my heart pounding in my temples. I was on a floor, a cold hard floor.

My first thought was that I was dead. Because no one can have a headache like that and still be alive.

My second thought was of *him*, the Man, and the castle on the hill. This thought was immediately followed by the realization that despite my best efforts to stay awake, I must have fallen asleep.

My eyes popped open, and a rush of panic slapped the grogginess away. My head whipped around as I frantically searched the kitchen, the living room, the hallway.

No man. I was alone. *Thank God.*

I blinked wildly at what was surely a spotlight in front of me. Except it wasn't. It was floor-to-ceiling windows framing a winter wonderland that was reflecting the rising sunlight like fluorescent fire.

"Oh my God," I whispered.

The world was white. Everything. The whitest white I'd ever seen. Iridescent.

Beyond the windows, an endless field covered in virgin snow stretched to white mountains in the distance. Dark clouds nearly obscured the rising sun, spitting snowflakes over sagging pines and oaks dipped in ice. Icicles sparkled from the awnings, creating a rainbow of colors dancing along the walls. It was breathtaking. I wanted to capture the image, but I had more important things to think about at that moment.

My mind raced as I desperately tried to replay the events of the night before through the dehydrated, hungover daze.

Car slid off road.

Ice. Snow. Lots of snow.

Idiot decides to take off into the mountains alone. The idiot being *me*.

The wine. *Jesus Christ*, the wine.

Castle on the hill.

Gun to head.

The Man.

I could have been dead. Either from the trek through the woods or from breaking into someone's house.

Not smart, Louise. Not smart.

I straightened, cringing at the pain in my back from sleeping upright on a cold slate floor. I didn't know bones could throb. At least my knee felt better now.

Holding my breath, I listened for any sound of the Man whatsoever, but there was nothing.

I looked at the kitchen where he'd stood, watching me for hours like a damn serial killer until I'd drifted off to sleep. With nothing but the dim light of a stove hood, he stood—never sat—leaning against the kitchen counter. He never spoke. Never moved. Like a statue, although most statues didn't give off vibes. And his vibe was pure disdain for my presence.

The minutes had stretched to hours. I'd eventually quit looking at him, mainly because it was so damn awkward. So, hammer in hand, I'd attempted to fade into the background. The darkness that had once scared me became my security blanket.

He didn't offer me water, food, hot tea, perhaps—and we all know he didn't offer me a drink, considering I already "smelled like a liquor cabinet." *The ass.*

He didn't offer me a bathroom, a shower. Clean, dry, warm clothes. No blanket, no pillow. The Man didn't even turn up the thermostat to normal human habitation level for the woman who'd walked a hundred miles in the snow. Dude didn't even start a fire in the fireplace.

Cold-blooded, I decided. Him. His house. That was the only explanation. I wasn't offered a spare bedroom, which the house had in spades, I was sure. I wasn't even graced with his name. Hell, I wasn't even graced with his face.

I tapped the screen on my cell phone that I'd kept at my hip all night, noting it was 7:07 a.m.

Reception? *Zip. None. Nada.*

I blew out a breath, recoiling at the smell. Wrinkling my nose, I smacked my lips in a feeble attempt to wet the cotton coating my tongue. No luck.

After wiping the drool from my chin, I raked my fingers through my matted hair, giving up midway through. I took a moment to wonder what I'd look like with dreadlocks, then wondered if I'd had dreadlocks, if I would have appeared more intimidating to the man with the gun. Because any woman with dreadlocks was surely a badass.

Once I'd added "try out dreadlocks" to my mental bucket list, I took an inventory of my body. I was wearing my puffer jacket, now with a few new stains and rips. My jeans had new rips at my knees. My boots were trashed. Duct tape dangled off the tip of one, the sole flapping like a hand puppet.

Summary? I looked like roadkill.

"You smell like a liquor cabinet."

What an asshole.

And . . . *what now?*

I remembered having shoddy reception before Ansel ran off the road. Maybe if I hiked back, I could call a tow truck that could haul Ansel and me to the resort I was supposed to be staying at. I'd figure out the rest later, as usual.

However, weather conditions were exponentially worse than the day before, so the odds of having reception was low, along with being able to drive anywhere.

I was stranded in a creepy dude's house.

What the hell *am I going to do?*

Movement in the corner of the framed window pulled my attention—a streak of black against the blinding white field. I pushed off the floor and crossed the living room, my gaze fixed on the movement in the distance. A horse as black as midnight trotted through the white snow, its mane and tail shimmering like ink. On it, the Man sat tall, strong, his presence somehow larger than the horse's.

He wore a cowboy hat, boots, jeans, and a brown leather coat with the collar flipped up. Snow speckled his shoulders and the top of his hat. I watched him for a minute, crossing the field, his head scanning from left to right. Checking the fences, I guessed. I took in the sweeping landscape of fields, woods, and mountains, wondering if it all belonged to him.

My palm drifted to the glass as I stared at him, heat blurring an outline of my fingers against the icy coldness.

His head turned toward the house, and I gasped. His hat sat low, the rim shielding half his face, but there was no question he was looking directly at me.

Sucking in a breath, I dropped my hand and took a few steps back, hoping to fade into the background. Something I was pretty good at, despite my best efforts.

Keeping my gaze on him, I slowly walked backward, expecting him to raise a pistol to the windows. My hands searched the air behind me until I remembered there was no furniture to worry about tripping over. I decided he must have only recently moved in, but even then, you'd think he'd have some folding chairs, at least.

His stare burned into me as I continued to back up across the room, although I was sure he could no longer see me. Finally, I turned and shuffled back to my spot by the front door.

My head was swimming with questions, the primary one being, *What the heck am I going to do?*

I shoved my phone and hammer back into my bag. I needed water, food, and a bathroom, but I didn't feel comfortable exploring the house. After all, that move had landed me with a gun to the back of my head not twelve hours earlier. What would the guy do if he found me in his personal space, like his bedroom or bathroom, trying to save the slaughtered lambs he kept in his shower?

I was wrestling with the zipper on my backpack when the front door blew open, sending a lightning bolt up of fear down my spine and my heart lodging in my throat. The Man breezed past me without so much as a glance, flinging dirt and snow all over me.

I swiped the ice from my left eye, the anger from the

night before reigniting as he strode through the living room, leaving a trail of wet footprints behind.

I was nothing but a dog to this man. An injured stray.

And I *still* hadn't seen his face.

"*Excuse* me." The attitude hurled out, despite my better judgment. I blamed the headache.

As usual, the Man didn't acknowledge me or my attitude, which somehow made me feel even more unworthy than a stray dog.

He disappeared into a room past the kitchen, rummaged around a minute, then came back out.

My pulse rate kicked up.

Although his face was still shielded by his cowboy hat, it was the first time I'd seen him in the light. The first thing I noticed was the thick chest underneath the coat, the way the T-shirt draped over his pecs. He strode across the living room with strong, quick steps.

While the world around us was glowing with virgin snow and sparkling ice, this man was dark and dirty with a swagger to his step reflecting a brooding irritation. Outside, an orb of magic; him, a stormy cloud, a gloom that even the brightest light couldn't penetrate. I found myself leaning forward, pulled to him like a magnet.

His face lifted, and my heart skittered in my chest. Sparkles from the icicles danced across a pair of eyes as dark as night, with a sharpness just as piercing.

My breath was taken away. Not by fear, but by the intensity vibrating off him in waves. He carried a kind of commanding presence that made you stop, watch, pay attention.

The laser focus he had on me combined with his quick steps made me press back against the wall, on pins and needles for what was about to happen next. But I couldn't stop staring at his face.

His skin was tanned but red from the cold, marked with fine lines that suggested hard living—or too many sleepless nights leaning against the kitchen counter, perhaps. Underneath a few days of stubble was a strong jawline that looked like it packed one hell of a bite. In contrast to this hard face was a pair of plump pink lips, the only softness about him.

He was the kind of striking handsome you only saw in old Western movies. The cowboys with the jilted past and revenge in their hearts.

We stared at each other. Mine, a wary curiosity. His, contempt.

A stray dog had nothing on me.

My thoughts immediately turned to my appearance, and embarrassment engulfed me. I ran my tongue over the corner of my mouth to erase any leftover drool—like that was the single most unacceptable thing about my appearance at the moment.

The Man stopped about two feet from me as if I were the epicenter of the black plague. Hell, I probably looked like I was. He thrust out a helmet that I hadn't even noticed in his hands.

"Where's your car?" he asked.

"It's a 4Runner."

"Whatever."

"Down the road."

"Where?"

"You want GPS coordinates?"

His eyes flickered with annoyance. "How long did you walk?"

"About a bottle's worth."

There it was, that good old Lou attitude, but he didn't laugh.

I cleared my throat, then remembered my breath. *God, can things get any worse?*

The helmet was tossed at my feet, missing the duct tape on my boot by a hair.

I cocked a brow.

"Come on."

"Where?" Annoyance colored my response, but I didn't care. Still, no inquiry of how I was doing, or offering me a bathroom. Thank God I wasn't on my period.

Ignoring my question, he grabbed my backpack and duffel bag and stepped out the front door. He smelled like clean soap and cedar.

Helmet in hand, I pushed myself off the floor and followed my bags outside.

I lifted the helmet. "This isn't exactly biking weather."

"We're not biking."

My gaze landed on a massive brown horse standing in the middle of the driveway. This was a different one than I'd seen him on in the field minutes earlier. Bigger. A shovel and several bags of something were hooked onto the saddle.

Helmet. Saddle. Horse.

I stopped in my tracks. "We're taking a horse to my car?"

He nodded, checking the straps on the saddle.

My heart kick-started into panic mode. Truth? I was terrified of horses.

I was six years old. It was the Carroll County Fair. My cousins forced me to go on a horseback ride with them. I did, and two minutes in, my horse decided to go apeshit, bucked away from its handler and took off in a sprint with me like a rag doll on its back, hanging on for dear life. Once the beast made it onto the track—with a full audience awaiting the demolition derby to start—I was bucked off, landing on a hubcap and breaking my right arm and collarbone.

I gripped the helmet. "Um . . . don't you have a truck or something?"

"I have lots of trucks."

"Can't we take one of those?"

"Do I need to remind you what got you into your current circumstance in the first place?"

Ice, got it. Condescending prick, definitely got it.

I chewed my lower lip as I walked over, my legs like lead weight. I looked back at the garage with its four doors.

"What about a tractor or something?"

"Nothing on wheels is making it down that hill. I'm sorry, princess, would you like to handle this yourself?"

"Listen," I snapped back. "I know this is an inconvenience for you, but I didn't plan this. I'm sorry I landed at your house. Believe me, I am. If you're too busy . . ." I paused to ensure the smartassery didn't go unnoticed. It wasn't like the guy had a family of six to care for . . . unless they were locked in the basement. "I *can* handle this myself. I made it here last night, and I can make it back to my car again."

"And get yourself out of the ditch like you did last night?"

"Maybe. Now that the sun's up."

He pulled the helmet from my hands and strapped it on my head with quick, jerky movements. I held my breath and avoided eye contact.

After the helmet was secured, he stepped behind me and gripped my waist, sending a lightning bolt through my body. Without a warning or the grace of a countdown, I was hoisted into the air.

Panic blew through me and I locked up like a plank. Arms froze at my sides, legs locked like four-by-fours.

He dropped me to the ground. "What the hell are you doing?"

I said nothing, staring in panic at the saddle in front of me.

"Hang on. Have you never . . ." He paused as if the question was too painful to even finish.

"Yes, I have," I croaked, staring at the horse. "And broke two bones in the process. I'm not exactly the most coordinated person. I can dance, though. Go figure."

Shut up, Louise.

A moment passed with one beast staring at the back of my head, and the other impatiently stomping its hooves in front of me.

The Man tapped my elbows. "Move these next time." Then he knocked the back of my knees with his. "And these. Grip the saddle horn and pull yourself onto the saddle. You're not going to fall. I'm right here. Now, let's go."

Birds scattered from a nearby tree at the squeak that came out of me as he hoisted me into the air again. Madly grasping at anything, I pulled myself onto the saddle, flung my leg over, and wrapped my arms around the horse's neck for dear life. My chest heaving, I twisted my head to look at him, a few strands of the horse's mane sliding into my mouth.

I swear I saw the corner of the Man's lip curl up.

Closing my eyes, I prayed for the good Lord to take me right then and there.

"Louise."

I spat out the horse's hair. "What?"

"I'm going to need you to release my horse's neck and scoot to the second seat on the saddle."

I didn't move.

"Now, Louise."

I hated him. God, I hated him.

My heart pounded, but *dammit*, I could *not* release my grip from around the horse's neck.

The Man stared at me, and I closed my eyes.

A moment passed. When I opened my eyes, he was gone. I didn't dare raise my head for fear of spooking the horse.

Three grueling minutes ticked by before a black horse trotted up from the side of the house, the Man sitting on top. It was the same horse he was riding before.

He pulled up alongside me, grabbed the reins from my horse, and slowly tugged. I squeezed the horse's neck tighter, my breasts smashed against the back of its neck.

A blanket was wrapped around my back, a thick, wooly plaid blanket. It smelled like him.

"What's mine's name?"

"Prudence." He side-eyed me. The name of the horse he'd given me to ride meant caution, good judgment, and common sense.

Ironic? Absolutely not.

"She has a good temperament," he said. "Smart."

I bit the inside of my cheek as Prudence began to walk, my body swaying from side to side with each step.

Oh my God, oh my God, oh my God . . .

If the Man said anything to me, I didn't hear it. I was too busy repenting my sins.

It took a while.

Eventually, I realized there was a rhythm to the move-ment, and because we were going so slowly, it was easy to anticipate each sway. I also began to realize that although there was a dip with each step, I wasn't going to fall off. The saddle felt solid between my legs.

I took a deep breath, then another, and another.

My gaze shifted to the man in the black cowboy hat. Snowflakes swirled around him, fading into the white landscape that was slowly closing in around us.

"What's your name?" I asked, almost in a whisper.

His steely gaze remained fixed ahead. "Ryder."

*I*t was breathtaking. Magical.

There was something about being in nature that always stirred my soul. But seeing that nature draped in inches of snow and glittering ice was like stepping into a different world.

The animals and birds had taken shelter from the falling snow, so the only sound was the crunching of our horses' hooves through the snow and ice. Everything was covered in white, and snow-laden trees sagged over the road, giving the impression of a tunnel. The dirt road was nothing but a white blanket.

Thick clouds had moved in, hiding the rising sun and muting its rays. For that, my headache was eternally grateful. About thirty minutes into our journey, the flurries turned into a steady snowfall, around the same time I finally got the balls to lift my chest off of Prudence's neck.

Ryder and his horse never left my side, my reins securely in his grip. True to form, not a word was spoken.

While I was beginning to relax, entranced by the beauty around us, Ryder remained hyperalert, as if he were expecting the boogeyman to jump out. Every snort of the horse, every pop of a twig breaking, he was attuned to, although never moving more than a slight turn of his head.

His gaze never met mine, not once, and I found myself staring at him. There was a quiet confidence about him that pulled you in, making you want to know more. Even the way Ryder rode the horse was skillful and competent.

I'd noticed the gun holstered on his hip before we were even down the driveway. Instead of making me fearful, it made me feel safe. The Man was always in control.

I wondered if he had a family somewhere. Divorced, perhaps. And how did he make his money? Ryder didn't have the entitled attitude that came with old money, so I assumed he'd achieved success the old-fashioned way—with hard work. And what the heck was up with the lack of furniture in the house? No pictures? And the coldness to it?

Why didn't he speak?

And who *the hell* forgot to teach him manners?

As I watched him, he was completely unreadable, his face frozen in a brooding expression that kept you on your toes. He was beautiful, though. There was no doubt about that.

Despite the snow, I was warm. The blanket he'd given me was thick wool, impervious to the frigid temperature. The blanket had been his first offer, which was nice, but there was no question he'd wanted me *out* of his home. Like a bad case of termites.

I wondered why.

What felt like an hour passed by, still without a word spoken, when I began to recognize my surroundings. A fallen tree limb, a sharp bend in the road. And finally, a burst of burnt orange through the white.

"There he is," I said, straightening my spine for the first

time since the journey began. Two minutes left, and I finally grew a pair. And *ouch*, by the way.

I'd never been so happy to see Ansel in my life. Mounds of snow stretched up to the floorboard. The roof and hood were covered. But he was in one piece.

Ryder slid off his horse with the grace of someone who'd done it a million times.

After unthreading the shovel from his saddle, he grabbed a few bags and walked over to the SUV, then began shoveling. He didn't tell me to *come*, or offer to help me off the horse, so I stayed put and watched him work.

Small puffs of breath escaped with each scoop as he shoveled in smooth, quick, efficient movements. I expected no less. Ryder was the type of guy who got the job done. I imagined him as someone who took pride in doing manual labor, and considered it an insult to hire anyone to do something that he could do with his own two hands.

As the mound of snow behind him grew, I began to feel useless. Jerk or not, the Man was helping me out of a jam, and I didn't feel right just sitting there watching him. Unless I had popcorn and a glass of wine, because if I'm being totally honest, the view was *not* bad.

"Do you need any help?" I cringed at my voice, a fake sugary-sweet with a twinge of hesitation. What was it about this guy that made my IQ drop twenty points?

He just grunted in response.

I looked at the ground, a thousand feet below. After convincing myself that snow provided adequate padding, I wrapped a death grip around the saddle horn, lowered my torso against the horse's neck—my safe place—and slid my leg over the side.

Don't look at me, don't look at me, don't look at me was all I could think as I slid off the horse in slow motion like a blob of slime. By the time my boots hit the snow, my heart was pounding.

I made it.

Thank you, thank you, thank you.

I peeked around the horse's neck, ensuring Ryder didn't witness my epic dismount. With a fresh burst of confidence, I squared my shoulders and walked over to the SUV.

"How can I help?"

A whoosh of the shovel passed inches from my face, followed by a plop of snow.

"I said no."

"No?"

"No."

"No to what?"

"To your first question."

"Oh. I didn't hear you."

I shoved my hands in my pockets and took a step back, giving him the few feet he demanded remain between us at all times.

Once the snow was cleared, Ryder grabbed a bag—that he could have asked me to hand to him—unlaced it, and dumped the sand inside it behind the tires.

He stood up straight and held out his hand, palm up. "Keys."

"Keys?"

"To your car."

My eyes slowly rounded in horror.

"Keys," he said again.

Heat shot to the tips of my ears as I looked at my backpack and duffel bag that he'd grabbed before storming out and had secured to the saddle.

No purse.

Oh. My. *God.*

"I . . . I'm *so* sorry . . ."

His lips pressed into a tight line, the muscles in his jaw twitching.

Babbling, I said quickly, "I didn't grab my purse on the way out. I didn't realize we were leaving. And then the whole horse thing threw me off. My keys are in my purse."

Die. That's what I wanted to do. For, like, the third time that day.

His nostrils flared. It was the nail in my coffin.

I looked at the gun on his hip. *Just do it. Might as well get it done now.*

He looked back at Ansel, then at me, and I stiffened.

Scowling, he stalked over to Prudence, yanked the wool blanket from the saddle, and tossed it to me. The corner caught my hair, pulling half over my eyes. I was swatting away the strands as he jumped onto his horse and yanked the reins as it danced in place.

"I'll be back in twenty minutes. Think you can stay alive?"

I shrugged, meaning it.

"Try." He flicked the reins, and the black horse took off like a bullet through the snow.

I watched the flash of dark lightning until it disappeared through the trees, taking a different route than he'd come with me. A shortcut that I must not have had the skill to maneuver.

Wrapping the blanket around my shoulders, I blew out a deep breath.

What a freaking day.

What a freaking week.

I turned to Prudence, who appeared bored.

"Your boss doesn't like me very much." She snorted, and I stroked her mane. "I'll bet he likes you, beautiful girl."

I unstrapped my duffel bag from her saddle, retrieved my toothbrush and toothpaste, and brushed my teeth in the snow. Next came a few yanks of a brush through my hair, and a dab of concealer to cover the dark circles under my eyes, sure I looked like the walking love child between Uncle Fester and Cousin It.

Digging in my duffel, I found a perfume sample, a locally made organic oil I'd gotten when I purchased my coveralls from the feed store. After smearing some on my wrists, neck, and for good measure, my armpits, I felt half human again.

Turning back to Ansel, I decided to make myself useful.

I was busy smoothing the third bag of sand around the back tire when the ground shook beneath me. I looked over my shoulder as Ryder pulled his horse to a stop nearby, snow exploding into a cloud around them.

He dismounted and his gaze raked over my body, changing the energy around us instantly. What was once calm, silent nature was now charged with an electricity that seemed to accompany him. All that testosterone.

I scrambled to my feet while Ryder stalked over. His head tilted to the side as he frowned at the daisies I'd traced in the sand somewhere between the second and third bag.

"They're flowers," I told the King of Darkness.

"Thought you threw up."

"Because vomit sprinkles out of my mouth in perfectly formed daisies?"

He ignored the quip and handed me my pleather purse that somehow looked even smaller in his hands. I was busy searching through the contents when he jingled the keys in the air.

"Hey, you went through my purse."

"You broke into my house." He strode to the driver's door.

Touché.

I shrank in embarrassment at the orgasm donor condom sitting on top, right next to the hammer. *Of course.*

Ryder pried open the driver's side door. Seconds later, Ansel fired up with a cough, and I stepped back.

The reverse lights came on, and Ryder slowly pressed the gas. The back tires spun wildly, but my attention was pulled to the front tire that only sort of spun. I was no mechanic, but it didn't look good.

Ryder unfolded himself from the driver's seat. "Your visor's broke."

"I know."

When he frowned, I shrugged. "I've tried to fix it. Duct tape, superglue, gum."

He squatted in the ditch next to the front tire, closely looking it over. With a grunt, he flung off his cowboy hat and lowered onto his stomach, his body sinking into the snow.

I cringed. Ryder was a jerk, but I felt terrible about all the trouble he was going to for me.

"Your axle's broke," he muttered.

"My what?"

"Axle."

"You mean, it can't drive?"

"Not unless you want to drive around in circles all day."

"You're kidding."

He pushed to his feet and brushed the snow off his coat and jeans.

We stared at each other for a moment, and I got the vibe he was thinking, *"Well, your turn. I've done all I can do here, sweetheart."*

I glanced at Ansel. "Are you sure it's broken?"

"Pretty sure."

"Pretty, as in—"

"Yes. I'm sure."

I blew out a breath, fisting my hands on my hips. "I'll call a mechanic."

"No mechanic's coming out here today."

Ignoring him, I pulled out my phone. *No reception.*

"Dammit," I muttered and began pacing. *Shit, shit, shit.* Again, I was left with no options. I looked back at my car. "Ansel's a tough beast. We'll figure this out."

"Who's Ansel?"

I thrust a hand toward the 4Runner as if he should know.

"You name your cars?"

"You name your horses."

"That's different. They're animals."

"So is Ansel. Trust me." I checked my phone again, willing one bar of reception to appear.

"Why Ansel?"

"Ansel Adams, American photographer and environmentalist, famous for his black-and-white images of the West."

"That's weird."

"Not really."

"What were you doing out here?" he asked, watching me pace.

"Going to my hotel."

"There are no hotels down this road."

"Yes, there is."

"No, there isn't."

"Yes, there *is*. According to my map app, Shadow River Resort is down this road."

His eyelids fluttered in what I assumed was as close to an

eye roll as the guy got. "Shadow River is on the other side of the mountain."

I stopped on a dime, stared at him a moment, then tipped my head back and laughed, because that was all I could do at that point. Not only had I run off the road, but I'd been going in the wrong direction.

I threw my hands in the air. "God, this is just so . . ."

He plucked my purse from the rock I'd set it on and began resetting the reins on the horses.

"You staying here?" he asked when I didn't move.

"Where the hell am I going?"

"To your hotel."

"How? I thought you said the roads were impassable?"

"I'll get you there."

The horses.

Relief washed over me. Food, water, shower, shelter, no sidelong glances that made me feel an inch tall. A minibar. The light at the end of the tunnel.

"What about Ansel?"

"I'll get him taken care of."

"No. I'll handle it. I'll call someone—"

"I know a guy. I'll have it towed to Frankie's as soon as someone can get out here."

"Who's Frankie?"

"Frankie's Auto Shop. Off Main Street."

"You know this town is kind of like a modern-day Mayberry."

"You have no idea, sweetheart."

Sweetheart.

"Okay. Well, thank you. I'll call Frankie from Frankie's Auto Shop and give him my information as soon as I get to the hotel."

"Let's go. This snow isn't going to let up."

I jogged over to the horse. When Ryder lifted his hands to my waist, I swatted them away. "Don't. I've got it."

I was hell-bent on showing Ryder that I wasn't totally incompetent. I was also done accepting the man's help that he served up on a block of ice.

Gritting my teeth, I grabbed the saddle horn, my boot fumbling with the stirrup. I pretended not to notice Ryder steadying it.

One. I inhaled.

Two. I bit my lip.

On *three*, I hurled myself onto that damn beast like I owned the bitch, my pulse racing. I quickly assumed my safety position—my arms wrapped around the horse's neck.

"Sit up. You can do it."

I ground my teeth. *Sit up, you pansy.*

Slowly, I raised myself from Prudence's neck, keeping my focus on the horse's mane.

Don't look up, don't look down.

When I was fully erect, Ryder disappeared for a moment, then reappeared on his horse.

"It's going to be a two-hour trek on the horses. At least." He tossed me the blanket. "Can you handle it?"

"Yes." Hell yes, I could. I could handle anything that led to wine, a shower, and food. In that order.

"Hold the reins, if you'd like, but you don't have to do anything. The horse will ride right behind me. If you need to stop for whatever reason, pull them."

"Okay."

"Okay. Onward then. *Hup.*"

With a nudge of his heels, Ryder pulled ahead, my horse falling into step behind his as we began what would be the journey that would forever change my life.

LOUISE

*I*t was almost noon by the time we finally reached Shadow Creek Resort. It had taken over three hours with all the stops we had to take for Ryder to clear fallen limbs and debris. I was starving and so thirsty, I'd considered sucking the ice off of Prudence's mane. My headache had reached epic proportions.

I was dreaming of funnel cakes and hot chocolate spiked with peppermint schnapps when we finally crested the hill and I saw the resort. My salvation—and it was *glorious.*

The main building was a multistory log cabin with soaring peaks under blankets of snow. Around it, dozens of small log cabins nestled between the trees, gray smoke rolling from the chimneys. A river split the grounds, feeding into Otter Lake not far away, according to the website. Cars and trucks were barely visible under the snow, and based on the lack of tire tracks, no one had come or gone from the resort since the snow started.

Ryder led me to the freshly swept stone steps at the entryway. This time, I didn't hesitate or wait for help. I threw myself off the horse with the enthusiasm of a toddler at Disney World.

Remaining on the horse, Ryder bent over, unclipped my bags from the saddle, and handed them to me.

"Thank you."

He dipped his chin.

We stared at each other for a moment, but when neither of us spoke, I mirrored his manly chin-dip thing, squared my shoulders, and started up the steps. As I pushed through the lobby doors, I looked over my shoulder and met Ryder's gaze as he watched my every move from atop his magnificent black horse. I stumbled over the threshold.

"Howdy-do there, miss."

I turned my head to the barrel-bellied receptionist wearing a pair of coke-bottle glasses and a dip in his lip.

"Name's Earl." He gave me the once-over, slow and steady like his accent.

I glanced over my shoulder again. Ryder was gone.

"I take care of the grounds around here," Earl said. "Helping out at the front desk 'cause Paula's stuck at home on account of the weather. Her kid's sick too. So she says, anyway. I swear that boy catches everything under the sun. Anyways, what can I help ya with?"

"I've got a reservation." *Mister Too-much-information.*

"Well, that's good 'cause we're booked solid. Even got a couple staying in one of the owner's personal rooms. Name?"

"Louise Sloane."

"Louise. My great-granny was named Louise."

Of course she was.

"Louise Sloooane," he said as he punched the keyboard with one finger. *One. Finger.*

I'd plotted Earl's death, resurrection, and then death again by the time he finally looked up.

"Well, Lou, hate to tell you this." He sucked back a spit. "Your room was given away this morning."

"What?"

"Yep." He tapped the computer screen that I couldn't see. "'Cording to this, your reservation was for last night, and you didn't show. We had two people stranded here on account—"

"Of the weather, yeah, got it. Are you serious?"

"'Fraid so. One got your room, and the other—"

"The owner's personal room. Got it. Do you have *any* other rooms available?"

"No, ma'am. Booked solid."

"Are you sure?"

"I'm sure."

"Earl, I'll sleep in a broom closet. I'm not kidding." Which would be more comfortable than my accommodations the night before.

"No, ma'am. We got nothin'."

I covered my mouth with my hand, trying to process the amount of shit that had been dumped onto me in the last twelve hours.

"Earl . . ." Desperation thick in my voice, I said, "There's got to be something. Do you have any place I can stay here at all? Anywhere?"

He shrugged. "You can stay with me."

"No." *Jesus.* "No, thank you. I mean, do you have any place for me to sleep here at the hotel? Is *anyone* leaving today? I'll wait. You don't even have to clean the room. I'll take it as is."

"Ain't nobody leavin' today. Roads are too bad. Supposed to get another few inches on top of what we already have."

"Oh my God," I muttered, shaking my head.

I had no car, no hotel, no cell-phone reception, nothing.

"You can use the office bathroom back here to, uh, do whatever women do in bathrooms."

"Earl." My head tilted to the side. "Be honest. Do I really look that bad?"

"Kinda."

I sighed.

"And the restaurant's open, of course," he said. "Maybe git you a bite to eat until someone can come git ya."

Right. Whoever can come git me. Thanks.

I inhaled deeply. "Thank you, Earl. I'll take your kind offer to use the bathroom for now."

I'd sleep in the damn lobby until a room came available, because, what were my other options?

Earl led me behind the counter to a short hallway lined with offices. I glanced in each doorway, casing each room for a spot to sleep if I needed to. He motioned to the door at the end of the hall.

"Have at it. Spray is under the sink."

"Thanks." I rolled my eyes.

I locked myself in the bathroom, leaned my weight against the door, and began to cry. I wasn't a crier. Usually, I got mad when I was upset. That day, though, I'd reached my breaking point. I wasn't good on little sleep, and I certainly wasn't good on little food. I also wasn't good at pushing the visions of dead bodies out of my head.

My hands curled to fists at my sides. Determined, I pushed off the wall, sucked back the snot, and made my way to the mirror. Bracing myself on the sink, I loathed the reflection staring back at me.

Puffy bags accompanied tired brown eyes—the color of poop, I'd been informed by a pair of mean girls in the elementary school cafeteria. It was true, though. I wasn't blessed with that deep chocolate brown, alluring and sultry. And they weren't a vivid blue like Disney characters—pre-political correctness, when they all had blue eyes. Mine were good old dirt brown.

I ran my fingers through my boring straight hair, frizzed with tangles and knots, its color similar to my eyes. I flicked the damn bangs I'd cut weeks earlier. *What the hell was I thinking?*

I wasn't thinking, and that's the point. I never thought things through. And it was exactly that kind of carelessness that landed me in my current predicament.

Dammit, Louise. Grow up.

Streaks of dirt marked my neck, and I wondered how long they'd been there. My puffer coat swallowed my body, making my curves appear thicker than they already were. *Note to self: get new jacket.*

As I gripped the sink, staring back at myself, I thought of my life. I was thirty-one years old, living paycheck to paycheck in a one-bedroom apartment that smelled like cheese. *Okay, fine, that last part I didn't mind so much.* No husband, no boyfriend, no fuck buddy, no kids, no dogs, no cats. No book clubs or wine clubs.

My days were spent alone, working tirelessly to keep my photography business afloat. I loved what I did, but where was I going with it? How was this job ever going to pay for a house? When was I going to turn into a real adult?

I never went to college, mainly because at eighteen I had no direction. I still didn't. I also grew up dirt poor, the only child of an alcoholic father who lived off the government, and a mother who'd waitressed at the same diner for two decades. Spending thousands of dollars on a college educa-tion with no end goal, or going into debt to pay for it, seemed incredibly irresponsible at the time. So I got a job at the local newspaper, which turned into a career in photography.

Somewhere over the years, my life had turned into the same boring routine. Morning . . . work. Night . . . work. Later night . . . wine, then bed. Repeat, repeat, repeat.

I loved my job, was proud of my business, but over the last few years, that fulfillment only went so far. I was no longer content with the mundane life I'd created for myself. The world seemed to be spinning around me while I stayed in one place. My friends had gotten married, had kids, started making real money, while I sat still.

Sure, I wanted more out of life, but the thing was—I didn't know what. That's what was so frustrating about it all.

I'd thought about getting a dog to talk to, or maybe a cat, but I figured I'd either talk them into oncoming traffic, or my life would bore them into, well, oncoming traffic. Either way, it would be messy.

Then I thought of the way Ryder had dismissed me at first glance.

Why did that bother me so much? Why did I care?

Maybe because I hadn't been on a date since stonewash denim was in style. That's the thing about small towns. Not a lot to choose from, and when you do, gossip runs rampant.

But let's be honest here. It wasn't like the guys were knocking down my door, anyway. I was never the girl who oozed the sensual confidence that drew men like flies. I was always the wallflower who tripped over the chair on the way to get there.

I'd had sex with two men in my life. One time each.

The first, the loss of my virginity, was in the back of an extended-cab Chevy during a drive-in movie. It took four trips to the chiropractor to get rid of the crick in my neck, and one trip to the doctor to make sure I wasn't pregnant. Turned out to be bloat from eating too many nuts. Needless to say, having sex was no longer on my care-to-do list.

The second time was a decade later, after my landlord came in to change a lightbulb. I made a joke about how many landlords it took to screw a light bulb, and five minutes later, I was flipped over the countertop. Got twenty bucks off my rent that month, though.

This was the extent of action in my life, until the day I found Kara Meyers murdered in the mountains of Berry Springs.

With that morbid thought, I pushed away from the sink, my thoughts narrowing onto one focus. The entire reason I was in the small redneck town of Berry Springs.

Find the bastard who did it.

LOUISE

I yanked up my hood as I stared out at the lake, watching the snowflakes swirl in the icy breeze before melting into the water. The late afternoon had darkened under a brooding sky, adding to the chill and gloom and doom I was feeling.

After brushing my teeth for the second time and washing my face, I'd changed into a clean pair of jeans and the thickest sweatshirt I'd packed, a red hoodie with bleach stains at the bottom.

Laundry wasn't my strong suit.

Unfortunately, there was no shower in the bathroom so I did what I could with a roll of toilet paper and hand soap. *Ouch.*

I'd cleaned the mud from my boots, then applied superglue to mend the flapping sole. It was beyond duct tape at that point. Then I pulled myself together the best I could with a sweep of mascara, a swipe of lip gloss, and a little blush to brighten my sallow skin. A five-star hotel meant rich people, and I wasn't in the mood to get any more side-eyes of disapproval.

Earl let me use the phone. I called every hotel in the phone book, but none had a vacancy.

Then I called Miles, no answer, and left him a message. I called Margie, no answer, and left her a message. I called Frankie at Frankie's Auto Shop, no answer, and left him a message with my contact information. After that, I found my way to the restaurant and inhaled a bacon-double-cheeseburger, large fries, and a Coke. Diet, of course.

After that, I was . . . lost. No hotel room, no car, no one to call. So, bags in hand, I meandered through the hotel, walking up and down the halls, pretending to be taking a late-afternoon stroll. When I reached the roof, I made my way back down and outside to take some photographs.

An ornate hand-crafted gazebo next to the lake called to me. Once inside, I recognized it from the website as an option for weddings. I took a few pictures, then sat cross-legged on the wooden slats and watched the snow.

An hour had gone by when a fishing boat slowly made its way out of a cove. A lone man stood at the helm with two fishing poles in the water, a snow-speckled black cowboy hat on his head.

I squinted, leaning forward. There was no mistaking that body, the size of the man. It was Ryder. And dammit if my stomach didn't dip.

My first thought was to run. Spin around and run far, far away from the guy I'd made such an ass out of myself with. Instead, I lifted my camera and took a picture. Zoomed in and took a few more.

His boat drifted closer to the shoreline, close enough that I could make out his face. His cheeks and nose were a ruddy red from the cold, his expression as dark and intense as when I saw him for the first time. He stared out at the water as if he carried the weight of the world on his shoulders.

Click, click.

What made this man so unhappy?

His gaze lifted from the water to the mountains, where it remained as if he was lost in his thoughts. The camera slowly dropped from my face as I stared at him, his expression suddenly so sad, so sorrowful, a ripple of goose bumps popped up on my skin. I wondered what someone could be thinking about to evoke a reaction so strong that it gave someone else the chills.

Who is this man?

I took a few more pictures, completely lost in my subject, Ryder. It was as if my camera had a mind of its own. And it liked him. Very much.

His head turned in my direction. Wide-eyed, I lowered the camera as our eyes locked. He stilled.

Shit. I was busted. So, what did I do? Flashed a lopsided smile and waved like an extra in *One Flew Over the Cuckoo's Nest.*

Ryder frowned, his usual expression, and jerked the wheel to guide the boat toward the shoreline. "Were you taking my picture?" he hollered.

"No," I lied.

Raising a brow, he nodded to the camera in my hand.

"I was photographing the lake."

"Why were you taking pictures of me?" His voice was sharp. Not annoyed like our previous interactions, but pissed now. "Are you with the paper or something?"

What the hell? Why would anyone from the paper want to photograph him?

"No, and I wasn't taking pictures of you," I said, lying

again. I gathered my bags and walked down the short hill to the shoreline.

He nodded to the bags. "Why do you have your stuff out here?"

"No vacancy at the hotel."

"You told me you'd booked a room here."

"I did. They gave up my room when I didn't show last night."

He frowned. "You sure?"

"Pretty sure, according to Earl at the front desk."

"Earl does the landscaping."

"You know Earl?"

"Everyone knows Earl."

"Well, no landscaping for Earl today. I called every hotel in the area. Booked solid. Also called your boy Frankie. No answer. Everything's closed down. Did he get my car towed?"

"No. Tomorrow."

Ryder looked at the hotel, back at me, back at the hotel, back at me, then scratched his head, tipping up his cowboy hat. "So, where're you going to stay?"

"I'll figure something out."

"Meaning you'll find someone else's house to break into?"

My eyes narrowed. "Yep. But this time I'll be damn sure to choose a house whose owner was raised with manners. And has a working heater."

"You're planning to sleep in that gazebo, aren't you?"

I shrugged.

"You'll freeze to death if you sleep out here tonight."

"I'll sleep in the lobby. Wouldn't be the first time I slept next to a front door."

Boom.

His eyes narrowed. "They won't let you sleep in the lobby."

I blew out an exasperated breath. "Then I guess I'll sleep out here, freeze to death, then come back as a ghost and have them charged for involuntary manslaughter for forcing me to sleep outside during Winter Storm Asshole."

Ryder stared at me a moment, then turned away. "Come on."

I blinked.

"Come on," he repeated.

"Come where?"

He shook his head and leaned over to shift things around in his boat. "Here. My boat."

I didn't move.

"Miss Sloane, I'm not going to beg you. Trust me."

The engine growled, and he maneuvered the boat closer to shore.

"I appreciate the sentiment," I called out, "but the gazebo would probably be warmer."

He didn't answer. Instead, he tossed his cowboy hat in the back of the boat, shrugged out of his coat, gripped the edge, and dropped himself into the lake, fully clothed. The water was up to his waist. The man didn't even cringe as he walked through the lake, ripples flowing behind him.

Once on shore, he gathered my bags, tossed them into the boat, then walked back, quicker this time. Before I could speak, I was swept into his arms like a new bride—an arranged marriage, perhaps.

I wrapped my arms around his neck, although I didn't need to. Ryder carried my dead weight like it was nothing. I yelped as he released one hand to steady the boat.

"I won't drop you."

My weight was shifted, my heart lodging in my throat as

he lifted me into the air and set me into the boat. I crumpled to the floor and curled up, knees to chest, as the boat rocked back and forth. The smell of fish filled my nose.

Ryder hoisted himself inside without so much as a grunt. He handed me his coat.

"Thank you." I slipped it on.

We took off across the lake—Ryder, a tower at the helm, and me, hanging on for dear life on the floor. The icy wind whipped through my hair, pins and needles pricking my face. Like the ice sculpture he was, Ryder didn't shiver. I wondered if his wet clothes had frozen.

The snow picked up about five minutes in, a blizzard swirling around us. My teeth chattered, and I was sure my ears had frostbite.

I couldn't believe anyone would fish in this kind of weather without a gun to their head.

Finally, we rounded a bend in the lake and slowed as we made our way down a narrow cove. Snowy woods closed in around us, steep hills climbing up from the lake. Ice rimmed the shoreline.

Ryder steered the boat into a newly constructed covered dock and cut the engine.

I couldn't move. My legs, arms, and eyelids were frozen.

He secured the boat to the slip, grabbed my bags, and set them aside. When he offered me his hand, I clasped tough, calloused skin, and my body was propelled forward by his tug. Nothing was gentle or soft about this man.

I waited as he locked a few things in the boat, then secured his poles to a shelved cabinet on the dock. Finally, he hoisted a large cooler from the boat. Once I had my bags slung over my shoulders, we set off on a narrow path that climbed through the woods.

We walked, and walked, and walked, each yard steeper

than the last. My shoulders ached and my quads were burning, but I welcomed the increased body heat.

Clumps of snow fell from the trees around us, their gentle plops to the ground breaking the silence. The beauty of the snowstorm had shifted from magical and enchanting to dangerous and eerie. I kept thinking how crazy I was for walking through it alone in the middle of the night.

Finally, we crested the hill, and the back of his ranch came into view. The back was even more impressive than the front. What wasn't impressive was the fields we still had to cross to get there. Ryder had walked a half mile in a snowstorm to fish.

And I'm the crazy one?

An ear-piercing whistle startled me. Seconds later, the black horse appeared through the blur of the snow, galloping to Ryder's call. Prudence was nowhere to be seen, probably doing long division in the stable.

Ryder grabbed the black horse's bridle and walked him to me. "Get on."

"Please."

His eyelids twitched with the smallest flutter. "Please."

I dropped my bags, so excited that I didn't have to walk anymore that I forgot to get scared. As I grabbed the saddle horn and raised my boot into the stirrup, two hands gripped my waist and lifted me before settling me into the saddle. Ryder secured my bags and the cooler to the saddle.

"What're you—"

My question was cut off when he grasped the saddle horn and hoisted himself behind me, the saddle shifting as it took his weight. My heart rate kicked up and I swallowed a yelp, desperately grabbing at anything to steady myself.

Two thick thighs wrapped around me, his groin pressing

against my ass. His arms reached around me to grab the reins. I inhaled that smell again. *Him.* Fresh soap and cedar.

Butterflies fluttered in my stomach and I stilled, not knowing what to do next.

"You okay?"

The deep voice in my ear sent a tingle down my body that settled between my legs.

"Yes," I whispered, and meant it.

A click of his heels and we were off at a slow, steady pace that I was sure was because of me. I was nestled in his arms, warm and safe. I relaxed against him, feeling his breath on my neck, my heart a steady pounding. Jerk or not, the guy awoke every sexual sensor in my body.

As we slowly made our way through the snow-covered field, I took in the land.

The fields stretched as far as I could see through the snow, dotted in perfectly symmetrical zigzag patterns with countless hay bales. Beyond them loomed soaring mountains, and miles and miles of dense woods. It was beautiful land. Expensive land.

Spotting a herd of cows through the snow, I wondered how many he had. A large red barn sat in the distance with a greenhouse-looking structure next to it. Several sheds were scattered in the fields. And in the center of it all was the castle on the hill.

The house of ice.

"What's this horse's name?" I asked.

"Liberty."

Freedom. An interesting name.

"How many do you have?"

"Four. More to come."

"What are their names?"

"Majesty, Prudence, Bullet."

"So distinguished. Excluding Bullet, of course. The black sheep?"

"The horse can get out of any fence I build. He's stubborn, headstrong. Contumacious."

"Contumacious, huh?"

"It means—"

"Willfully disobedient. I know."

"Figured."

"Did you? May I recommend a name for your next horse? Pharisaic." I smirked.

"You think I'm self-righteous, judgmental, and hypocritical?"

"All signs point to yes."

"Good to know."

He leaned into me, and I was hot in seconds. Not warm, *hot*.

A few minutes later, we reached his house, dark in the gloomy late afternoon. It could be beautiful, but it wasn't. Everything about Ryder's home—and him—was cold and unwelcoming. I wondered if that was on purpose. I wondered why. I wondered if he was single, for the hundredth time.

And I wondered what the hell this man's story was.

Ryder unhooked my bags and the cooler as I dismounted—all by myself. Once again, I slung my bags over my shoulders and followed him inside, looking forward to the reprieve from the freezing temperature. *No dice.* The house was even colder than when I'd woken up next to the front door.

"Ryder, did you just move in?"

He breezed past me. "No."

"How long have you lived here?"

"Sixteen months, two days, eight hours."

I watched him walk to the kitchen and drop the cooler on the counter, no words, not a single glance in my direction. I was unsure where to set my bags, where to sit myself, what to do, what to say. And I had to pee. And that was it— the straw that broke the camel's back.

"To be clear, you picked me up from the resort, invited me onto your boat and to your house, to offer me a place to stay for the night, correct?"

His brow furrowed as he looked up. This question confused him.

"So, yes, then?"

"Yes." He refocused on the cooler.

"Well, thank you," I said, my tone similar to the temperature.

I was grateful, but going through another night like the one before made my stomach sink—and made me a bit irritable.

"Shall I resume my place by the front door?"

A moment passed before he finally tore his attention away from the cooler and crossed the room. "This way."

I followed him past the front door and down the hall.

The house was beautiful. Soaring ceilings, arched entryways, sweeping windows that made you feel like you were outside. An open, airy floor plan. Exposed beams lined the ceilings, and earthy colors reflected the nature outside.

I glanced over my shoulder. Behind me was another long hallway. The house was endless. Much like the living room, each room we passed was bare. Not a stick of furniture, no pictures or paintings. The kitchen appeared to be the only room used in the entire house. Room after room, beautiful and vacant.

Cold.

It was spotless too. Not a speck of dirt anywhere, not

even in the corners or windowsills. I wondered if he had a maid, or if he actually cleaned it all himself.

Finally, we reached the end of the house, marked by two large wooden doors, arched at the top. My eyes rounded as he pushed them open and we stepped into the master bedroom.

The first thing I noticed was the light. Walls of windows allowed for daylight to seep into every corner of the room. It was warmer too, I noticed.

Log beams supported a tall ceiling with an iron chandelier hanging over a four-poster bed. Like the living room, a rock fireplace split the windows that looked out to the fields. A brown leather chair and footstool were tucked in the corner, next to a floor lamp and a stack of books two feet tall. Bindings out, perfect ninety-degree angles. Double doors led into a masculine slate and copper bathroom with a soaking tub to die for. Still, no pictures, plants, or furniture other than the chair, the bed, and the books.

"Closet's over there, if you want to hang your stuff."

"No. No, I won't take your room. I'll—"

"It's the only one with a bed."

"Really? In the entire house? You have *one* bed?"

He blinked.

"Well, thank you, seriously, but no. I won't take your bed. I'm more than happy to sleep—"

"Take it."

"But what about you? Where will you sleep?"

"I don't sleep much."

"Why?"

Ryder didn't answer, simply took the bags from my hands and set them on the bed, their weight sinking into a lush dark-green plaid comforter that I imagined was down.

The guy had no manners, no social skills, no desire for

human interaction of any kind, but he took his bed seriously. His bed, his kitchen, and most importantly, his space.

"Bathroom's in there." He stepped past me, avoiding eye contact.

I watched him pull logs from a crate next to the fireplace and stack them strategically into the box. In under a minute, a fire was going.

"Thank you."

He mumbled something about the comforter, then breezed past me again. And with the click of the doors closing behind him, Ryder was gone.

I darted across the room on tiptoe and bolted both locks on the door. As I blew out a breath, a wave of relief washed over me. I had a locked door between me and the Man, a fire in the fireplace, and a bed. I could drink the water from the faucet and gnaw on the bedposts if I had to.

I spun slowly in a circle, taking in every inch of the room. The fire popped and hissed in the silence, and that's when I realized there wasn't a television in the room, and I also hadn't seen one anywhere in the house.

Who is *this guy?*

With that thought, I did what any warm-blooded woman would do. I went snooping.

I peeled off my coat and toe-heeled out of my boots— God forbid I get dirt on the gleaming floor. Then I padded into the bathroom.

I started with the drawers first. Toothpaste, shaving cream, a razor, a few bars of soap—actual bars, not body wash—and foot powder. *Gross.* Maybe Ryder wasn't perfect after all.

I made my way into the closet and had a mini orgasm. My entire apartment could fit inside the room. And what did Ryder have in it? Five plaid button-ups, a row of T-shirts

—ironed, a stack of jeans folded into perfect squares, two pairs of cowboy boots, a pair of hiking boots, and three cowboy hats.

That. Was. it.

After sniffing one of the T-shirts, I gathered my bags and placed them in the closet. I checked my camera, pulled out my laptop, and downloaded the images from the day, as I did every day. After that, I made my way back to the bathroom.

With a wicked grin, I stripped bare and started filling the tub.

I heard the bathroom door shut as I paced the hallway. Like the caged rabid animal I was, I stared at the closed door of my bedroom.

My bedroom.

I didn't even know her. Didn't know a thing about the woman who would be sleeping in my bed tonight.

My skin started to itch as I wondered what she was doing in there. What she was touching, what she was thinking. If she was using my things. If she was undressing. If she was showering.

Cupping my hands over my nose and mouth, I inhaled deeply. Again, in through the nose, out through the mouth, and again. And again.

I could *feel* her in my house. The presence of another body, her lungs breathing my air.

I could smell her. Her scent lingered like dust after a nuclear bomb, settling into my hair, my skin, spreading to every corner of every room in my house.

My space.

Visions of the last woman who'd been in my house

flashed through my head, followed by murder and death. I squeezed my eyes shut, shoving the images away.

No, Ryder, she's safe, I told myself. Promised myself.

My pacing increased with the beat of my heart, my fists clenched at my sides despite the deep breaths. Pacing, pacing, pacing, I stared at that goddamn door, feeling that tornado begin to spin inside me, the anxiety that had taken years to learn how to tame.

Louise Sloane.

I had no patience for simpleminded people. No patience for people who indulged their impulses without premeditation or any thought whatsoever. I'd lived that life once, and it had sent me to federal prison for ten years.

Louise Sloane was my walking antithesis. Everything I'd pushed out of my life. Everything I couldn't tolerate in another human being. Everything I'd spent the last twelve years avoiding.

Listening to the five-foot-two train wreck's story was like taking one hit after another. I'd struggled to keep my mouth shut.

Louise Sloane had made the decision to travel during one of the worst snowstorms to hit Berry Springs in years, in an SUV as shoddy as her boots. A storm that had been forecast for weeks.

The woman had packed only three bags, none of which contained a blanket, an emergency pack, water, or food that provided any sustenance but did ensure clogged arteries. Clothes, toiletries, a box of wine, a bottle of wine, a hammer, and an expired condom were Louise Sloane's necessities. To no one's surprise, she'd slid off the road.

Yet despite this, and despite the blizzard around her, Wonder Woman here decided to take off on foot—in the middle of the night—and break into a stranger's house. A convicted felon's house.

Fool.

The woman had been two seconds from losing her life when I caught her snooping in my library. The only thing— I repeat, the *only* thing—that saved Louise Sloane was her height and small frame. I'd instantly known my intruder was a woman, and therefore easier to disable if the situation called for it.

Little did I know the woman was like a bad rash that never left, a rash that made me itch long after she'd gone.

It was remarkable she'd made it as far as she did, really. The mountains around my land were inhabited by a pack of coyotes and an elusive mountain lion I'd been stalking for weeks. They were also filled with dead bodies, according to the gossip. The body of a young woman had been recently found not far from my house. "The String Strangler strikes again," this according to the gossips who knew nothing of the case.

I knew about the notorious serial killer who preyed on young women, rumored to live in the area. Everyone around here knew the story. And the fact that Louise Sloane could be so careless made me sick to my stomach.

I knew what evil could do to someone. I knew the merciless, blind rage. I knew the feeling of blood on your skin, the adrenaline rush that came from incapacitating someone. The moment of watching someone take their last breath. The power of knowing you'd delivered that final blow.

There were monsters in the world, and this woman had already crossed paths with one, unbeknownst to her.

Fool.

This was exactly why I'd built a fortress around myself.

To keep everyone out. Not her, though. Louise Sloane blew through my front door, all train wreck and temptation.

A broken soul.

An invitation to danger.

I reminded myself it was only temporary. The drifter would be gone and out of my life before I knew it. I'd burn the comforter, buy a new one, buy new sheets and a new bed. Build a new master suite. I'd add three more locks to my front door. Maybe a trip wire.

It was only temporary.

Only temporary, Ryder. Temporary.

Another breath, then another.

Then I heard the water kick on. She was in my shower or bath.

I stopped in my tracks, turned toward the door, fantasies of that curvy body flashing through my head. The water sluicing over her body, her hand drifting over her breasts, her stomach . . .

Fuck. Shit. Goddammit.

My heart racing, I stalked to the kitchen, grabbed a towel and a bottle of bleach, and sprayed down the outside of my bedroom door. The knob, the floor, the hinges. For good measure, I sanitized the front door again, the windowsill, knobs, hinges, and the single tile she'd slept on the night before, as I'd already done. Twice.

I took a few steps back, staring at the entryway. Then down the hall, then back at the entry.

Pacing again, I stared at that goddamn tile she'd slept on. The tile that I'd spent the entire day staring at, long after she was gone. The tile that reminded me of those deeply hooded brown eyes with little gold specks around the irises. That bedhead sexy hair that I wanted to tangle my fingers in. That little dip at the end of her nose. The dimples that deepened with her disdain for me. That round, pouty mouth, and those goddamn red lips and the little dent in the bottom one.

Louise Sloane.

Who is she?

Back and forth, I paced. Back and forth, my pulse increasing and adrenaline building.

My hands shaking, I stalked to the utility closet, grabbed a hammer, and stomped back to the entryway.

With a guttural groan, I raised the hammer and destroyed the tile Louise Sloane had slept on.

14

LOUISE

*a*n hour later, I pulled myself out of the tub, my insides toasty warm, my limbs languid and relaxed. For the first half hour, I'd simply soaked, feeling like a princess in the castle on the hill, held captive by an evil beast. A very sexy beast.

I'd washed my hair, my body, and even shaved. Not surprisingly, there was no hair dryer, so I combed my hair and scrunched it, hoping for the beachy wave look. My bangs curled up, as usual, in annoying waves above my brows.

No bangs, ever again.

My stomach grumbled loudly. I considered the bed posts, then reconsidered when I imagined Ryder's disapproval.

I smoothed on a dab of tinted moisturizer, more concealer, and more mascara. When I applied lipliner *and* lipstick, a little red flag flipped up in the back of my head.

Although I was as emotionally attracted to Ryder as one might be to a seventeen-foot python, I was unquestionably physically attracted to him. I wanted that reciprocation. Craved it, for some reason. From him.

With one more sweep of lip gloss for good measure, I took a step back and looked at myself in the copper-trimmed full-length mirror. I studied the curves of my body, my breasts, my waist.

I was a solid C-cup, with a little sag over the years. A good handful, though. Not too bad. I turned, glancing at my ass. Big, sure—not Kardashian big, for the record—but it was plump and firm. Not too bad either, but I couldn't ignore the fact that my body could use some work.

I took a deep breath. *If you don't like it, change it.* I made a vow, right then and there, to lose that damn fifteen extra pounds.

Rummaging through my duffel bag, I found my cleanest pair of boyfriend jeans and a beige corded sweater that resembled my grandmother's afghan. Next, my superglued boots. Second vow? *New clothes, new shoes.*

I checked the mirror again.

It would have to do. *Que sera sera.*

After wiping down the counter, I ventured out of the bathroom. The sun had set, the white wonderland outside now dull and gray, soon to fade to blackness. I clicked on the floor lamp next to the leather chair, zeroing in on a stack of books.

I'd expected smart stuff like biographies and memoirs, maybe some historical fiction about World War Two. Ryder seemed like one of those guys. But what I found was fiction —spies and espionage, thrillers, mysteries, action and adventure, and toward the bottom of the stack? Romance. My brows popped and a grin spread across my face.

Ryder reads *romance*? Dark, brooding, manly Ryder

reads romance? And not just any romance, but romantic suspense.

I stifled a laugh, flipping through a paperback with a shirtless man on the cover. I felt like I'd uncovered his deepest, darkest secret. Little did I know what the day had in store for me.

Seconds became minutes as I skimmed the book, stopping on a particularly steamy sex scene.

Holy shit.

I imagined Ryder reading it, sitting in the chair and sipping brandy. Then I imagined him as the hero in the scene, me as the woman, as he spread my legs open and devoured me in front of a fire on a snowy night. Warmth pooled in my gut, a rush of tingles below that. Short of breath, I slammed the book closed, heat warming my cheeks.

Good Lord.

I quickly replaced the book into its previous spot at its ninety-degree angle.

Fanning my face, I crossed the room and quietly opened the door, peeking into the hallway. No noise, no lights, no shirtless Ryder. My stomach growled again, for food or man, I wasn't sure.

Best go with food.

I padded quickly down the hall.

Still no lights in the house. I peeked into each room as I passed, half expecting Ryder to jump out with a gun. I scowled at the front door, my previous sleeping spot, then paused and frowned at a missing tile.

The tile I'd slept on the night before was now missing.

What was *I* missing?

Still frowning, I turned and stepped face-first into a rock-hard chest. I squealed, stumbling back, and slammed my hand over my racing heart. "You scared me."

Ryder scanned my wet hair and freshly bathed body with an expression I couldn't quite read. I realized it was the first time he was seeing me without a jacket that hung past my knees. Insecurity swept over me, and I hated that.

Yep, fifteen pounds. Gone.

"I was just going to the kitchen . . . to grab a snack. If that's okay."

"Okay."

Ryder turned and strode into the kitchen. It was the only room with lights on, although barely lit. Dimmable lights, I guessed.

What was his deal with light?

First, the smell hit me. I stopped dead in my tracks, gaping at the bloodbath on the counter.

"Oh my God."

Ryder wiped his hands on a towel and flipped it over his shoulder. In front of him lay dozens of fish bones—the full spinal cord, plus fins, fish guts, and other fish organs. For the grand finale, fish heads. Huge fish heads with long whiskers and beady black eyes stared right at me. The cooler from the fishing boat sat to the side.

"Dinner," he said casually.

"Dinner." Saliva pooled in my mouth, and not the good kind. I fought the urge to cover my nose with my hand. "You caught all this today?"

He dipped his head in response.

"It's . . . a lot."

"I've got a solid route."

"What are they?"

He glanced at me from under his lashes. "Fish."

"I *know* that. I mean, what kind?"

"Catfish."

"Oh." Memories flickered through my head, and suddenly the smell wasn't that bad.

"You like catfish?"

I nodded. "When I was little, my mom and dad would take me to a catfish place on the outskirts of town. It was the only time we ever went out to eat. Once, the beginning of every month, after payday. I hated it at first, but I grew to love it." I smiled. "I think because it was the only quality time I got with my folks. Catfish brought us together."

His gaze stayed on me as he listened intently.

"Can I help?"

"You can take the bones and stuff to the trash."

"Bones and stuff. Stuff being heads and guts." *Ugh.*

Time for redemption. You can do this.

I squared my shoulders and popped my neck from side to side like a wrestler before a fight.

"Trash bags are in the utility closet behind me."

"What about a hazmat suit?"

One corner of his lips lifted. *Dammit*, I wanted to see a full smile. Fifteen pounds gone and a full smile. I wondered which goal would be more difficult to achieve.

I crossed the kitchen and stepped into the utility closet. It was easy to find the bags because the closet was impeccable, clean and organized by shape and color. The man would have a coronary if he saw my closet. I pulled out a black bag, careful not to move the box from its designated spot, and then made my way back to the island.

Clearing my throat, I stared down at the blood and gore.

My gaze lifted and met his. I got the feeling this was some sort of test. Never was good at tests.

"Okay, here we go." I pulled back my wet hair with the

rubber band around my wrist, and after a quick inhale, I dove in.

A chorus of screams rang out in my head as I scooped the icy flesh and bones into the bag, goo sliding between my fingers and under my fingernails. My mouth went bone dry —pun unintended—as I reached for the first head.

No, no, don't do it! I imagined the fish screaming as I gingerly grasped its head.

The slippery son of a bitch slid from my fingertips, shooting across the counter. Blood splattered as the head hit the floor and bounced a few times. I released the girliest scream ever, dancing on my tiptoes.

Pick it up, pick it up, pick it up . . .

I swooped down, grabbed the head, and gagged. Not cute, little playful gags. Guttural gags.

"Jesus, Louise." Ryder dropped the knife onto the counter.

"No." Breathing through my mouth, I groaned in the most masculine voice I'd ever heard come out of me. "I've got this."

He watched me in disgusted awe as I shoveled the rest of the heads into the bag, gagging profusely. I spun the top in a twist and extended my arms, holding it out in front of me as I bounced on my toes.

"Where do I put it? Where do I put it?"

"Just . . . the trash. Good Lord. The trash."

I swear I heard him chuckle as I jogged to the trash, shoved the bag inside, and slammed the lid closed. When I turned, he was wiping the blood from the floor—along with the specks of dirt that had fallen off my boots.

"Sorry," I mumbled, grabbing a paper towel and attempting to wipe the caked dirt from my boots. "Damn fish heads. Get me every time."

"It's okay. I'm just glad I didn't decide to leave them on."

"Oh God."

He grinned. Not a full smile, but close.

"Well. What else can I—"

"How about you have a seat?"

"That I can do."

I walked over to the breakfast nook, but instead of sitting, I looked outside into the darkness. Swirls of snow spun in front of the window, reflecting in the light. My gaze shifted to Ryder's reflection in the glass—staring directly at me. At my *ass*.

I blinked. When I turned, his focus quickly shifted back to the fish.

Hmph.

I pulled out a chair from the breakfast nook, the legs squealing across the slate floor, and sat. In silence.

Awkward.

I noticed a highball glass on the counter filled with a few ice cubes and a deep amber liquid. I wasn't much of a whiskey drinker, but I'd give my right arm for anything that involved alcohol at that moment.

"Drink?" he asked, as if he had eyes in the side of his head. Wouldn't put it past him.

"Sure."

"What would you like?"

"What do you have?"

"Everything."

"I'll take it," I said with a laugh.

"The wine cellar's in the basement."

"You have a wine cellar?"

He nodded and slid me a glance. "Sorry. I'm all out of boxed."

Smartass. "Boxed wine isn't that bad, you know."

"Neither is common sense."

"Or manners. Listen, Ryder, I'm not going to apologize for leaving my vehicle and finding my way to your house last night. Yeah, in retrospect, it wasn't the best judgment—or *prudent*, you might say—but news flash, I'm not perfect. And I'm not going to thank you again for helping me. I genuinely appreciate it, and that's the truth. Thank you for giving me shelter last night, and thank you for offering your bed to me tonight. But for the record, I'm not thrilled to be trapped alone with a total stranger who pulled a gun on me."

"You're lucky that's all that happened to you."

"What's that supposed to mean?"

"It means that not only did you put yourself in a dangerous situation, but you were impaired, unlikely to respond with a clear head to any situation that you might have come across."

I jerked my chin to his glass of whiskey. "Those who live in glass houses shouldn't throw stones."

"I like a drink at dinner."

"And you also like judging others, if I had to guess."

"What's that supposed to mean?"

"Uh, 'you smell like a liquor cabinet.' You judged me for having wine last night."

"You did have wine last night."

"Well, apparently you drink too."

"Not stranded—alone—on the side of the road during a snowstorm. Are you aware that drinking lowers your internal body temperature?"

"Tell that to my drenched panties halfway into my hike."

His gaze flicked to my pants. "You were sweating because your liver was working overtime, therefore making you sweat and feel warm. But in reality, your temperature was decreasing."

"Thanks for the science lesson. You learn that in one of your romance novels?"

His brow quirked. "The point, Louise, is that in a situation where hypothermia was a very real possibility, you might as well have stripped out of those drenched panties and hiked naked."

I wasn't sure what I liked most about that sentence. The sound of my name rolling off his tongue, or hearing this six-foot-four-inch stoic mountain man say the word *panties*.

"I'll keep that in mind for the next house I break into. Maybe that would have gotten me an invite to sleep in a bed instead of the floor."

"Only if you could find it."

"You're kind of a jerk, you know that?"

"I'm sorry. Is my king-size bed and soaking tub not up to your standards? I'm sure I could throw a few pieces of duct tape on them to make you feel more at home."

I cocked my hip. "The only person that could feel at home in this house is the devil himself. Now, where's the wine cellar, so I can get *really* drunk and make some more bad decisions?"

"Thanks for the warning. Down the hallway to the right, past the library, at the end of the house. Door's on the left."

He eyed me as I sauntered past, the corners of those lips quirking.

I stomped my way down the hallway, leaving a trail of dirt in my wake. *That'll teach him.*

Pushing through the doorway, I switched on a light that illuminated a steep, curved staircase. I crept downstairs, and at the bottom found an enormous basement with rock walls, a full bar, and a kitchen to the side.

It was the man cave of all man caves. However, like the rest of the house, it was totally bare. It was also ten degrees colder than the rest of the house, which meant my blood would freeze in exactly eight minutes.

I spied a curved archway with ornate rock work. *Bingo.* Inside, the walls were lined with rock shelves holding hundreds—*hundreds*—of wine and liquor bottles. These were no eight-dollar bottles. These bottles were imported, likely hundred-dollar bottles of wine, a few of which I recognized from the top shelf at bars. Half were in different languages.

One caught my eye, decorated in gold ribbons and twine. A French wine, best I could tell. *Expensive.* With a grin, I reached up on tiptoe and plucked it off the shelf.

Don't mind if I do.

Smiling, I danced back up the steps with my prize where the scent of Cajun spices mingled with baking bread. As I walked into the kitchen, Ryder was pulling golden-brown hush puppies from the oven. Catfish sizzled on the stove's grill top.

Hush puppies? I was in love.

He glanced at the bottle in my hand and popped a brow. Yep, definitely expensive, and nope, I didn't care one bit.

"Wineglasses are in the cabinet to my left."

"Thanks." I breezed past him, running my fingertip along the countertop, taking care to spread my germs all over the place. I pulled open the door and retrieved the largest glass I could find, a copper goblet with antler ears shooting out the sides.

Grinning, I lifted the cup. "Is there a sense of humor here that I'm not aware of?"

"Absolutely not. I got it for free with a bottle of whiskey. Not wine." He slid me the side-eye.

"Thanks, Emily Post, but I think it's perfect for wine. Actually . . . wait." I sauntered into the utility closet, found the duct tape, tore off a piece with my teeth, then went back to the kitchen and wrapped it around one of the antlers. "Now it's perfect."

Ryder cleared his throat.

I wanted to yank out the cork with my teeth, but since that wasn't possible, I found a wine opener with the wine-glasses. That chore done, I poured a third of the bottle into the cup and held it up in a toast. Ryder was giving me his full attention now.

"Cheers." I sipped. "Holy *smokes.*"

He nodded, pleased with the reaction, then went back to cooking the filets.

The wine was like nothing I'd ever tasted before, smooth and smoky with a chocolate finish. Not bitter or tart, simply perfection in a bottle. I began to wonder if the gold strings around the neck were real.

I watched him set the first batch of catfish on a cooling rack, then drop a few more into the pan.

"Are you sure I can't help with anything?"

"Yes."

"Okay." I didn't sit but stayed next to the breakfast nook, which was where I felt like he wanted me.

An energy seemed to bounce between us now that I couldn't quite put my finger on.

I took another gulp. "Where did you learn to cook?"

"I feed myself."

"That doesn't answer the question."

"When you feed yourself, you cook."

"Hush puppies and catfish from scratch isn't just feeding yourself. I don't know how to make either of those things. Shocker, I know."

"Well, you might want to sit down for this, Louise, because you're about to watch me make a salad from scratch."

"*That* I can do." I set down the wine and stepped over to the kitchen, eager to do something. I turned on the faucet. "Don't worry, I'll wash my hands *real* good for you. And I'm up to date on all my vaccines."

"It's fine. I can handle it."

"Let me help. What's wrong with you?"

I wiped my hands on the towel, watching him. What an interesting creature he was.

I pulled open the refrigerator door. "Whoa . . ."

Much like the utility closet, the refrigerator was spotless and organized by size and shape, but it was the fact that everything appeared to be homemade or harvested that made my jaw drop. Nothing was factory-packaged with a name brand. The fridge was filled to the brim with stacks of glass containers, plastic containers, and jugs of liquid.

"Where do you get all this food?"

"Like I said, I feed myself."

"How?"

"My land."

"All this comes from your land?"

"Did you sleep through Agri in high school?"

"I slept through a lot of things in high school."

He grabbed his whiskey and sipped.

"So, you hunt and fish for all your food?"

"And farm. Do you understand how refrigerators work?"

I realized I was standing there with the door open. Rolling my eyes, I muttered, "It's not like there's a bunch of heat getting in."

"What was that?"

"Nothing."

"Good. If you really want to help, grab the lettuce, tomato, cucumbers, and peppers."

I piled the ingredients in my arms. "I'm assuming you grew this stuff?"

"I have a greenhouse."

I dumped them onto the counter, kicking the fridge door closed with my boot. "Are you some sort of survivalist or something? Where are your bowls?"

"No. Cabinet next to the wineglasses."

I grabbed a knife and a cutting board, and began chopping the salad.

The oven dinged.

"I've never had baked hush puppies before."

"They're healthier."

"But are they as good?"

"I'm on pins and needles for your review, Louise."

I grinned. "I'll bet you are. I tried the organic thing once. Didn't stick." I pinched the fat around my stomach and jiggled it.

"Try growing the food yourself. There's pride in it. Makes it taste better."

"Okay, but that only gets me fruits and veggies. You saw how I handled fish heads."

"There used to be a great meat market in town. You should check it out while you're here. They have catfish too. You could stock up and freeze it."

"Where is it?"

"Used to be off the square."

"Used to be?"

"Not sure if it's still there."

"Don't you ever go into town?"

"No."

With that single word, the conversation died.

A few minutes passed as I made the salad and Ryder finished grilling the fish. As I worked, I inventoried everything I knew about him.

Antisocial hermit? *Check.* Jerk? *Check.* Arrogant? *Check.*

The guy appeared to be a minimalist living off his land, with no furniture, electronics, or clothes. Yet he appeared to indulge in luxuries such as a bed to rival the queen of England's, a wine cellar to rival Mel Gibson's, and a million-dollar house.

Nothing about Ryder added up.

I added the last of the cucumber slices to the salad. "Done."

"Good. Sit."

"You're welcome."

He rearranged my salad, not pleased with my toss. Next, he plated the fried catfish and hush puppies. One by one, he brought the plates over, including a side dish with sliced lemons. Catfish wasn't catfish without lemons.

Lastly, he placed a glass jar on the table. "Lemon vinaigrette for the salad."

"Homemade?"

"Yes, ma'am."

Ma'am. I stared at him a moment. There appeared to be little flashes of chivalry in the man, buried deep inside as if he'd either intentionally pushed the manners away, or had simply fallen out of practice.

Ryder didn't serve me. Instead, he slipped an empty plate and silverware in front of me.

When he nodded for me to go ahead, I loaded my plate with a third of the amount I really wanted. He, on the other hand, loaded his to the rim.

Leaving me at the table, Ryder took his plate to the counter, leaned against it, and dug in. *Message received.* And just as well, because now I didn't have to worry about him judging how much I ate or how much I drank.

I gulped my wine and bit into a hush puppy. When I looked up, he was eyeing me over his whiskey.

"Okay," I mumbled around chewing. "That's damn good." It was. No lie.

"Told you."

I grabbed a lemon slice and squeezed it on my fish. This also seemed to please him. The fish was delicious, light and flavorful.

A few minutes passed while we ate in silence. Ryder was a hell of a cook. I noticed that he ate slowly, as if savoring each bite. This surprised me, but worked to my favor as I slipped seconds onto my plate without him noticing.

He even used a napkin.

"What kind of wine is this?" I asked, the buzz beginning to kick in.

"A fifteen-hundred-dollar one."

"*What?* You let me drink a fifteen-hundred-dollar bottle of wine with river fish?"

"Don't insult my fish."

"You should have said something. Jeez, I feel terrible."

"You should. Catfish are some of the best fish to grill."

"I meant about the wine. I didn't realize I'd grabbed the most expensive bottle."

"You didn't. The row above is the twenty-K bottles."

"You have twenty-thousand-dollar bottles of wine?"

"Those are reserved for crawdad legs," he deadpanned.

I laughed. "Can I ask you something?"

"You already have."

"You said you've been here for almost two years, right?"

His only response was to pop a hush puppy into his mouth.

"What's with the lack of furniture?"

His Adam's apple bobbed as he chewed and then swallowed deeply. Finally, he said, "I like my space."

"Why?"

He picked up his drink and drained the contents. It was the first time I saw something other than cool confidence in the guy. He was immediately uncomfortable.

"And why no TVs?" I asked.

"I don't like background noise."

"So keep them off. Don't you care to watch the news? Check it from time to time, at least?"

"I despise the news."

A moment stretched out. He caught me staring at him and began to eat faster.

I drained my wine.

"Okay. One more question. I'd like to know what it is about me that bothers you so much."

He narrowed his eyes, his head tilting to the side. "My turn to ask the questions, Miss Sloane. I'd like to know what brought you to Berry Springs in the middle of a snowstorm."

15

LOUISE

I grabbed the wine bottle and poured myself another glass.

"What brought me to Berry Springs in the middle of a snowstorm? An eighteen-year-old girl named Kara Meyers."

"The girl who went missing and was found in the woods."

"You know about that?"

He nodded.

"How? You don't even have a TV."

"Small town."

"You don't go into town."

"My brother, a former detective, visits occasionally. Was she your sister?"

"No."

"Relative?" he asked.

"Not really."

"Not really?"

I began spinning the antler mug between my fingers. "Kara lived with me for almost a year."

"When?"

"A couple years ago. She was sixteen and had recently gotten her license."

"Did her mom kick her out?"

"No. No, it wasn't that. Her home life wasn't a good environment . . . and I remember being so proud of her for realizing that at such an influential time in her life."

"What was wrong with her folks?"

"Her mom was a drug addict. Coke, heroin, you name it. Her dad was in prison; I'm not sure she ever met him. Her mom had a different guy every night."

"That's extremely careless of her mother."

"Tell me about it. Child protective services had been to the house three times that I know of, but nothing was ever done. A common story, by the way. Anyway, I just . . . became her friend. She was hesitant to open up at first, but after time, she started to relax. No one knew she was living with me. No one knows even today. She didn't want it to get out because she was embarrassed. Embarrassed that she didn't have a solid home life and had to crash at someone else's house to survive."

A sad smile crossed my face. "She was a good cook, like you. She cooked every night. It became a thing. We'd go to the grocery store together, pick out the food, and she'd cook while I pretended to help. We'd play music. It was fun. I tried to introduce her to new hobbies, things she could focus on. Build her confidence. Before I knew it, she'd become like a sister to me. She . . ." I felt the sting of tears and sucked them back. "She had a lot going for her despite the trouble she got in. I could see it, you know? The good in her. Deep down, she was good."

Something flashed in his eyes.

"I still have pictures of her, in an apron, cooking brownies in my tiny kitchen. She was happy. Hopeful. Light.

You could see it written all over her." I shook my head. "So tragic."

"Were you the one who found her?"

"Wow. Gossip really does spread quickly. I thought I knew small-town gossip until I came to Berry Springs."

"Why do you think I live all the way out here?"

"I get it."

"Why did she come to you?"

"When she ran away?"

"Yeah. What's the connection?"

I explained the Sunshine Club to him. "The program would set up the kids with a mentor to help keep them on the right path and give them insight into life that didn't revolve around chaos. Someone to talk to other than what was, in most cases, an abusive mother or father."

Snorting, I said, "Yeah, I know, they let *me* in the program."

I forced a laugh, but it didn't feel funny. I'd questioned my role in the program a million times over the last few days. The girl who'd been paired with Lou Sloane was found rotting in the woods. Didn't bode well for the mentor, did it? The guilt was overwhelming. My self-doubt at an all-time high.

"You're too hard on yourself," Ryder said.

"I always have been." I inadvertently looked down at my body. *That damn fifteen pounds.*

"Stop."

"Why?"

"You're beautiful." He said it so matter-of-factly that it didn't feel like a come-on, or even a compliment. Like it was a simple fact that I needed to accept.

"Thank you."

"Look at me," he said, and my gaze lifted. "You're beautiful. But you've got terrible judgment."

This time, I laughed. "Wow, you're one with the compliments, aren't you?"

"You don't think things through. If I had to guess, you move from one thing to the next without giving it full commitment or thought. You're impulsive and reckless. You need to fix this."

"Oh, well, thanks, Dr. Ryder. Anything else you'd like to diagnose from your high horse in the clouds?"

"Try routine. Structure. Make a list. Tackle the things you hate most about your life, or the things you worry about the most. Start there."

"You mean like color-coordinating my utility closet?"

He ignored the dig. "It will help, trust me. You just need someone to kick you in the ass. Kind of like you were doing for Kara."

I stilled, the words settling in my stomach like a greasy meal. I'd never had someone try to better me, call me out on my faults, take me to the carpet, so to speak.

My mom and dad were good parents. I had a roof over my head and food in my stomach, but that was about it. They let me figure out life on my own. I'd never had someone care enough about me to try to better me.

"You still haven't told me why you're here," he asked.

The conversation was giving me whiplash.

"A few months after Kara's seventeenth birthday, she told me she was going back home. Give living with her mom another shot. I think she wanted to try to help her mom. I didn't want her to leave, but I had to let her go. Kara wasn't mine, wasn't my family, and I couldn't make her stay. To this day, I wonder if I would have demanded she stay with me, if she would still be alive." I took another sip, noticing a slight tremble in my hand. "Anyway, she packed up and left the next day. I cried. And I'm not a crier, believe it or not."

"I believe it."

"Then I stopped hearing from her. I'd text but she wouldn't respond. I didn't want to press. Next thing I knew, she'd gotten arrested for drunk driving. She'd found the wrong crowd. Boys, drinking, drugs . . . that was the rumor, anyway. I hadn't heard from her in over a year when I got the call from a Berry Springs detective asking if I'd heard from her. That's when I found out she was missing. The next day, a friend of mine, Miles, and I drove up to join the search. Met two others from Ponco a few days later, Austin and Margie. Then I found her."

I picked up my wine, sloshing it as I sipped. A few drops dripped onto my sweatshirt. I didn't care.

"She was murdered. Her body dumped in the woods for the animals to eat. And the worst part is that the cops aren't giving the case their full effort. Kara has a bad reputation and is from a family with a history with the police. The cops don't care. They want it to go away."

"That's a big statement."

"It is. And it's bullshit. She's nothing but an out-of-town drifter to them. Not important. The bastard that killed her is still out there, and I get the vibe the cops are on to bigger and better things."

"Why are you so sure she was murdered?"

"It's the only thing that makes sense. She came to Berry Springs to meet someone to go camping. No one knows who that person is. And I think that person killed her."

"What about boyfriends? Do you know anyone she was hanging out with?"

"No boyfriends. I spoke with a few of her friends."

"Bet the cops liked that."

I laughed. "Let's just say you're not the only one annoyed by my presence. Anyway, Kara didn't have any boyfriends, but a lot of 'male friends,' if you catch my drift. I'm assuming they've been interviewed."

"Have they retraced her last twenty-four hours?"

"You mean have I, because who knows what *they've* done? I know that Kara intended to go camping, and also to visit that famous haunted house, Hollow Hill. And let me tell you, that place is creepy."

"You went?"

"Yep. And to every campground in the area. I wanted to personally retrace her steps. Have you been?"

"A few times when I was a kid. Not recently. It's not a common place for thrill seekers anymore."

I heaved out a breath. "Well, I've been trying to help in any way I can. Do anything to find her."

"You feel like it's your responsibility. It's personal."

"I'm the only one with a personal connection with her who's searching. I'm the closest thing to family she has. Her mom doesn't care. I'm the only one who will press the cops to keep going. So, yes, I do feel responsible. I even involved a private investigation firm."

Ryder's fork froze in midair, halfway to his mouth. "Which one?"

"A local firm I overheard about at the diner. Astor Stone, Inc."

He stilled. "You went to Astor Stone?"

I nodded. "Figured between them and the cops, Kara would have her best shot at getting justice. I'm not stopping until she does, Ryder."

"Who did you see there?" he asked, a sudden sharpness to his tone.

"A bunch of beefed-up rednecks."

"Did they agree to help you?"

"They said, verbatim, they'd 'look into it.' They're supposed to send me an email before they get started."

"So, what?" he asked, irritation thick in his tone. "You're going to camp out in Berry Springs and keep lighting a fire under the PD's ass until they find the guy?"

"Yes."

"Not smart, Louise."

"Why? And who are you to judge my decisions? Kara deserves justice, and I—"

"Have you heard of the String Strangler?"

My gut clenched. "Yes. A serial killer who rapes and tortures young at-risk girls before strangling them to death. I know all about the String—"

"Kara's cause of death was strangulation with a thin ligature. She was also raped and beaten."

I gaped at him. "How do you know this?"

"Her autopsy began this morning. My brother spoke with the detective on the case. He stopped by before I went fishing and updated me."

"Oh my God." I put my hand over my heart. "I remember noticing a mark around her neck, on the skin that wasn't ripped away, anyway. I remember because I thought she was wearing a choker necklace . . . So she was definitely murdered. It's proven now."

He nodded. "The ME also suggested she was a chronic drug abuser, but toxicology tests will confirm that."

My heart sank. Although I wasn't surprised, hearing it confirmed still stung. "Will the test confirm if she was using the night she died?"

"I think the assumption is that she was."

"Hang on," I said, my wheels turning. "So if she was partying right before she died, that means whoever she was camping with spent time with her. Maybe wined and dined her, so to speak." I popped my fist on the table. "She met him somewhere. Where? He invited her camping, got her drunk and high, won her trust, then went in for the kill."

Ryder nodded.

"Why is that somehow creepier than just being snatched off the street? Being tricked first . . ."

"A woman being snatched off the street screams and fights, but a woman having a good time is blindsided. Easier to incapacitate. Kind of like a desperate woman stranded on the side of the road."

My blood chilled at the thought that the String Strangler could have driven up on me.

"I need you to be—you need to be more careful, Louise. The Strangler has killed five women the authorities know of, his confidence and skill building with each one. And there you are, Louise the Punisher, bulldozing your way into a case that possibly links to him. Getting stranded on the side of the road, breaking into strangers' houses. The Strangler outsmarts these women. He's smart. Determined."

"He has an ego."

"I believe so, yes."

"Not all of his cases are close to Berry Springs, right? I read his attacks are within a hundred-mile radius."

"Right. Some have been around Berry Springs. One was in Missouri, and one in Oklahoma."

"So he travels to pick his victims."

"Or finds them on the internet."

"I read somewhere that he's believed to be a regular joe. Someone with a normal job, possibly doesn't have a record."

Ryder shook his head. "But he's not. My guess is he's got a job that requires some sort of skill that he applies to his other work."

"Other work, meaning his victims."

"Right. His job requires him to think and solve problems. It's likely a regimented job with structure and routine. This guy isn't a grocery clerk or a carpenter."

"Hang on." I held up my hand. "Does this mean the cops will involve the FBI? If they suspect the Strangler is involved?"

"My assumption would be yes, but the official autopsy isn't complete."

"When will it be?"

"Maybe now, maybe tomorrow."

"Call your brother."

"He's on his honeymoon. Left two hours ago."

I sat up straighter, relieved that there might be some movement in the case. "Well, maybe I can—"

"No, you can't, and you won't. Louise, you are aggressively inserting yourself into an investigation that potentially involves a serial killer. A *rapist*." Ryder spat out the words with venom, the most emotion I'd seen from him. "You need to let the cops handle this. Think, Louise. *Think*."

He started to take another bite but dropped the fork on his plate with a scowl. He set the plate on the counter and began cleaning up with swift, jerky movements.

Dinner was over.

I cleared the table, stacking everything on the counter while he turned on the faucet in the sink. "Can I help?"

"No."

I cleared my throat and took a step back. "You won't have to worry about all my bad judgment soon. I'll find a place to stay tomorrow."

His jaw clenched, a flush coloring his neck. He was so *mad* all of a sudden.

I picked up my wine from the table. "Well, good night. Thank you for everything."

When he didn't respond, I turned and retreated to the master bedroom.

As I kicked the door shut behind me, I heard the click of the heater turning on.

16

LOUISE

I shot up in bed, frantically blinking the grogginess away. My head spun as I tried to figure out where I was. I rubbed the gunk from my eyes, and the room began to take shape . . . along with my memories.

Ryder.

"You're beautiful. But you've got terrible judgment."

You're beautiful . . .

I pulled my legs into a crisscross and swiped the drool from my chin as I looked out the window.

The fields beyond the windows were still blanketed with snow, the mountains solid white. More snow had fallen overnight, maybe as much as a foot. The sun was peeking out from behind big white clouds. In the distance beyond them hovered more menacing gray clouds. I wondered if we'd be able to make it down the driveway.

God willing.

I blew out a breath and relaxed back into the pillows, taking a moment to get my bearings. I hadn't slept that hard since eighth-grade church camp. I also hadn't gone to bed fantasizing about a man since then either. Well, a boy, back in the day. His name was Gerry, with a G. He played the flute.

My hand swept over the down comforter as I imagined Ryder in the bed. He probably filled it, while I was swimming in it. I stretched my arms over my head and popped my neck. I could definitely get used to the bed.

The man was an entirely different story.

A crackle pulled my attention to the fireplace, where a fire was roaring.

I stilled. I'd gone to sleep with a buzz, but I was ninety-nine percent sure I didn't start that fire. Which meant Ryder had. Which meant he'd been in the room while I was passed out and drooling like a baby.

Christ. Can the guy give me a break?

I ripped off the covers, searching the walls for a clock. None, of course, because Ryder probably woke up with the sun. With perfect hair and perfect breath.

Wearing a long nightshirt that read save the winos, I padded to the closet, fumbled through my bag, and pulled out my phone. *Still no reception.*

Assuming Ryder didn't have any either, this meant that calling either Miles, or Frankie at Frankie's Auto Shop, or every hotel in the area wasn't happening.

Frustrated, I crawled back into bed.

"What?" I gasped, embarrassment shooting up my neck like a torch when I woke up again and checked the time on my phone. Eleven forty-four a.m.

Holy crap. I'd slept until noon—in someone else's house.

Noon? What am I, a freaking college kid?

I couldn't remember the last time I'd slept until noon.

Not even at church camp. I groaned, rolling my head. A *lazy* drunk. Was there anything worse? Two points for the rude houseguest.

Resigned to the fact that there was absolutely no redemption for me now in the eyes of the Man, I rolled out of bed and shuffled into the bathroom.

I did what I could with my hair, wetting it again and scrunching. Frowning at my reflection, I clipped back the damn bangs. I brushed my teeth and skipped the makeup because, at that point, what did it even matter? I yanked on the same jeans I'd worn the day before, along with a gray Hanes sweatshirt I'd picked up in the discount section of Walmart. Bypassing my boots, I tugged on a pair of socks.

By that time, I was feeling the beginnings of a headache from being deprived of my morning coffee addiction. I pushed open the bedroom door, peeked out, and listened.

Nothing.

Biting my lip, I quietly padded down the hallway. The first thing I noticed was how warm the house was. Ryder had left on the heater for me after turning it on last night. It felt like a small victory, and somewhere deep down inside, approval.

The house looked different in the sunlight, still cold and unwelcoming, but open and free. I imagined myself running naked through the wide hallways with earbuds in my ears and a tumbler of wine in my hand, screaming the lyrics to the latest Lady Gaga song. I was sure Ryder never did anything like that.

Shame.

I glanced in each room as I passed by, looking for the Man. *No dice.* The house appeared to be vacant. Pleased by this, I relaxed my shoulders as I walked through the living room, admiring the breathtaking view outside.

I didn't have to search far for the coffee and fixings. True to form, Ryder had everything organized and stacked perfectly in a cabinet above a simple coffee machine. A few minutes later, I leaned against the counter and sipped fresh —organic—coffee.

It was so quiet, I couldn't stand it. I wanted to scream at the top of my lungs—*really* dirty curse words—simply to hear them echo off the walls. How could someone live in such silence? Why would they want to?

I scanned the kitchen, taking in every inch and corner. The minimalism, the cleanliness, the organization. I inwardly laughed, imagining him in my apartment.

Then I noticed a small black device in the corner. A phone. Ryder had a landline and hadn't even told me or offered it to me.

I hurried over and picked it up—*yep, dial tone*—then jogged back to my room and retrieved my cell phone. I wasn't someone who memorized phone numbers.

I dialed Miles. *No answer.* I tried again. *No answer.* I tried one more time and left a voice mail. Next, I tried Margie with the same result.

What the hell are they doing? I assumed they were as snowed in as I was.

I called Shadow Creek Resort, where I was informed that there was still no vacancy, but they'd call immediately when something opened up.

Lastly, I tried Austin's number.

"Hello?"

"Hey, Austin, it's Louise."

"Hey. You make it home all right?"

"No, I left a voice mail yesterday with Miles. From a number at Shadow Creek Resort. He didn't tell you?"

"Guess not. You all right?"

"Yes. Well, no. I slid off the road and banged up my car on the way to the hotel. I had to crash at someone's house."

"Someone's house?"

"A friend." I lied because I didn't want to rehash the story of me hiking through a snowstorm and breaking into a stranger's house.

"Okay. How's the beast?"

"Not good. Getting it towed today. Hopefully."

"So, are you at the resort now?"

"No, they're booked. I'm still staying with my friend."

"You all right? You sound kinda wound up."

"Yeah, yeah, I'm fine. My friend's place is a castle. Plenty of room. I call it the castle on the hill. It's on the opposite side of the mountain from the hotel, down county road 2355, not far at all." I was rambling. I ramble when I lie.

"Okay, well, glad you're all right. We're still snowed in here at the Towering Pines Inn."

"I assumed. I tried to call Miles. Where is he?"

"Not sure."

"I tried Margie too." When Austin didn't respond, I asked, "Do you know where she is?"

"Nope."

"Did you go to their rooms today?"

"Yeah, well, I tried. Knocked. No answer."

"Is your truck still there?"

"Yep."

"Then they didn't leave in it, and they don't have another vehicle so they couldn't have gone far." I frowned. "When was the last time you saw them?"

"Can't remember."

Really?

"Well, would you mind telling Miles everything I just told you? I don't have reception out here. If he can catch a ride with you guys back home as soon as the roads clear, that would be great. I'm not sure how long it will take to fix my car."

"Will do."

An unease settled in my stomach. I wasn't sure why.

"Okay. Thanks, Austin. Stay safe."

"You too."

I replaced the phone on the charger.

Where would Miles and Margie go in this weather? Perhaps hooking up somewhere? Wouldn't surprise me. Everyone knows pastors' kids can get wild, and who can resist Miles's Cool Water cologne?

I sipped my coffee and settled against the counter again. My gaze landed on the library, my thoughts going to that secret door I'd found after breaking in.

Feeling the buzz from the caffeine, I decided to explore.

First, I searched for the Man because I didn't care to start the day with another pistol to the neck. After that fruitless search, I assumed he was doing cowboy stuff outside, so I made my way to the library.

Unlike the other rooms in the house, the sun seemed to hide from this one, dissolving in shadows that stretched to every corner. The room was also a few degrees colder than the rest of the house. I hugged myself, rubbing my arms as I slowly walked across the floor, admiring the books. Thousands and thousands of books.

I stopped in the middle of the room, feeling like a speck in the ocean. I couldn't remember where I'd found the secret door, so I decided to start from the right and work my way around.

An hour had gone by with me trailing my fingers along the shelves, getting lost in reading the titles on the leather bindings, alphabetized by section and dust-free. The library had everything from encyclopedias to biographies of dead dudes I'd never heard of, to educational books, to thrillers.

Somewhere around the letter R, I hit the jackpot. My finger bounced over a crack in the shelf, and my heart skipped a beat.

I looked over my shoulder, then out the window, before refocusing on the shelf with the secret door. I traced my finger along the crack. It was definitely a door, but not a large one. Ryder would have to crawl to get inside, which made me think it wasn't so much a room as a hidey-hole, perhaps.

What is Ryder hiding?

I ran my finger under each shelf, looking for a shiny red button that screamed push here. No luck. I ran my finger along the outline of the door again. No button, switch, or flap. No antique candleholder that doubled as a doorknob. Nothing, and this only made my resolve stronger.

After another glance over my shoulder, I began pulling the books from the case, tossing them on the floor until the stack reached my knees. Once the shelves in that area were bare, I ran my hand along the dark, cold wood until my finger slid over a dip with a tiny hole. Impossible to see unless you were feeling for it. Still, no button.

Chewing on my lower lip, I scanned the room for something long and sharp that I could jab inside it. After finding nothing, I sprinted back to my room, grabbed a bobby pin and the flashlight from my purse, and ran back.

I jabbed the pin into the hole and—*click.* The door popped open slightly. I straightened and stepped back, my heart pounding as I wondered what I was about to discover.

Stolen cash? Gold? Guns?

Drugs?

A stack of human skulls?

A pile of dead puppies?

Did I want to see?

Yes.

My knees popped as I squatted down. Clutching the flashlight between my teeth, I slowly pulled open the small door.

The flashlight illuminated a black-walled compartment that resembled the inside of a large safe. I guessed it was about five feet square. Not quite tall enough to stand up in, but enough to hunker down. Stacks of small storage bins lined the back wall. Gun cases sat in front, and to the left, a large metal box.

No dead bodies. No dead puppies.

I lowered to my hands and knees and, ignoring the warning bells in my head, crawled into the room.

It smelled like leather, oil, and money.

After propping the flashlight in the corner, I squatted in front of the box that drew my attention the most, the metal one. I opened the lid and my jaw dropped.

Stacks and stacks—*and stacks*—of bound hundred-dollar bills lay in perfect rows with *$10,000* printed on the bindings. I counted ten stacks with ten bundles in each stack. One million dollars. In *cash.*

I'm not going to lie. For a solid minute, I considered filling my duffel and making a run for it. But I figured I'd only get halfway down the driveway before slipping and breaking an ankle, getting frozen in place by hypothermia, or finally catching that bullet from Ryder, slowly dying while hundred-dollar bills rained down on me.

An epic ending to my not-so-epic life, but I passed.

I'd closed the lid and was shifting to the storage bins when—

Click.

The secret door shut behind me with a deep suction-like sound.

"No, no, no, no, no!" I crawled across the safe and desperately grabbed at the door, but there was no handle on the inside.

"Shit! Shit, shit, shit, *shit.*"

Frantic, I scanned the walls for another exit. There was nothing, of course.

My pulse roaring in my ears, I pressed my back against the wall, breathing in short, quick pants. Knowing I was on the verge of a panic attack, I closed my eyes, took a deep breath, then another. Once I felt my heart rate dip below heart-attack level, I opened my eyes.

Ryder would find me; I had no doubt about that. It was hard to miss stacks of books scattered on the floor of a pristine, alphabetized library.

While that thought calmed me a bit, I wasn't sure how long it would be until he realized I wasn't in my room. Tomorrow?

Then another terrifying thought grabbed hold of me. *Is the safe airtight?*

Followed by another. *How long will I have oxygen?*

But worse than those thoughts was the realization that I had to pee. I groaned and bounced the back of my head against the wall.

Dammit, Lou. Why am I always so . . . me?

What would Ryder do once he found me, locked in his hidey-hole? I imagined the extent of damage would equal the depths of secrets hidden in this room.

So . . . let's find out, shall we?

I took a deep breath, repositioned the flashlight, and crab-walked over to the plastic bins, already devising a blackmail plan in my head.

One bin was filled with stacks of passports, each containing a different name, address, and other information, but all featured Ryder's brooding face. He looked a little different on each ID. Darker skin, lighter skin, long hair, short hair, beard, no beard. Black eyes, blue eyes. There were a few where he appeared to have a fake nose, and in one, lifted cheekbones.

Holy shit.

Among the passports were driver's licenses to match, concealed-carry licenses, stacks of foreign money, credit cards, and keys.

The Man, whose house I was trapped in, had eleven separate identities.

Eleven.

Goose bumps prickled my skin as I flipped through the stamps on the passports.

Egypt
Iran
Russia
Sudan
Kenya
Somalia
Mali
Greece
Spain
Morocco

The stamps went on and on, but I noticed all were dated no later than twelve years ago. There wasn't a single stamp beyond then. Ryder's international travel seemed to have stopped abruptly.

I set that box aside and opened the next. This one contained dozens of files, most containing reports that I didn't understand, some in foreign languages. Was Ryder multilingual? Many of the documents appeared to be official, with stamped letterheads and logos at the top.

One caught my attention—

Astor Stone, Inc.

My brows popped up. Ryder was involved with the private investigation company?

As I flipped through the papers, I realized that the work Astor Stone, Inc. did went well beyond US borders, and appeared to be much more than a run-of-the-mill private investigation firm like its letterhead stated.

Another file contained groups of stapled photos, each featuring a different "target," per the label. The last photo of each stack was stamped deceased, depicting images of the target dead, bloodied, beaten, or shot between the eyes.

My hands trembled. *What have I gotten myself into?*

I set the box aside and reluctantly picked up another, this one buried in the back. It seemed that secrets in the bins only got worse the deeper they went, so I decided to flip to the final chapter.

This bin was lighter than the others, with only a single folder inside. Anticipation snaked up my spine as I pulled out the papers and stared down at a black-and-white mug shot of Ryder.

Inmate number 730576
Forrest City Federal Prison
Jagger, Ryder T.

I gasped.

I knew the name. Dear God, I knew that name. Everyone knew the name. I realized I hadn't even bothered asking Ryder what his last name was—I would have known then.

And I would have run.

It happened twelve years ago. The story dominated state-wide headlines for weeks and had even made national news.

Ryder Jagger brutally beat and murdered a nineteen-year-old man.

I couldn't believe I didn't put it together, but it was so long ago.

The story was so shocking that it quickly became sensationalized, the details leaking to the public because of the sheer brutality of the crime. Rumor was Ryder had waited outside of Leon Ortiz's house for days, waiting for him to return from what would be his last camping trip. Once Ortiz got out of his truck, Ryder jumped him, and using nothing but his fists, beat Ortiz so badly, he broke eight bones and cracked Ortiz's skull.

The man's face was so unrecognizable, they had to use his fingerprints to identify him. But the beating wasn't what killed Ortiz. Before he fell unconscious, Ryder cut off his balls with a rusty switchblade. The autopsy confirmed Ortiz was awake during this. Then Ryder shoved Ortiz's balls down his throat, plugging his nose while he choked on them. And for the grand finale, while Ortiz gagged on his own balls, Ryder strangled him to death.

Ryder was found hours later with Ortiz's blood all over his face and body, lying on a cliff not far from the scene, his legs dangling off the side as he stared up at the sky.

The reason why Ryder killed the man was never released, but it didn't matter. The public deemed Ryder an evil monster who should be locked away from society.

The mug shot slipped from my fingers and fluttered to the floor.

I covered my mouth. *Do not puke, do not puke, do not puke . . .*

I was trapped in a house with a psychopath. Had slept under his roof for two nights.

Then all my thoughts suddenly coalesced into a single epiphany.

Kara was eighteen when she was brutally beaten and murdered. And she was strangled.

Could Ryder have killed her too?

I looked at the bin with the passports and the money.

Could Ryder *be the String Strangler?*

An icy chill swept over my skin. In my gut, I didn't believe it. I felt safe with Ryder. Or maybe I just didn't want to believe it.

But one thing was for sure. Ryder had many secrets.

And I was *not* going to be the next.

With that thought, I crawled to the gun cases and began unloading them one by one.

17

LOUISE

The flashlight—the only light I had—dimmed to a dull orange somewhere between the third and fourth hour of my being locked in the safe. I figured I had another hour before I was left in complete darkness.

On the upside, I'd managed not to wet myself, although that miraculous well of strength only had another hour, at most. I also still had oxygen. I wondered, though, was that an upside? Or would it be better to simply drift away in an unconscious state, as opposed to being strangled to death?

I'd had three legitimate panic attacks as I waited for Ryder, the convicted murderer, to find me in his secret room. It was what I imagined waiting on death row felt like.

I'd pushed aside the gut feeling that Ryder was *not* the devil, allowed myself to get consumed by fear, and fully convinced myself he was Kara's murderer. That Ryder T. Jagger was the String Strangler himself.

Perhaps he preyed on young, helpless victims. Was that why he offered to help me? Was he only waiting for the right time to strike?

Then a more unsettling thought crossed my mind.

Was I at risk in my own way? In a less obvious way? In an I-apparently-can't-make-a-single-good-decision kind of way?

I'd pondered that thought for a good hour, thinking of my life. My boring, unfulfilling life, and all the mistakes I'd made in it. I wondered if all my spontaneous, shortsighted decisions were the cause of my discontent.

And I wondered if that life were about to end.

I'd never fired a gun before, but I passed the time checking them out—pistols and rifles, one a really scary-looking one with cool sights. Then I fiddled with bullets, figuring out how to load each gun, assuming I was doing it correctly. I wondered how many men, or women, Ryder had killed with these guns.

I didn't go through any more of the folders. I couldn't. I'd seen enough to know that I was dealing with someone who wasn't who they appeared to be. Someone capable of lies, manipulation, and murder.

And I was trapped in his fucking library.

My head snapped toward the sound of books being shuffled outside the door.

He'd found me.

It's time.

I whimpered, blinking away the tears threatening to creep up. Not tears of sadness . . . tears of terror.

The String Strangler had found me.

I gripped the gun I'd chosen for our little reunion, a small pistol with big bullets. It was the only gun I felt like I could manage. Aiming at the door, I silently asked for forgiveness for my sins.

After a faint click, the door slowly opened.

"Stop." My voice shook along with the barrel I had pointed at Ryder's face.

He was squatting, sitting back on his haunches. Melting snow covered his dark hair and the shoulders of his plaid button-up. Mud spattered his jeans and boots. His brows drew together in confusion—a seemingly natural response to a gun in his face.

Before I could take another breath, he moved like a rattlesnake with lightning-quick strikes. The gun was slapped from my hand, and a fist wrapped around the collar of my sweatshirt. He dragged me out kicking and screaming.

I clawed at his forearms. Once my body was out of the secret room, I twisted and bucked, managing to catch him somewhere between the legs. His grip loosened with a grunt, and I lunged for the door.

In two seconds flat, I was laid out like a ninety-pound red-shirt freshman, then flipped onto my back, my arms pinned above my head as he straddled me.

"You went snooping."

"You killed Kara!" I spat out the accusation, my chest heaving and legs flailing.

Ryder didn't budge, didn't flinch. "What the hell are you talking about?"

"Kara. My friend. You killed her."

"What the hell gave you that idea?"

"Leon Ortiz. You're a psychotic murdering bastard."

Ryder leaned down, inches from my face. "I didn't kill your friend." His voice was low. Menacing.

"You brutally beat and murdered Ortiz. Strangled him to death. Kara was eighteen, only a year younger than him, also beaten and strangled. I saw everything. Your mug shot and the news clippings."

Ryder's grip around my wrists loosened, but his gaze remained pinned on mine. Finally, I was released, and he pushed off me.

I shot up like a feral cat and bolted out of the room, my socks spinning out on the slate flooring like a cartoon character. Once I got my footing, I sprinted across the living room to the kitchen. I grabbed the cordless phone and fumbled, dropping it. Cursing, I swooped down and clicked it on.

My hands shook wildly as I dialed 9-1—

"Hang up the phone."

I spun around. "I'm calling the police."

Ryder crossed the kitchen in two steps. I was attempting to scramble over the island when his arms wrapped around me, pinning my arms at my sides. He bent me over the counter. The phone dropped to the floor and was crushed to pieces by his boot.

I fought, kicked, and wiggled. Bit his arm until I tasted blood.

"You will not call the police. Do you understand me?" His voice was commanding but eerily calm.

"Yes, I will!" I squeaked like a toddler.

"I didn't kill Kara."

"Liar."

"I don't lie."

"Why should I believe you?"

His groin pressed into my ass. "Because I don't lie."

"But you killed Leon Ortiz, didn't you?"

"Yes, Louise, I did. And I had a damn good reason."

"To kill someone?"

"The world is better without him in it. Trust me."

Trust me.

Did I?

Goddammit, I did. Somewhere deep in my soul, I trusted Ryder.

I stopped fighting against his hold, but his grip didn't

loosen.

"I want to know everything," I said firmly. "I want to know about the fake identities, what you do for Astor Stone. I want to know why you killed Ortiz."

Still holding me from behind, he froze like a statue, not even breathing.

"And let *the fuck* go of me."

The moment he released me, I whipped around and took a step back, my heels hitting the island.

He glowered down at me. "I didn't kill Kara, and I'm not the fucking String Strangler. You can believe me or not. But I want you to make the decision right now, because I'm not going to deal with this bullshit all night."

He stalked to the cabinet and pulled out a glass.

I looked down at the shattered phone on the floor. "You've got a lot of explaining to do."

"To who?"

I crossed the floor and jabbed my finger into his chest. "*Me.* Me, Ryder. The woman who's trapped in your damn house."

"My past is my business." He turned on the faucet and filled the glass with water.

"Your business was splashed all over the freaking news."

"I don't owe you a damn thing, Miss Sloane."

"You owe me common fucking curtesy."

He angrily chugged the water, then turned to me. "You're something else, you know that?"

"You'll hate me even more when I call the cops and tell them about all the passports and guns in that chest."

"Are you threatening me?"

"Yes."

"I wouldn't do that if I were you."

He stared down at me with a look that would send most

men and women running with their tails between their legs. But I wasn't scared. I knew he wouldn't hurt me.

Scare me, though? That was another story.

With a sudden guttural yell, he threw the glass against the wall, shattering it into a million pieces.

"God*dammit*, Louise." He raked his fingers through his hair and began pacing as if gathering himself. Then he looked at me, his eyes wild. "You want courtesy, huh?"

I swallowed the knot in my throat and nodded.

"All right." He jerked open the cabinet and pulled down another glass, filled it with water, and thrust it at me.

"I'd rather have a real drink."

"You'll do water tonight."

I took the glass from him, marched over to the sink, poured it out, and replaced it with the whiskey he'd been drinking the other night.

"You're gonna have to do better than that." I sipped as I leaned against the counter in front of him, eyeing him over the rim of my glass.

Ryder's nostrils flared as his chest rose and fell. Seeming to come to a decision, he plucked the whiskey from my hand, poured it down the drain, and jerked my chin to face him. His hands cupped my face.

My heart lodged in my throat, and before my brain could catch up, his lips were on mine.

Hard, greedy, hungry. Angry kisses as if his brain was telling him not to do it, but his body wasn't listening.

So raw, so intense, there was nothing else to do but give in.

The moment I opened for him, he devoured me as if he couldn't get enough. As if I were the single drop of water in an endless desert.

Fireworks? Mine were like a nuclear bomb. My entire

body tingled, every inch of my skin. Every follicle of hair stood on end. Butterflies erupted in my stomach.

The man could kiss.

With his hands still cupping my face, he leaned back slightly and stared at me. Our chests heaved. When he dropped his hands and took a step back, the heat between us was instantly replaced with ice.

I wanted it all back. The heat. And him.

"How's that?" he growled.

"Not bad." I swallowed hard. "But now I really need that drink."

He retrieved the antler mug, filled it with ice and water, then handed it to me. I was glad I didn't get the whiskey. No telling what I'd do after a buzz at that point.

I chugged, cooling my insides. Ryder watched me closely as if not quite sure how I was going to react to what just happened between us.

I set down the mug and took a deep breath. "Now that we got that out of the way, talk. What's with the fake identities? What's with Astor Stone?"

"Astor Stone is the devil's spawn. I worked for him before I went to prison."

"Astor Stone, Inc. isn't an investigation company."

"Incorrect. It is an investigation company."

"But they don't just follow around cheating spouses or investigate insurance fraud. What exactly does Astor Stone investigate?"

He grabbed the broom and began sweeping up the broken glass and remnants of the phone. "Foreign affairs."

"Okay. What did you do for him?"

"I was an agent. Took orders and implemented those orders."

"Those orders took you overseas?"

"Yes."

"Using fake identities?"

"Yes."

"What's overseas?"

"My targets."

"Elaborate."

"It's confidential."

"Not anymore. And the entire town will know if you don't come clean with me right now. I'm not kidding, Ryder."

"I'm not either."

"*Talk.*"

He propped the broom against the wall. "Dammit, Louise, you come into my house, into my space, and turn everything upside down."

"Didn't seem like you minded it too bad thirty seconds ago."

He took a deep breath, grabbed a dustpan, and swept the glass and phone shards into it. He spoke as he worked.

"Astor Stone is contracted by the US government to run black ops for them. It's all under the guise of a private investigation firm. Stone receives his orders from the DOD, and filters the orders down to his agents, who implement the ops."

"Kinda like James Bond."

"But secret."

"Now I know why the beefy rednecks were laughing at me."

He stopped cold. "They laughed at you?"

"No. I just felt out of place. I could tell what I was asking of them wasn't something they typically did."

"We take occasional local jobs to make it seem legit, but not many. Only a handful of people in the world know what

Astor and his agents do. We operate on foreign soil, cross restricted borders, work with whoever we need to in order to get our mission completed."

"Meaning bad guys? Terrorists?"

"We do whatever we need to do to get the job done. Period."

"Sounds dangerous."

"It is. If any one of us were exposed, if the world knew the US was behind half the things we did, it would cause a catastrophic international incident. World War Three. Not that any of us would be alive to see it."

"How many agents does he have?"

"Currently, three active agents here in the US. You met them all when you went, I'm sure."

I arched a brow. "I expected you to say twenty or something."

"More overseas, but not many. A lot of egos to control."

"How long did you work for him?"

"Years."

"Did you have a cover job?"

"Nope. No time. Working for Astor is constant. I was never home."

"Why did you do it?"

"I loved it. Astor recruited me right out of college. Like you said, it was very James Bond, and I couldn't ignore the lure of it. Paid damn well too. Six-figure bonuses on some successful missions. I joined them, signed my life away, and went through two years of training that I wouldn't wish on another human being. It only made me want it more. I was twenty-two when I took on my first op. Turns out I was a damn good agent."

"Good at killing people?"

"Yes," he said coolly.

"I'm surprised you're telling me all this. Why?"

"Common courtesy to the woman who's trapped in my house."

"Seriously."

"Two reasons. One, I don't care to have to explain this to the cops if you try to call them again. Two, even if you do, Astor will kill you if you talk. I'm warning you, and I'm not lying. He'd stage it as a car accident . . . you know, something believable."

I rolled my eyes. "I'm not that bad of a driver."

"Tell that to your axle."

"What's with the cash?"

"Go money."

"In case you have to leave the country?"

He nodded. "What Astor does for the government is completely off the books. If any of us were picked up during an op, Astor would deny any knowledge of our existence and throw us under the bus in two seconds flat. Kind of like what he'd do to you. But unlike you, I'd be one step ahead of him. I'd disappear and never resurface. A million bucks can help make that happen."

"Hence the secret room."

"Not so secret anymore," he muttered.

"So you did this for a while, and then everything stopped when you went to prison for killing Ortiz?"

A dark cloud swept over Ryder's face, and he looked away. A super-long minute passed as I waited on pins and needles for the story. What I got was—

"Your turn, Louise."

"My turn what?"

"Your turn to answer questions. Why do you drink so much?"

I blinked. "That's kind of personal."

"And going through my things isn't?"

Touché. I looked down the mug in my hands. "I don't know. I guess it helps me to relax."

"You ever try exercise?"

"You ever try *not* being an asshole?"

"That wasn't a passive-aggressive way of saying you need to lose weight. Because you don't."

I snorted. "Thought you said you didn't lie."

"I don't."

"I'm not going to say thank you because it doesn't feel like a compliment, but to answer your question, no, I don't exercise. And by the way, who the hell works out to relax?"

"Lots of people. Exercise releases endorphins that make you feel better physically, mentally, emotionally. Gives you clearer focus."

I stared at the antler mug.

"You seem wound up. Like a jack-in-the-box. Like you're searching for something, but you don't know what, and it makes you crazy."

"You seem like a neurotic, control-freak, germaphobe, coldblooded agoraphobic."

"I'm not coldblooded."

"Besides, you drink. You have an entire room dedicated to booze."

"I only drink when I'm at home."

I frowned, a little piece of the puzzle clicking into place. "Are you still on parole?"

"Six more months."

My eyes rounded. "I didn't realize. Okay, now I see why you didn't want me to call the cops."

"You don't get it, Louise. One misstep—one fucking misstep—and I'm back in a cage." He swallowed hard and focused on a spot on the slate floor. "When you're an ex con, cops will pin anything on you. You're a mark, a target, an easy arrest. You're always looked at as the bad guy. I'd be the first person they'd cuff if anything around me went to shit. One mistake, one 'being in the wrong place at the wrong time,' one fuckup, and I'll spend the rest of my life in prison."

For a moment, Ryder's expression went blank, and he left the room. Not physically, but mentally. Emotionally. Memories pulling him in back in time.

Something in my heart broke for him. There was such pain behind his eyes, and I knew, then and there, that whatever led him to kill Leon Ortiz must have been something horrific. I decided not to ask again, not to push.

Ryder was right. It wasn't my business. Ultimately, the reason made no difference because justice was served, and he paid the price. Ten years of his life.

Ten years.

I thought of what I was doing ten years ago and everything that had happened in between. The thought of spending it in a cage made my stomach roll. Ryder might have secrets, and he might be as emotionally available as a rock, but he had his reasons. And I'd leave it up to him to tell me why.

I set my mug on the counter. "I'll cook dinner tonight."

He didn't look up, didn't move. Just kept staring at that spot, lost in memories that I knew I didn't want to know.

I wasn't even sure if he'd heard me.

"Ryder. Sit down. I'll cook."

When I touched his arm, he flinched and jerked away, blinking. Without a word, he set down his water, stalked out the front door, and slammed it behind him.

I had dinner alone that night.

18

LOUISE

*a*fter Ryder stormed out of the kitchen, I waited for him to return. Night fell, along with the temperature and more snow. After an hour of silence, I assumed he wanted to be alone, wondering if that was the most he'd opened up to anyone in a long time.

I also wondered if he regretted the kiss.

I didn't. I couldn't stop thinking about it.

I made myself an organic chicken salad and ate at the breakfast nook, watching the snow whirl through the icy night. To my surprise, the low-carb, high-protein dinner was not only satisfying, but helped take the edge off the guilt from my confession that I didn't exercise.

Why didn't I exercise? I didn't know, other than I simply hated it. But had I really tried it? Gotten past that grueling first ten minutes that made you feel like you were going to die? No, because Louise Sloane never thought about the bigger picture.

Ryder was right. I was lost.

I didn't take another sip of alcohol that night.

After cleaning up, I retreated to my room—*his* room—

where I soaked in the copper tub that was quickly becoming my favorite place. I wondered how many other women had soaked in it.

I thought of the secret room, the passports, the money, the guns, all the people Ryder had killed. How different our lives were. How different *we* were. I thought about his time in prison.

Somewhere between wondering what he looked like in a jumpsuit and what kind of food they served behind bars, it hit me like a ton of bricks. Suddenly, all the pieces of the weird Ryder puzzle began to take shape . . . and I couldn't believe I hadn't seen it before.

Ryder wasn't an inherently odd, antisocial jerk. He was a victim of circumstance.

As I soaked in the bath, everything added up. The massive house with soaring ceilings and hallways as wide as a racetrack. The acres and acres of fields. The miles of woods, streams, and rivers.

Space.

The man spent ten years locked in an eight-by-eight jail cell. Ryder wasn't grandiose or overindulgent, he simply wanted space and fresh air. The minimal clothing and lack of furniture wasn't odd; it was because he simply didn't need it. He had chairs where he sat, and a bed where he slept. That was all he needed. His bed and bathroom were luxurious because he'd slept on a plank and showered with serial killers.

His indulgence in cooking, quality food, and expensive booze was because he didn't have a bit of good food or a drop of alcohol in ten years.

His ripped, muscular body (I imagined), was because it was his only weapon in prison. Ryder had probably spent every day pumping iron, not just to stay healthy, but more so to send a message to the other inmates.

His hermit lifestyle, his solitude—it was because he didn't trust anyone. Hell, he probably hated the human race. Ryder had spent a decade living with the scum of society, and I assumed before his conviction, he was labeled the scum of Berry Springs. In his own hometown. I couldn't imagine the gossip and sidelong glances he'd endured.

Wow.

The layers that made up this man were so deep, I wondered if anyone would ever get to see the real Ryder. His soul, who he truly was, deep down. And then I wondered if he even remembered who that guy was. The real Ryder, the one before he murdered a man.

The thought was so sad to me.

With Ryder, everything had a reason. You just had to find it.

That night, my view of him changed. There were reasons for the madness. I just wished I knew the biggest riddle of all.

Why did he kill Leon Ortiz?

After the bath, I'm not too proud to admit that I pulled on one of Ryder's T-shirts, crawled into bed, and attempted to sleep. Sometime after one in the morning, I got up and began pacing his bedroom, taking in every detail like the crown molding, and the intricate rock work around the fire-place. I assumed Ryder helped renovate the house. He took pride in it.

After I'd memorized every inch of the space, I crept into the hallway. I wanted to explore more. Learn more about the man who was slowly revealing himself to me.

I glanced into the first room to my left and stopped cold.

With no blanket, no pillow, Ryder was asleep on the

hardwood floor, fully clothed with his arms crossed over his chest like a pharaoh in a tomb.

I froze, staring at him, afraid that if I made the slightest sound, he'd wake. And also because I couldn't take my eyes off him. Although he was asleep, his face was pulled tight as if he were in a bad dream.

I wanted to hug him. Hold him. Tell him everything was going to be all right.

Didn't he have any other place to sleep? Not a couch, a cot, a sleeping bag? And why right next to me? To keep an eye on me? Or maybe to be there if I needed something? I craved the latter.

His shoulder jerked, and I spun on my heel and darted back into my room. I closed the door and jumped under the covers, where I remained the rest of the night.

It was day two of waking up in Ryder's glorious king-size bed, but night two was very different from night one. I'd barely slept a wink, tossing and turning, replaying the day before.

Yawning, I brushed back my bangs and looked at the window. Based on the lack of light behind the curtains, I decided it was still early morning. I gripped my pillow and rolled over, squeezing my eyes shut, but knowing I was past the point of no return. Last I'd checked the time, it was 3:40 in the morning. I must have drifted off after that, but it was that weird state where you didn't know if you were asleep or not.

Something pummeled into my stomach.

I shot up like a cannon, my pillow tumbling to the floor. Startled and confused, I blinked at the dark silhouette in front of me, then down at the pair of running shoes on the comforter, then back to the man in front of me.

"What the hell are you doing?" I rasped, sounding like a chain-smoking trucker.

"Morning jog. Let's go."

"Morning what? No. Those two words don't go together."

"They do in this house."

I looked down at my lap. "How did you get my shoes?"

"They were in your bag."

"You went through my stuff?"

"Doesn't feel good, does it?"

I rolled my eyes, then realized he'd opened the curtains. I looked out the window. "It's literally freezing outside. And still dark."

"It's eleven degrees, and the sun is coming up. It will be beautiful against the snow."

To hear him use an emotional word like *beautiful* proved to me how much he loved his nature. His space.

"I've already shoveled the trail," he said. "Wear those stained long johns you have under your blue sweatpants."

"No shirt?"

"Optional."

"I can't believe you went through my stuff."

"I can't believe you went through mine."

"Why the blue ones?"

"I like blue."

"Fine." With a groan, I ripped off the covers and flung my legs over the side of the bed, not remembering I was wearing only a T-shirt over a pair of pink panties. *His* T-shirt.

Heat rose to my cheeks.

If Ryder cared, he didn't show it. Something flashed in

his eyes, something that warmed my stomach. His gaze slowly slid from the T-shirt to my bare legs.

Humiliated, I yanked the sheets over my legs and fumbled to find something to say. I came up with—

"How do you look so perfect and put together for . . ." I looked around the room. "And why the hell don't you have a clock in this room?"

"It's five thirty-seven, and I have good genes. Let's go."

I sighed, then nodded. A moment passed.

"Can I have some privacy, please? Or is that something else that doesn't happen in this house?"

He turned and started for the door.

"Hey, Ryder," I called out after him. "Coffee first, then jog. Just so we're clear."

"Jog first, then coffee."

"No *way*. I can't—"

"It'll be the best damn coffee you've ever had. Get dressed. I'll meet you outside in three minutes."

"Five."

"Four."

"I'm growing to hate you as much as you hate me."

"Doubtful." He strode out of the room.

"Hey, Ryder?"

"What?" he hollered from the hallway without breaking his stride.

"It was fruit punch."

"What was fruit punch?"

"The stains on my long johns."

"I wasn't going to ask. *Believe* me."

~

Exactly ten minutes later, I stepped out the front door to a winter wonderland and the sight of Ryder stretching his quads.

Thighs as big as tree trunks stretched a pair of thin jogging pants. He wore all black—shoes, pants, and a pullover that draped over his muscular shoulders like silk. A black beanie was pulled low over his head, revealing wisps of that shaggy brown hair that curled out from underneath.

No layers or jackets for him. *Of course not.*

He looked up, alert and gorgeous.

I threw my arms out wide. "Gray sweatshirt and blue sweatpants, long johns underneath, per your request, Captain."

"I like it."

"Thanks. Your approval means everything to me."

"I meant you calling me Captain."

"Don't get used to it."

"What the hell is around your waist?"

"A fanny pack. Straight off the discount aisle at Walmart."

He blinked.

I fisted a hand on my hip. "They're so convenient. I don't know why they get such a bad rap."

"We're going on a simple jog. Not a trek through the Andes."

I shrugged.

"What do you have in it?" he asked. This fanny pack was really throwing him for a loop.

"My camera. And a stick of gum. I don't go anywhere without my camera."

He continued stretching. "I'm not holding it when you get tired."

"Are you familiar with how fanny packs work? The entire point is that you don't have to hold it."

"You know how to stretch?"

"I know how to stretch my liver."

He snorted. "Cirrhosis is no laughing matter."

"Another thing that's missing from this house."

"Cirrhosis or laughter?"

"Both."

"Stretch."

I mirrored his widened stance and bent forward. My muscles screamed. I stretched my left leg, then the right, and glanced over to find him staring at me.

Our eyes met, and his quickly shifted away.

"Ready?" he asked.

"As I'll ever be."

We took off across the driveway onto a manicured trail that led into the woods. As promised, the trail was shoveled, and I wondered how long he'd been awake. I also wondered if he'd only done it for me. I doubted he cleaned the trail for himself. The guy probably never fell down.

The freezing-cold air burned my lungs. My legs felt like rubber bands wound too tightly. True to form, I was sure I was going to die five minutes in, but dammit if I'd let him know that.

I picked up my pace, and Ryder matched my speed. He was pacing himself for me.

The woods closed in around us, a dim blanket of white beginning to lighten a little more with every few minutes that passed. Along the sides of the trail were mounds of snow two feet deep. The air smelled fresh, sharp with winter.

"You didn't have to shovel all of this for me."

"I didn't. I have a skid-steer loader."

"What's that?"

"A machine that clears snow."

"You're like a one-man town, you know that?"

"Two now." He gave me the side-eye.

"Speaking of, have you caught the weather on your *radio* today?" I side-eyed him right back.

"More snow is coming this afternoon. Supposed to get another inch. That's the last of it, though."

"Thank God." I glanced over, expecting him to say the same, but he didn't. "Any word from Frankie on towing my car?"

"No."

I scowled. "I hate it sitting out here on the side of the road. Bothers me."

Ryder glanced at me.

"I'll call the area hotels when we get back," I said. "Assuming you have a phone that isn't in a million pieces. There's got to be a room somewhere."

"Where are your friends staying?"

"They're at the Towering Pines Inn. They booked longer than I did."

"Thinking ahead."

Another eye roll. "Anyway, I considered asking Miles if I could crash with him—"

"Is he your boyfriend?"

"No."

"What about the other guy? Austin."

"You have a good memory. I just met Austin. I've known Miles for years. I'm sure he wouldn't mind—"

"No," Ryder said quickly. "It's fine."

I looked at him, but he stared ahead.

We ran in silence. My quads felt like someone had taken a blowtorch to them, and I realized we were jogging upward.

The sun was rising, a blazing orange invading the stars and igniting the tree trunks in sparkles of gold.

Ryder was right. It was beautiful.

The churning in my stomach, on the other hand, was not.

Do not puke, do not puke, do not puke . . .

We crested the mountain, and I stumbled as the view opened up. My pace slowed as my lips parted with a gasp. I looked over at Ryder. He was staring into the rising sun, and for the first time, his expression was soft.

"It's beautiful." I planted my feet, my chest heaving, a bead of sweat rolling down my temple. "I need to take a picture."

He stopped but kept jogging in place.

As I pulled my camera from my fanny pack, he shifted to the side, out of the frame. I took pictures from three different angles, capturing the streaks of color against the snow.

"Wow," I said softly. "I don't get a lot of sunrises."

"Why not?"

"I'm kind of a night owl."

"Mornings are the best part of the day."

I winked. "Nights can be pretty good too."

"Come on. Your muscles are going to tighten up. Let's keep up the pace. Your focus right now is fitness, not pictures."

Focus on fitness, focus on fitness, focus on fitness . . .

Fifteen pounds, fifteen pounds . . .

I shoved the camera back into my fanny pack, clenched my teeth, and pressed on, the brief stop giving me a rush of renewed energy.

Ryder wasn't even breathing heavily.

We descended the hill—a much-needed reprieve—and I

was awestruck at the beauty around us. A creek ran through the bottom of the mountain, ice clinging to its sides. We took a cute little curved bridge over it that appeared to have been built recently. My muscles had warmed, my breath evening out, and it seemed that the farther I ran, the easier it was. Perhaps if I would have pushed past that miserable first ten minutes in the past, maybe I would have become a real runner.

Maybe I still can.

We jogged along the fence line of the pastures. The horses, covered in plaid blankets, meandered through the field. One bucked as we passed, enjoying the rising sun shining on its back. Cows roamed the opposite pasture.

I was drenched in sweat when we finally made it back to the driveway. While Ryder paced a bit, hands on his hips, I doubled over, catching my breath.

"You did good," he said.

My brows raised as I glanced up, still gulping air. "Thanks. I'm going to be paying for this for days, though."

"Not if you stretch good enough."

His hands were suddenly on my lower back, his groin against my ass. I tensed, my eyes popping as I remained bent over.

"Take a deep breath."

His hands gripped my hips, yanking them back, against him. "Bend through your hips, not your back."

My heart beat faster—and that's saying something.

He released one hand and laid it on the small of my back, then pressed. "Bend deeper, like a hinge, from here."

With his other hand, he squeezed the crease in my hip, and I did as he asked, feeling myself open up to him.

A rush of warmth and wetness pooled between my legs. I wasn't sure if it was endorphins from the run, or because I hadn't had sex since fanny packs were in style. But if Ryder wouldn't have taken a step back at that moment, I would have climbed him like a spider monkey. Right there in the driveway.

At that moment, I wanted nothing more than to feel him inside me. All that intensity. All that *man*. I wanted to be on the receiving end of all that pent-up madness, because somehow I knew the pleasure would be explosive.

"Ready for coffee?" His voice came out gruff, low, as if he'd been thinking the same thing.

I slowly raised from the bend, my back still to him. "You promised me the best."

"It'll be nothing like you've had before."

The sexual innuendo heating my cheeks, I followed him inside.

The house was warm, the sunrise framed in the sweeping windows overlooking white pastures. I pulled out my camera and took a few pictures as Ryder made the coffee.

"I'm going to get my laptop to download these. Be right back."

I jogged to the bedroom and pulled out my laptop. By the time I returned, the house smelled like fresh coffee.

Ryder pulled down two mugs. "How do you take your coffee?"

"I'll give you two guesses."

"Lard and sugar cane?"

"And sprinkles."

He smiled. *Smiled.*

There it was. And it was magnificent.

I smiled back. He had dimples too, as if he needed anything else to be sexier. The guy could destroy a woman with only a glance.

He retrieved a small container from the fridge, poured a dash in the coffee, then something else I couldn't see from my angle. He handed me the mug, his gaze lingering as I sipped.

My brows arched. "Damn good."

The corner of his lip curled with satisfaction.

"What's in it?"

"Vanilla almond milk and honey."

"Healthy and healthy."

"Always." He sipped his coffee. "Okay, the agenda for the day."

He leaned against the counter while I settled into the breakfast nook. *Space.*

"First," he said, "we'll get your car out and get it to Frankie."

"I thought you said they'll tow it?"

"We'll do it."

I smiled. "Thanks."

He dipped his chin.

"Will he have a rental for me to use while he fixes it?" I asked as I powered up my computer.

"Doubt it. You can use one of my trucks. The visors work in all of them."

"My lucky day. What's your internet password?"

"Bobcats99."

"Really? I expected a seventeen-digit code from you."

"It's my high school football number."

"You played football?"

"High school and college. Berry Springs Bobcats, number ninety-nine."

"Wow."

"What?"

"Kind of surprises me."

"Why?"

"Well, you're built like an ox, so I get that, but football's a team sport. Social. You don't exactly scream 'team player.'"

Ryder looked out the window, again lost in thoughts that I wondered if I'd ever learn about.

"Anyway," I said, trying to clear the air that had clouded all of a sudden. "Okay, car towed. Then I'll find a hotel room, and then I'm going to head to Hollow Hill again."

Frowning, he refocused on me. "You're going back?"

"Investigating Kara's murder is the entire reason I'm here. So, yeah, I'm going back."

"You're not going back to Hollow Hill."

"I can drive in the snow. I promise."

"Can you?"

"The working visor will make all the difference."

His brows slammed down. "This isn't a joke. You're not going back."

"I am going back. And why not?"

"You're not going alone to the last place Kara was known to be before getting brutally raped and murdered. Why do you need to go back anyway? You already went. Leave this to the cops."

"If I'm stuck here, I'm going to make myself useful. *Period.*" My eyes narrowed. "I'm not asking for permission here, Ryder. You can keep your truck, if that's what this is about. I'll find another way to get there."

Scowling, I clicked into the pictures. I didn't hear him but could feel him behind me.

"Did you take all these pictures?"

I stopped scrolling, images from my last trek across Yellowstone Park filling the screen. "I did."

He zeroed in on the sunset, electric colors blazing over jagged peaks. "You're very talented."

"I'd better be. I own my own photography business."

"You do?"

"Believe it or not, yes. Sloane's Stills, at your service."

"Ah, that's why you named your car Ansel Adams."

"Just Ansel."

"Stop. I like that one. I want it."

"This one?"

"Yeah."

I enlarged an image of an animal skull on dusty ground. Soaring copper cliffs touched the stars behind it. I remembered taking that picture right at twilight. The last of that day.

"I want it framed," he said, and I grinned.

"It'll cost you."

"Name the price."

My head tilted to the side. "Another batch of hush puppies."

"Done."

He pushed my hand away and took over the control pad, slowly scrolling through my pictures. Instead of being self-conscious, I was proud. I was good at what I did, and I knew it.

After a few minutes, I resumed control and scrolled through the images I'd taken since being in Berry Springs.

Ryder's hand closed over mine, and I stopped scrolling. He pushed my hand away and enlarged an image. It was the one I'd taken of him fishing before he'd invited me back to his house. The one where he looked so sad, tortured, gazing into the mountains.

Instead of giving me grief for lying about taking his picture, he leaned in, staring at the image. I looked at him as he stared for what seemed like a full minute at the photo. Then he swallowed hard and pulled back.

I closed the photo and scrolled down to images of the search sites, the campgrounds, of my first trip to Hollow Hill. "It's creepy, isn't it?"

"It should be bulldozed down."

"Agreed." I clicked into a picture of the master bedroom. Rotted beams ran across a ceiling dotted with holes, planks missing on the hardwood floor. Spray paint on the stained, dingy walls. Cracked windows smeared with dirt.

He yanked the laptop closer to him and zoomed in on the fireplace.

"What do you see?"

He didn't say anything, just stared at the picture, the vein in his neck throbbing.

"Ryder. What do you see?"

He pulled away, blinked, then seemed to decide something. "I'll take you there. We'll go this morning."

"No, you don't have to. I can—"

"I'm taking you. End of discussion. Let's get moving. We've got a lot to get done."

As I watched him disappear down the hall, I wondered what the hell he'd seen in that picture.

19

LOUISE

*I*t was noon by the time Ryder had shoveled the snow away from Ansel, pulled him from the ditch, and loaded him onto the trailer. I'd helped where I could, but Ryder truly was a one-man show. There was nothing he couldn't handle on his own.

The snow had started again, its last hurrah, but this time bringing with it a blustery wind that could cut through steel.

The drive to Ansel wasn't as bad as anticipated, thanks to the cherry-red diesel dually Ryder had chosen for the occasion. It was the meatiest vehicle I'd ever seen. Even had chains on the tires, as if I'd expected anything less from Ryder. I also got the impression he had many cars to choose from.

In complement to the manly truck, Ryder looked as alpha as ever, wearing a pair of charcoal-gray all-weather pants that hugged his ass like a glove, a red and navy pullover under a thick Carhartt jacket, combat boots, and a beat-up baseball cap. I, on the other hand, was officially out of clothes. Boyfriend jeans again, red sweater, and my good old superglued boots. This was topped with the glorious puffer jacket.

Although the truck had six tires and four-wheel drive, we'd slid several times on the way into town—which was terrifying when you were towing a trailer. The roads hadn't seen a plow since Winter Storm Barron started.

Berry Springs was a ghost town, as was the only mechanic shop in town. Frankie's Auto Shop was locked up, no lights, not a human in sight. Ryder called Frankie, who'd advised him to unload Ansel, and promised he'd take a look as soon as he could dig himself out of his house.

After unloading the 4Runner, Ryder shook the snow from his hat and climbed into the truck. He shoved the truck into reverse.

"I'm hungry."

He hit the brakes. "Me too, actually," he said as if suddenly realizing it. "The diner is right there."

I followed his gaze to Donny's Diner, two doors down. Blue-and-white checkered curtains framed the daily specials written in window paint. Next to that, cartoon images of pancakes, plates of fried eggs, and bacon looked delicious. I licked the drool from my lips.

He grinned, watching me. "Donny's, then?"

"Donny's."

"All-righty then."

I grabbed my purse from the floorboard, and before I could reach for the handle, Ryder had rounded the hood and opened my door. His hand stretched for mine. I smiled, and he helped me out.

"The sidewalks haven't been salted." He lifted his elbow, and I looped my arm around his.

"Ryder, if you're not careful, I might start to think there's a gentleman buried deep inside that black soul of yours."

He chuckled. I loved that chuckle.

A gust of wind whipped around us. When I shivered, he pulled me closer.

"You need a new jacket."

"I need a lot of new things."

He frowned, looking down at me. "Do you need some help?"

I cackled, gaping up at him. "You mean money?"

He nodded, serious as a heart attack.

"No. God, no. I might not own a castle on a hill surrounded by a million pristine acres, but I get by."

"Selling pictures?"

"Yes. It's not a lot, but it pays the bills."

"Do you like it? What you do?"

The question surprised me, and I hesitated. "Yes, I do. I opened my own business because I loved photography. I'm good at it."

"But you're not content."

"You're observant." I slipped on a patch of black ice, then steadied in his firm hold.

"Add new boots to the list."

I kicked out my right foot. "Hey. These are comfortable. Broken in. What's wrong with them?"

"The flapping sole is what's wrong with them, Louise. The first night I met you, they were covered in duct tape. They make new shoes that I guarantee you are just as comfortable."

"All right. I'll add that to my list of things to pay for after I get the bill for Ansel."

His hand dropped to mine and gripped it.

Only three trucks other than ours were parked on the town's square, two in front of the diner. We pushed through the front door. A warm blast of air scented with bacon and coffee made my stomach rumble.

A lone cowboy sat at the counter, nursing a cup of coffee. A husband and wife, I guessed in their mid-seventies, sat in a booth by the window. An old Tanya Tucker song blared from the jukebox.

Heads turned as we walked in.

A coffee cup slipped from the waitress's hand, shattering on the floor, her face paling as if she'd seen a ghost.

"Oh, silly me." She bent down, a strand of gray hair falling over her face as she picked up the shards. When Ryder knelt down to help, she froze, staring at him.

"Ryder Jagger," she whispered.

"Mornin', Mrs. Booth." He avoided eye contact as he picked up the remaining pieces.

"I haven't seen you in . . ."

"Twelve years."

They stood, her wide eyes never leaving his face as if he were the second coming of Christ. Or the devil himself, I wasn't sure which.

"It'll be two of us," he said, breaking the awkwardness. His easy demeanor had tightened. He was uncomfortable.

"Ah, sure, son. Pick where you'd like."

Ryder motioned for me to choose, and you could cut the tension in the place with a butter knife.

"Are you okay?" I whispered as we slid into the booth.

"Fine."

I dared a look at the elderly couple, who were also staring at us, but with very different expressions than the waitress's. Instead of shock, their reaction was unmistakable disgust for the former inmate. I glanced at the cowboy at the bar top, whispering with Mrs. Booth.

"Ryder." I leaned in. "We can go."

"No," he snapped. "You're hungry. I'm hungry. We're eating here."

"Is this your first time here since being out?"

"Yes."

An argument broke out in the kitchen, an old man in a hairnet peering out of the window at Ryder. A minute later, Mrs. Booth walked up.

"We're, uh, thinkin' about closing down early today, on account of the weather."

"Not until you serve us, Mrs. Booth. Louise, what would you like to eat?"

Holy shit. I gripped the menu and rattled off the first thing I saw. "Uh, I'll take the western omelet, wheat toast, and coffee."

"I'll have the same." His tone was as cold as ice as he pushed the menus to the side.

Mrs. Booth dipped her chin and scurried back to the kitchen to try to convince the cook—who didn't want to cook for Ryder, apparently—to make our food.

A second later, the couple in the booth next to us gathered their plates, their coffees, and slid out of their booth.

"God bless your soul," the woman said in a whisper as they passed, scowling.

I wanted to slap the brooch from her plaid jacket. They reseated themselves two booths away from us.

"Ryder, I didn't realize. We can get the food to go."

"Are you embarrassed to be seen with me?"

I gaped at him. "No. No, not at all. But this is *bullshit*. You don't des—"

"Stop. It is what it is. I'll have to deal with this the rest of my life."

"It's bullshit. I'm going to say something to that cook."

"No, you're not. *Sit*, Louise."

"Why? You shouldn't have to deal with this."

"Why? Because if that man says one cross thing to you, I'll bust out his teeth. And guess why that's not a good idea?"

I blew out a breath. "You're still on parole."

"Exactly."

I shook my head, frowning at the waitress who was staring at us. The cowboy at the counter paid his bill and left.

My heart broke for Ryder. I felt defensive on his behalf. Protective.

He sat stoic, expressionless. For the first time, I wondered if he was embarrassed.

I slid out of the booth, and he grabbed my hand.

Tugging out of his grip, I said softly, "I'm going to the bathroom."

I didn't go to the bathroom. I paid our tab and asked good old Mrs. Booth to box up our food to go. Five minutes later, our grease-stained paper bags were delivered to us. I winked at Ryder, grabbed the bags, and slid out of the booth.

"What did you—"

"Let's go. Come on."

As we pushed out the doors, I glanced back at the table where Ryder had left the waitress, who'd asked him to leave, a hundred-dollar tip slid beneath the salt shaker.

We stepped onto the sidewalk and Ryder grabbed my hand. Although he tried to hide it, I heard him take a deep breath.

I now completely understood why he avoided *all* human contact.

When he pulled me off the sidewalk and onto the street, I glanced up at him. "Where are we going?"

"Pit stop."

We crossed the street without bothering to check for cars. The town was dead. All the storefronts on the square were dark, except for a flashing open sign on a small store on the corner. The sign above the door read damsel in a dress.

Cowbells jangled as Ryder opened the door for me.

"Howdy, there," a woman's voice called out from the back. "Be right out."

The store was warm, scented with spicy cinnamon and leather. Racks of cowboy hats lined the back wall behind a cabinet filled with turquoise jewelry. To the right were rows of coats, sweaters, pants, and dresses. To the left, a wall of shoes. A saddle on a wood-carved horse sat in front of the window. In the center of the store were two rocking chairs and a table over a Navajo rug.

This was no discount thrift shop.

A woman, five feet tall and maybe a hundred pounds, shuffled out of the back. She was dressed in a cashmere sweater, skinny jeans, and ski boots, her glasses perched on the end of her nose. Her gray hair was pulled into a messy bun on the top of her head. She smiled, lines creasing around friendly blue eyes.

I liked her instantly.

"Well, I just lost a bet with myself. Didn't think I'd get a soul in here today. I live above the store," she said, pointing to the ceiling. "I open, no matter the weather. My name's Mary Anne. What can I help y'all with?"

I assumed she didn't know or recognize Ryder.

Ryder grabbed my hand. "We're going to need everything in your store, Mary Anne."

Her face lit up and her eyes sparkled. "Sir, *that* I can do."

I squeezed Ryder's hand. "What are you doing?" I mouthed between gritted teeth.

Ignoring my question, he said to Mary Anne, "Louise here is a little shy. Can you help get her started?"

"Oh yes, yes. My pleasure."

Mary Anne grabbed my arm and pulled me away as I mouthed obscenities to Ryder, who grinned and took a seat in the center of the store.

Ten minutes later, the dressing room was a tornado of shirts and pants being tossed in, then tossed out. Dresses, sweaters, slacks, a suit that I'd never wear—all came over the curtain. I recognized half the brands from fancy magazines I'd perused while waiting in line at the grocery store. *Expensive* brands.

I got lost in it, feeling like a princess while Mary Anne styled me. Reminding myself I needed new clothes, I quit looking at the price tags.

You only live once, right?

Ryder left us alone, taking no interest in two women chatting about fabrics. Instead, he sat patiently in the chair, buried under stacks of *National Geographic.*

An hour later, I met Mary Anne behind mounds of clothes and coats stacked on the counter. Boxes of shoes sat on the floor. My hand trembled as I handed her my credit card.

"Oh no, it's already been paid for. Go sit up front, and I'll bring out your food."

"What?"

"It's been paid for, dear. I'll get your food."

"Wha—and food?"

"The food y'all came in with. Your husband asked me to put it in my oven upstairs until you were done. Made you two a fresh pot of coffee too. Stay as long as you'd like." She beamed up at me. "You guys just made my year. Literally."

Speechless, I smiled back.

"And, ma'am, if you don't mind me sayin', he is *one* looker. *Wowie.*" The shop owner fanned her face.

My smile widened. "He sure is, isn't he?"

"You're a lucky girl." With that, Mary Anne scurried off to get our food.

I met Ryder in the center of the store. "You didn't have to do that."

"You didn't have to do what you did in the diner."

I smiled, staring down at him as he grinned up at me. "Thank you, Ryder."

"Thank *you*. Let's eat."

Surrounded by piles of shopping bags, we ate our western omelets peacefully in the rocking chairs, watching the snow fall outside. Mary Anne waited on us hand and foot, thanking Ryder profusely for coming in. She even sent us on our way with a homemade apple pie she'd baked hours earlier.

Ryder took the bags to the truck, then came back for me. As my hand slid into his, I savored the closeness, the feel of his skin against mine. The warmth of his hand. Of him.

I *was* lucky.

If only for one more day.

*I*t took us almost two hours to get to Hollow Hill. The snow was falling quickly, sheets of ice against gray. I suggested turning back, but Ryder was hell-bent on carrying on.

I asked him what he'd seen in the picture, a question he sidestepped, reminding me that he didn't like the idea of me going back out to the estate alone. I didn't push. Figured I'd find out soon enough, because whatever was in that picture, Ryder would find it. And I'd be right there next to him, in my brand-new down winter jacket and hiking boots.

"Turn here." I leaned forward, squinting. "I think this is it."

"Nope. Next road."

"You sure? I think—"

"It's the next road. I've been here before."

"Yeah, but I was here days ago."

"It's the next right. I checked the map before we left."

"Why can't men take directions from a woman?"

"Why can't women read maps?"

I rolled my eyes and looked out the window, pretending he wasn't right. I was the worst at directions. Obviously.

We turned onto a narrow dirt road with sagging trees overhead. Dead, ice-covered branches littered the unplowed road. There were a few tracks, from coyote or deer, but no tire tracks.

When we rounded a curve, the house came into view, and a chill snaked up my spine. In contrast to the sparkling snow around it, the house looked darker and more menacing than the first time I'd seen it.

Dead trees pressed in on the old colonial-style mansion, built in the late eighteen hundreds. Four columns stretched from a decrepit porch to a crooked roof pockmarked with holes. A balcony hung over the front door, several slats of wood missing. At some point, someone had painted the house white, but the color had faded to varying shades of browns. Mounds of snow piled along the sides.

The house must have been luxury at its finest when it was built. Not anymore.

Ryder parked next to the front steps, careful to avoid the trees and their weak branches.

I zipped up my new coat, secured my camera into the pocket, and hopped out, my boots sinking six inches into the snow. The heavy snowfall created a hush around us. I yanked up my fur-rimmed hood.

Ryder was already on the porch by the time I made my way around the truck, and I met him at the front door.

"Tell me again why Kara was here?" he asked.

"Her friend said she wanted to check it out while she was here camping. Like a tourist attraction."

"And still no idea who Kara was meeting to go camping?"

"Nope."

The door creaked loudly as Ryder pushed it open. The house was dark, but with enough daylight to see your way around.

We stepped inside. It smelled old and musty, worse than I remembered. An iron chandelier lay broken in the middle of the floor, covered in spiderwebs. A steep black staircase faded into the darkness of the second level. Graffiti covered the walls—obscenities, anarchy, Wiccan symbols, a few gangly penises. The entryway was littered with sticks, toppled-over chairs, trash, and a few beer bottles from brave teenagers who'd used the place to party. Shards of glass from the busted windows covered the floor.

I shivered, not because the house was freezing, but because of the feeling I got when I stepped inside. It was one of those weird feelings that convinced you to your bones that something bad had happened there . . . maybe recently, maybe long ago. Regardless, it was the type of feeling that told you to turn round and get the hell out.

Evil lurked in Hollow Hill. There was no doubt about it.

"Did the cops find anything here? Any trace of her?" Ryder asked.

"Not that I'm aware of. I'm hoping to find something they missed. Any clue to help put this damn puzzle together."

We stepped around the fallen chandelier, and I turned to go into the next room.

"Stay with me," he said, taking it all in. "Please."

Turning back, I wondered if Ryder felt the same evil I did.

I pulled my camera from my pocket and took more pictures, paying attention to every nook and cranny as we walked through the first floor. Ryder was looking for something too, but his search was different from mine. I just didn't know why.

The staircase creaked and groaned as we walked up it. Ryder reached back and grabbed my hand.

Midway up the stairs, my heart beat faster. Irrationally, I had the urgent compulsion to turn and *run*.

I gripped his hand tighter as we took the curve in the stairs and stepped onto the second floor. Mounds of snow from the holes in the roof littered the hardwood floors. There was little trash and graffiti upstairs, as if the party-goers knew to avoid it. I wondered why.

Gripping my hand, Ryder quickened his steps. He pulled me along, glancing into each room until we came to the master bedroom at the end of the hall.

The room was large with a fireplace and a small balcony. There were only a few holes in this part of the roof and most of the floor was still intact, along with the two windows. It was warmer too, and I noticed the faint smell of ash. He dropped my hand and scanned the room.

"Ryder, you have to tell me what you're looking for. Maybe I can help."

Laser-focused, he ignored my question as he clicked on his phone, using it as a flashlight. He walked to the fireplace, crouched down, and leaned forward. I squatted next to him, following his gaze into the ashes. Something small and colorful sparkled in the beam of light.

"What is that?"

His eyes widened as he stared at it.

"Ryder?"

"It's a pendant. From a necklace," he whispered, his tone chilling me to the bone.

We both stared at the dirty oval blown-glass pendant with a rainbow of colors swirling inside. It was beautiful, like a million flower petals had been captured in glass. The pendant was caught under the corner of the iron grate, as if it had been tossed and forgotten.

I put my hand on his shoulder. "Is this what you saw in the picture this morning?"

He looked toward me, not at me so much as through me. He seemed to be somewhere else.

"Ryder. You're kind of freaking me out. Are you okay?"

He blinked, shook his head as if shaking away memories, then pulled a baggie from his pocket that he must have brought from his house. I watched him carefully remove the pendant from the ashes and zip it in the bag.

"What are you doing? Do you think that's Kara's? If so, we need to call the cops."

"It's not Kara's."

"How do you know? This could be evidence. You have to leave it. It could be Kara's—"

"It's *not* Kara's."

"Whose is it then?"

"It's mine."

o say the drive back to Ryder's castle on the hill was hair-raising is an understatement. We ran off the road once. Ryder handled it, of course—and had to make two additional stops to clear fallen branches. A drive that should have taken twenty minutes took over two hours. Winter Storm Barron was going out with a bang.

Like a stubborn child, Ryder made it clear he had no interest in discussing the pendant on the way back.

It was past seven o'clock and dark by the time we reached his house. Once inside, he immediately disappeared into the library.

I didn't follow. Whatever the story was around that pendant put him in a vile mood. So I went to the bedroom, changed out of my wet clothes, and threw on a pair of new skinny jeans and a fitted cashmere sweater, both courtesy of Ryder and Damsel in a Dress.

It was officially the tightest outfit I owned, and as I spun in front of the mirror, I surprised myself by liking the view. The jeans lifted my ass like no boyfriend jeans could do. Who knew? After that, I journeyed to the kitchen, glancing into the library as I passed. Ryder was gone. The house was dark.

I bypassed the wine and made myself a cup of tea, contemplating if I should wait for Ryder for dinner or not. Minutes ticked by, becoming an hour as I stood, leaning against the kitchen counter, watching the snow outside and waiting for the master of the house.

At nine o'clock, I set down my tea and decided to go on the hunt. He was nowhere in the house or in view of the windows.

Finding a flashlight handy in the utility closet, I stepped out the front door. Faded boot tracks in the snow disappeared around the side of the house.

I grabbed one of Ryder's coats from the coat rack, zipped up, and followed the tracks. Leaving the house in the distance, I made my way along the fence line of one of the pastures. The footprints led me to a stable, where Liberty was missing. Prudence snorted as I walked inside.

"Hey, girl. Made any good decisions today?" I rubbed her white-striped nose. "Have you seen the king of the castle? Did he come in here?" I asked, and she nuzzled against my hand.

I looked around. Liberty's saddle was missing. Prudence's hung in the back of her stall.

Considering, I tilted my head to the side. "Wanna go for a ride?"

Prudence let out a snort that I took as a solid *yes*.

It took thirty damn minutes to figure out how to strap on the saddle, and I had no idea if I'd done it correctly. Then I grabbed the bridle and convinced her to take it, arranging the reins on her neck. Thank goodness she knew what she was doing.

Stepping back, I studied my work. *Looks right to me.* I

grabbed the saddle horn and tested my weight on the stir-rup. When it held, I figured it was good enough, and I pulled myself on.

It took a few deep breaths to settle my heart.

I grabbed the reins. "You probably remember me clinging onto your neck for dear life during our first moments together. Not anymore. I'm going to be strong, and you're going to walk as smoothly as you did the first time. Got it?"

The horse dipped its head.

"Good. Because something is wrong with your master, and we need to figure it out."

I tapped my heels against her sides, and as slow and steady as before, Prudence stepped out of the barn. Grip-ping the reins with one hand, I pulled the flashlight from my pocket and aimed it into the darkness with the other. Hoof tracks led into the woods.

"We're going to follow these tracks, okay?" I tugged to the right and tapped my heels again.

We set off, following the tracks along the field and even-tually onto the trail that led into the trees. The woods were an inky black and icy cold. The beam from my flashlight illuminated only a few feet ahead, just enough to continue following the tracks.

What the hell is Ryder up to?

Upward, upward, upward we climbed, and I realized it was the same mountain he and I had jogged that morning. Finally, we crested the top. A thin beam of yellow light penetrated the darkness in the distance.

Ryder.

I pulled Prudence to a stop, slid off, and tied her reins to a nearby tree. Keeping my light low, I slowly stepped through the snow, following the hoof tracks as my heart raced.

Liberty was also tied to a tree, and I ran my fingers along his side as I passed him. The hoof tracks turned into boot prints. Whatever Ryder was doing, he obviously meant to be alone. I had no idea what I was about to walk up on.

I followed the prints through the clearing where I'd captured the sunrise on my camera hours earlier. The prints cut through a small patch of trees to a smaller clearing, this one with unobstructed views of the surrounding mountains.

I froze.

With the light of a single flashlight behind him, Ryder sat in the snow in front of two gravestones, his legs folded underneath him, holding his head in his hands. His shoulders shook.

My instinct was to turn and run back to the house, pretending that I didn't see him, but I couldn't. I couldn't move. My feet were pinned to the ground.

He lifted his head, and I held my breath. Slowly, he looked over his shoulder.

I will never, ever forget that moment, the moment our eyes locked and we stared at each other with snow and darkness between us. At that moment, I saw the real Ryder.

A broken man. A lost soul.

He turned back to the gravestones. I slowly walked forward, stopping behind him to silently pay my respects to the two souls I didn't know, but somehow knew had shattered this man's life.

I put my hand on his shoulder. He didn't flinch, didn't move.

We stood that way for a few minutes until Ryder broke the silence and told me the story that gives me nightmares to this day.

"I asked her to marry me, twelve years ago. She said yes." His voice was raw. Weak. "Her name was Maci. The next day, she moved in with me. The day after that, I left for a job in Colombia. I remember smiling the entire flight, feeling like my life was finally mapped out. I was one of those guys, those old souls, who always wanted to be married, have kids, the white picket fence. To me, the idea of a family was the key to success in life. That, I thought would be real happiness. I felt lucky, relieved, happy. I felt like I had something to build on, if that makes sense. Something bigger than me.

"When I came back from Colombia, things were different. She'd rearranged my house, thrown out half my stuff. Redecorated. We started arguing." He paused. "We'd only dated six months before I asked her to marry me. It wasn't long before I left for another trip. This time, I was gone for three weeks. I came back and found her in bed with the guy she'd dated before me. I kicked the guy's ass and told him if he ever touched her again, I'd kill him. She groveled, begged me to stay, so I did. I wanted to make it work. I wanted the dream of a wife, kids, dogs. I wanted it all, and I thought she did too.

"I took time off away from Astor to try to make things work between us. Things were good for a while. Five months. We even set a date. Then we started arguing again. All the time. Nonstop. I couldn't take it. I broke the engagement hours before I left for another job. Told her we'd discuss our relationship and living situation when I got back. I didn't want to throw her out with nothing.

"The job was in Venezuela. I called her when I landed, but lost reception not long into the trip. That mission was tough. I spent six nights in the jungle, tracking the leader of a militia group who was plotting an attack on the US. The mission was successful, and after a week, I was on the next flight out. Called her from the airport before I left but didn't get an answer. It was late, though, so I assumed she was asleep.

"It wasn't until she didn't answer when I landed that I remember something in my gut twisting, an instinct that something wasn't right. I called her over and over the entire drive home, each mile feeling like ten. It was exactly nine fourteen when I pulled up to my house."

His head dipped.

"The door was unlocked. She always locked the door. I raced up the stairs to the bedroom . . ."

He paused, his shoulders rising and falling with deep breaths.

"She was on the floor, in front of the bed. Her skin was ghostly pale. Her eyes were open but there was no life in them. Her head was turned toward the door, like she'd been waiting for me to save her when she took her last breath. Her nightgown was around her waist. She was naked underneath, her legs spread apart. Her neck was covered in purple bruises, and so were her fucking hips. Maci had been raped and strangled to death in my bedroom."

My entire body froze as my heartbeat roared in my ears.

"I checked for a pulse." He shook his head. "Stupid. Anyway, I checked for a pulse and called the cops. The rest is kind of a blur. I remember watching Jessica, the medical examiner, check her over, so methodically as if Maci weren't even human. Just an object to search. I watched them zip her into the body bag. That was the last time I saw her face, exactly twelve years ago today. Five days after that, I murdered Leon Ortiz, the man who raped and murdered her. I was arrested hours later and thrown into jail, where I remained for the next ten years of my life.

"The headstone on the left is hers. The headstone on the right is for the baby she was carrying in her stomach when she was murdered." His gaze shifted to mine, the pain so vivid that goose bumps broke out over my skin. "Maci was nine weeks pregnant. I didn't know. She'd kept it from me because we were so volatile. She'd had the blood test and everything to confirm the sex. I found the papers. She was pregnant with my baby. My son."

Uncontrollable tears rolled down my cheeks as I looked at the small gravestone that honored Ryder's baby boy.

"The night I asked her to marry me, I gave her a ring and a necklace. The ring is in my safe. The pendant that we found in Hollow Hill, the pendant that's now in my pocket, is hers. Was hers. I gave it to her."

22

LOUISE

fter placing flowers he'd picked from his greenhouse by the gravestones, Ryder and I rode Liberty and Prudence back to the house in silence and went our separate ways. I tried to offer him my bed—*his* bed— but he wouldn't have it.

I was so worried about him, I couldn't sleep. So I took a hot bath, then spent some time stretching and doing a few relaxation poses I saw on a yoga program once.

Sometime around midnight, I tiptoed to the kitchen and made myself a cup of chamomile tea. Sipping, I slowly walked around the house, looking for Ryder. I found him in the library, with only a dim light on, sitting in his leather chair as he stared into the darkness outside.

I hesitated, knowing that he wanted nothing more than his space at that moment. But then I wondered, would the old Ryder want his space? I padded across the room, noting his eyes were puffy and shaded. When he looked at me, his drawn face revealed not only his sadness and pain, but also his emotional exhaustion.

I handed him my tea, plucked a book off the stack next

to the chair, and handed it to him. It was one of his action/adventure books, this one featuring a couple running out of a cave on the cover. Very Indiana Jones.

He took the book, staring at me.

"May I read with you?" I asked.

"Yes."

I chose a book with a shirtless man on the cover and settled in next to him, tucking my legs under my body. He stood, pulled the folded plaid blanket from the back of his chair, and draped it over me.

"Thank you."

His eyes met mine. "Thank *you*."

With that, he sat, opened his book, and with the snow falling outside, we read together for an hour in a comfortable silence. A companionable silence.

I fell asleep after the first few chapters.

I pretended not to wake when Ryder gently lifted me from the chair and carried me down the hall. I pretended not to wake as he laid me in his master bed and pulled the covers to my chin. I pretended not to wake as he stroked my head. When the warmth of his skin left mine, I opened my eyes as he quietly slipped from the room.

Ryder slept on the floor again in the same room as the night before. Right next to mine. Sometime after two in the morning, I covered him with a blanket.

I was awoken the next morning the same way as the morning before—with a pair of running shoes pummeling my stomach. This time, though, I didn't groan and piss and moan. I was dressed and jogging through the snow with Ryder four minutes later. We didn't say much the first mile or so, same as the night before after he'd poured his heart out to me.

The first mile of our morning jog was rough. My legs were sore and stiff, but like the day before, the muscles seemed to loosen about fifteen minutes in. It felt good.

It was the first clear day in weeks, a big, bright sun beginning to peek over the mountains. As we jogged next to each other, I felt a newborn bond between us. I was one of the few, maybe the only one, who got to see the *real* Ryder. The man behind the armor.

I waited until we were into the second mile before bringing up what I'd spent the evening thinking about.

"Hey, Ryder?"

"Yeah?"

"I've been thinking . . ."

He flashed me the side-eye. "Oh yeah?"

"You're sure the pendant is, was, your former fiancée's, right?"

A moment passed as he seemed to mull over the question, as if he'd thought about it all night too.

"I bought it at a little art shop in town called Magic Mavens. It was one of many, so, technically, I can't guarantee the one we found was the one I gave to her. Although it was exactly like I remembered when I picked it out. And each one was a little different."

"Was she wearing it when you found her?"

"No."

"Do you remember finding it in your house after you packed up her things? Assuming you did?"

"Yes, I packed up her things and sent everything to her folks, and no, the necklace wasn't there."

"Could she have lost it?"

"She wore it every day."

"So she was wearing it the day you left for your job in Venezuela, and when you returned and found her, it wasn't around her neck?"

"Right."

I looked at him. "Ryder, you can't ignore the coincidence here. We found the pendant you gave Maci in one of the last locations we knew Kara to be. And Kara was raped and strangled to death by a string, like Maci." I cringed at my bluntness. "Sorry. That was insensitive."

"No, it wasn't. It's a fact."

"Yeah, but I should have chosen my words more carefully. I need to think before I speak more."

"I like it."

"You do?"

"Yeah. Never was a fan of people who beat around the bush or don't say what they mean, or vice versa. Just say how it is."

"Okay then, buckle up. Here I go. You asked for it."

"Go for it. Say what's on your mind."

"I think you—*we*—should consider the idea that Kara's murder and Maci's might be connected. I know they were twelve years apart, but you can't ignore the fact that the women were killed the same way, and that your pendant somehow made it to Hollow Hill."

"I killed Maci's murderer, Louise. It's the entire reason I spent a decade in jail."

"You're sure you killed the right guy?"

He planted his feet, stopping on a dime. I stumbled as I halted.

"Yes. I am one hundred percent sure I killed the man who killed Maci, and don't ever question that again, all right?"

"Okay. But lay it out for me. Let's talk about it."

He began pacing. "Lay what out?"

"How you found out it was him. How it was confirmed that Ortiz killed Maci."

Ryder stopped pacing and aggressively flicked the snow from a branch. "They found his pubic hair. *Inside* her. He wore a condom, and also gloves, but they were still able to pull his DNA from the hair. The hair was found during the autopsy and was sent to the state crime lab, where they got the hit. Ortiz was already in the system for multiple offenses. It was a slam-dunk case."

"But how did you get his name before it was released? According to the gossip, you killed Ortiz before the cops even had a chance to arrest him."

"I drove my ass to the crime lab and slept in the parking lot until the tests from the autopsy were completed. After a little asking around, I found out the lab tech's name who recorded the results. I paid off the man's house and his child's college tuition in return for being the first to see the results." Glancing at me, he said, "Close your mouth."

My mouth snapped shut. "Does anyone know?"

"Nope. Only me and the lab tech."

"Didn't the police ask how you knew before them?"

"I waited until literally the minute the tech emailed the results to the chief. We communicated through burner phones. When the cops asked, I told them they had a leak in the department."

"They didn't ask who the leak was?"

"Of course they did. I didn't talk. I was already going to be convicted of first-degree murder. What the hell difference does a little lie make?"

He began pacing again, clumps of melting snow falling around us.

"Is that why you . . . killed him the way you did?"

Ryder's gaze narrowed as he looked at me. "Yes, Louise. That's why I cut off his balls. So he could never rape another woman in his life. So he knew his most prized fucking possession was gone. And that's why I watched him choke on them before strangling him to death. Like he did to her."

"I don't blame you. I want you to know that."

"Let's keep jogging."

I nodded and we took off together again, this time at a slower pace.

"Okay, so considering you definitely killed the right guy . . . there's something else we need to consider." I looked at him, the clenched jaw telling me he knew exactly what I was about to say. "We need to consider if there was another person involved in Maci's death, the man who took the necklace. My thoughts? It's the man who would become the String Strangler. The timing adds up. Maci was killed around the time the Strangler killed his first victim. Or second, I might say."

"There couldn't have been another person there. There was no trace of anyone else."

"You said it yourself you think the Strangler is smart. Maybe he and Ortiz were buddies." When Ryder didn't respond, I continued. "We have to go to the cops."

"We're not going to the cops. *You're* not going to the cops. I can't go digging around murder investigations, don't you get that? I can't have my name associated with a recent murder. Hell, I don't even leave my house for fear I might get into a freak accident and hurt someone else. Even if it wasn't my fault, it could easily get pinned on the ex con who's still on parole. I'm not going back to jail." His voice shook. "I'm not fucking going back to hell."

"Yeah, but there could be a link somewhere that might help us find Kara's murderer. We have to explore it. If these cases are somehow connected, that means we're close to the Strangler. If we don't explore this, he's going to keep raping and murdering young women."

"Which is exactly why *you* need to drop this, Louise."

The woods opened up and we skirted the fields, the snow beginning to melt with the rising sun.

"I'm not dropping it. How can *you* drop it?"

"The guy who raped Maci was taken care of. That's all I care about. And I paid for it, for ten goddamn years. His debt was paid, as was mine."

"But what about Kara? Where's her justice?"

"Not my problem."

"Not your *problem*? How the *hell* can you say that?"

"You need to stay out of this, Louise."

"But what about the pendant? Aren't you the least bit curious to know why it was at Hollow Hill?"

"I can't afford to be curious!" he yelled, his voice echoing through the trees.

Frustrated, I pressed my lips into a thin line. I understood Ryder, but it bothered me that he wouldn't even entertain the idea of exploring my theory if it would bring Kara justice. It felt like no one was helping me. No one was giving Kara's case their full energy.

I pushed into a sprint. Ryder hung back, giving me space for a change. By the time I reached the house, I made a promise to myself that I wouldn't leave this town until the man who killed Kara was brought to justice. Help or no help.

I'd just stepped out of the shower when Ryder burst through the bedroom door. I squealed like a toddler and spun around, water from my wet hair splattering the wall. The towel I'd haphazardly wrapped around my body fell to the floor.

He froze in midstride, his eyes locking like laser beams on my breasts.

"Ryder!" I shrieked.

He snapped out of it. "Oh. Shit. Sorry."

I dropped to the floor in the fetal position, wrapping my arms around my legs. "Don't just stand there! *Jesus,* get me a towel!"

The Neanderthal finally sprang to action, covering his eyes with one hand while hurrying into the bathroom. I squeezed my eyes shut in pure horror. A towel was dropped over my face.

I yanked it off my head, wrapped it around my body, and jumped to my feet, my cheeks scorching with embarrassment.

"You good?" Ryder asked, his hand still covering his eyes.

"Yes."

He dropped his hand, and I glared at him.

"Don't you knock?"

He dared one more glance at my chest before he turned and sauntered out of the room, turned back, and knocked on the door frame.

I rolled my eyes. "Come *in.*"

He stepped inside. "Thanks for allowing me in my own room."

"You're welcome. Jerk."

"Hey, I can't help it that you didn't lock the door."

I wanted so badly to deliver an earth-shattering smartass response, but I was too flustered. Ryder smirked as he continued to stare at me. He liked me flustered. And in a towel, I think.

"Well." I casually swiped my hand through my hair, gathering the last shred of dignity I had in me. "What did you want, anyway?"

"Get dressed."

"I'd planned on it. What else you got?"

"I mean, we're leaving. Come on."

"Is this how you operate? Waking me up by hurling shoes at my forehead? Demanding morning jogs, demanding that I do this or don't do that? Demanding that I leave with you without giving me the courtesy of telling me where we're going?"

"Yep."

"Where are we going?"

"A few places. Come on."

"Does this have anything to do with Kara's murder?"

"Maybe. Come on."

"Tell me where we're going first."

"To talk to some friends."

"You don't have any friends."

"You coming or not?"

"Give me ten minutes."

"Five."

"Ryder, a woman needs ten minutes. I'm not asking. You will give me ten minutes. You can't control everything on the planet."

His brow slowly lifted, and after one more scan of my body, he left the room. But this time, he left the door open.

23

LOUISE

Thirty completely intentional minutes later, I made my way out of the master bedroom.

I'd taken my time for two reasons.

One, Ryder needed to understand that although he controlled every aspect of his own life, he couldn't control mine.

Two, after a man who looked like Ryder saw you naked, you put your best effort into your appearance for the next meeting.

I spun my hair into a sexy, bed-head-tousled knot at the top of my head, and combed my bangs until they were sleek and straight. I applied makeup, and even a little eyeliner, and lots of lip gloss. After considering my new clothes, I pulled on a pair of Damsel in a Dress skinny jeans and another cashmere sweater, which was quickly becoming my favorite fabric.

I looked good. Big ass and all.

Ryder was in the kitchen, wearing his usual jeans and untucked plaid button-up under a thick jacket. He turned as I walked in, scanning my body, and heat rose to my cheeks.

He handed me a mug. "You're twenty minutes late."

"And the world is still spinning, isn't it?" I took the mug. "Thank you, gracious and thoughtful host."

I expected a smartass response, but instead, he continued to stare at me with a look that had me shifting my weight.

"Well, you ready?"

He tore his gaze away and grabbed his mug. "Where's your coat?"

"In the bathroom."

"How's it going to keep you warm in there?"

I raised an eyebrow. "Are we going on a hike?"

"It's thirty-eight degrees outside. You should always be prepared."

"It's got to be exhausting being you."

"Not too bad."

"Don't you ever want to be spontaneous?"

"If spontaneous is walking through the middle of the woods during an ice storm while drunk on wine, no thanks."

"Brought me here, didn't it?"

He blinked.

"Meaning," I said quickly, following up, "because of my stupid decision to drive to Berry Springs in the middle of an ice storm with not much more than a box of wine, we might have found a link between your past and Kara's murder that could help find her killer. That's something." I sipped the coffee, eyeing him over the rim. "See, Ryder, sometimes unexpected blessings can happen in chaos. Sometimes throwing caution to the wind can lead you to things you never knew you wanted."

His head slowly tilted to the side. "What do *you* want, Louise?"

Butterflies flapped in my stomach as I tried to decide how to answer a question that I was sure had hidden meanings.

"I meant . . . it can lead you to things you wouldn't have seen before. You know, like the link in these cases."

Ryder released a throaty *hmph,* then nodded. "On that note, let's get going."

• • •

Thirty minutes later, we turned onto a barely there dirt road that I wouldn't have noticed driving by.

"Where are we going?"

"You'll see."

"Will I? Because all I see right now is millions of trees and not much else."

"Exactly."

About that time, the woods opened up to a clearing, where three trucks were parked under the trees.

"These trucks were parked outside of Astor Stone's PI firm the other day."

"Yep."

He rolled to a stop and parked.

"These are your former coworkers, right?"

"Yep."

Ryder shut off the engine and pulled the keys from the ignition. "Grab that coat you said you didn't need."

I slipped on my new leather coat and got out. Shouts and loud banging echoed in the distance, followed by a few gunshots.

"Where are we?"

"Training facility."

"You're joking."

"Nope."

He led me down a path flattened by boot prints and not much else.

"Why is it all the way out here?"

"Privacy."

The woods opened up, and my eyes rounded. A massive field had been cleared, the snow plowed. Where once was thousands of trees was now a massive military-style obstacle course, a shooting range, and a long black building that resembled the office I'd visited days earlier.

"Wow. This really is very James Bond."

Ryder laughed at this, the sound settling warmly in my stomach.

"That building looks like the office I went to. What's with the prison compound look?"

"The buildings are built for security. Think of them like bunkers. They're soundproof, bombproof, fireproof, and totally off the grid."

"What do you mean, off the grid?"

"Meaning, all communication inside that building is basically hack-proof. If you didn't notice, your cell phone stopped working the moment you walked onto the property. All signals are blocked. No one outside any one of Astor's buildings can track or see any communication or signals inside. If a drone flew over, it wouldn't pick up any technology, not even heat signatures of the people inside. The place runs solely on a secure satellite connection and generates its own power."

"Are these his only two offices?"

"No. Astor's main office is in New York. He chooses Berry Springs solely for the location. It's in a landlocked state in the middle of the country—less likely to be a target of terrorists—and in a small, unassuming town in the middle of the mountains. He's got offices on both coasts, London,

Paris, Tokyo, and I think he recently opened in Dubai, although I'm ninety percent sure that's just because he likes vacationing there."

"Does the government pay for all this?"

"God, no. They send us target packets and pay a fee for each completed mission. A lot of money."

"Failed or not?"

Ryder nodded.

"Why would they pay for a mission that failed?"

"Astor's a hell of a businessman."

"Still . . ."

"We're—" He caught himself on the word. "They're the best in the world. Astor trains his agents for years before they're released into the field."

"Do you miss it?"

Shrugging, he glanced down.

"You think you'll ever work again?"

"My ranch is my work."

"I get that. But, Ryder, for the rest of your life, you're just going to spend every day, all day, on that ranch by yourself?"

He opened his mouth to respond but was cut off when someone jumped out of the woods, startling a squeak out of me.

Ryder didn't flinch.

"Well, holy fucking shit." Mack spat out the toothpick that was hanging from his mouth. "Either I've had too much to drink or I'm staring at the man, the myth, the legend himself, right here at our training facility."

"You shouldn't be drinking at nine in the morning, Mack."

"Louise Sloane." Mack cocked his head. "Quite the surprise. How do you know this asshole?"

"My car broke down and he helped out. Have you found out anything about Kara's case yet?"

"Workin' on it."

Just then, another super-silent ninja emerged from the woods.

"Well, holy shit."

"Seems to be the general consensus," Ryder muttered as Justin stepped onto the path. The two men shook hands, and I could tell they were closer than Ryder and Mack.

"Knew you'd come to your senses." Justin slapped him on the back. "Glad you're back, bro."

Mack laughed. "Astor's gonna shit when I tell him you're back."

"I'm not back."

Mack frowned. "What do you mean?"

"I'm here because I need a favor."

"Stone won't do shit for you unless you sign on the dotted line. You know how he is."

"Then I need a favor under the table."

Justin's brow furrowed as he looked back and forth between Ryder and me. Ryder shifted closer to me, angling his body between me and the two men.

"Well, come on then." Justin eyed me, obviously picking up on his former partner's protective body language. "Let's head to the range."

Ryder motioned me ahead of him as we fell into step behind Mack and Justin. I felt him close at my back as we walked along the obstacle course, and finally into the shiny black building.

The inside resembled the office I'd visited, with sleek black walls, no windows, and endless security and palm-print locks. Wires ran across the ceiling.

Once we passed through two doors of security, the

building opened up to an enormous room. To the left was an indoor shooting range with four lanes. To the right, an expansive gym and two boxing rings. In the back, a few chairs gathered around a big-screen TV that I assumed was for mission research and updates.

My body jerked as the sound of a rapid succession of gunshots ripped through the air. A hand softly squeezed my waist, sending a different kind of reaction through my body.

Justin led us past the range, where the tattooed agent, Roman, lowered his gun, his gaze fixing on Ryder. There was no acknowledgment between them, unlike with Mack and Justin.

"Do you know him?" I whispered.

"No. He's new. Former SEAL, discharged for fighting."

"He's kinda scary."

"Then stay away from him."

"You don't trust him?"

"I don't trust anyone I don't know. He's from Ireland and moved to the US when he was a teen. Lived in Missouri, I believe, before moving to the area not long ago."

As we were led farther into the building, I glanced over my shoulder to see Roman still watching us. Ryder's presence seemed to rattle everyone.

Justin pulled open a door hidden in the back wall. This led us down a short hall and finally into an impressive kitchen, considering how undomesticated the place was.

"The boys like to eat," Ryder whispered in my ear.

"Well, that's one thing we have in common," I said with a wink.

He grinned, his hand finding my waist again as he gently guided me toward the table. I sat, but Ryder didn't. Instead, he stood a few inches in front of me, again angling his body where I was shielded from the constant glances. He was like a drug dealer guarding his loot, or a king guarding his queen.

"Coffee?" Mack asked as he poured a cup for himself.

Ryder looked at me, and I shook my head.

"No," he said.

Justin sank into the chair across from me while Mack leaned against the counter in front of Ryder. Both men eyed me, their curiosity palpable.

"Okay, talk." Justin crossed his arms over his chest. "What do you need?"

"I need you to pull Maci's files from BSPD. The crime scene photos, the official report, interview transcripts, autopsy report, forensic reports, everything. Everything the cops have."

"Why?" Mack demanded.

"I think there might be a connection to the recent murder on Summit Mountain."

Four eyes shifted to me.

"Ah," Mack said. "So that's where little Louise here comes into play."

Ryder's voice turned cold. "Miss Sloane."

Mack's brows slowly lifted. "Miss *Sloane*." He glanced at Justin.

Justin jumped in. "Ryder, don't you think you should stay out of—"

"I just want the files. To read over them. That's it."

"So you've come all the way here, asking us to hack into BSPD's files and pull your girl's file?"

"Maci's," Ryder said tersely, correcting him.

"Dude." Justin spread his palms. "You're trained, just like we are. You're one of our best hackers. Why can't you do it?"

"He's still on parole," I blurted. "He could get in trouble."

Mack and Justin's gazes narrowed, assessing.

"Why, man?" Justin asked. "Why now? It's been twelve years. You got the guy. Why open it back up?"

"To close it."

The room fell so silent, I swear I could hear my heart beating.

"I'll do it."

My head turned toward the doorway where Roman was standing. I didn't even hear him come in.

"When do you need it?" Roman asked.

"Now."

"I'll have it by this time tomorrow."

As Ryder dipped his chin in thanks, Justin shook his head.

Mack pushed up from the table. "That's it?"

All eyes locked on Ryder.

"That's it."

When I stood, Ryder grabbed my hand. He took a moment to look at each man before leading me through the doors, clearly telegraphing *she's mine*.

"I thought you said earlier that you didn't want anything else to do with this? Why the change of heart?" I whispered as Ryder pulled me through the building.

"You're not going to drop this, and I won't let you do it alone."

I squeezed his hand. "Thank you. For Kara, and for every woman whose life has been destroyed by the Strangler, thank you."

Ryder nodded.

"Where to now?"

"The one place I promised myself I'd never go again."

24

LOUISE

$\mathcal{M}$y heart pounded as we pushed through the doors of the Berry Springs police station. Although Ryder tried to conceal it, I could tell he was nervous.

Me? I was a wreck.

Ryder was about to walk into the last place he'd been as a free man, the last place he'd been before being thrown in an eight-by-eight cell for ten years. The place where his life changed forever. And he was doing it for me, for Kara, for every woman who'd been raped and murdered and whose case was sitting in an evidence freezer somewhere.

The receptionist, Ellen, looked up from her cell phone and flashed a welcoming smile at me. Then she looked at Ryder, blinking a few times, paling much like Mrs. Booth had at Donny's Diner. The cell phone slipped from her hand, clattering onto the desk, but she didn't notice.

"Afternoon, Ellen."

"Heyyy . . . Ryder."

Apparently, the two knew each other, as did everyone else in this small town. It was like I no longer existed.

Ryder squared his shoulders. "Is Chief McCord in?"

"Uh, let me check. Reason?"

"I'd like to talk to him about Kara Meyers." His voice was level but loaded.

Her eyes widened more. Yep, the convicted murderer was here to talk to the chief of police about a woman who'd been murdered weeks earlier.

Ellen refocused on her computer, rapidly typing over what I assumed was an internal instant message system. After a minute, she looked up. "He'll be right out."

"Thought so."

The minutes waiting felt like hours as I sat in a cold plastic chair while Ryder stood next to me, his hands in his pockets, staring at the door that led into the station. I reached over and lightly grabbed his forearm. The touch seemed to startle him, and he looked down at me.

"Everything's going to be okay," I whispered. "We're doing the right thing."

The door opened with a loud beep, and I shot to my feet.

Dressed in a navy dress shirt under a wool vest, a pair of starched jeans, and cowboy boots, McCord locked on Ryder as he crossed the floor, the click of his boots echoing in the silence.

The air was instantly sucked from the room.

"Ryder." McCord reached out his hand, but Ryder didn't shake it.

"Hi, Chief McCord," I said quickly. "Thanks for seeing us."

The balding chief shifted his attention to me. "Miss Sloane, I don't have any new information about the Kara Meyers case."

"We do," Ryder said.

McCord's brow cocked. "Do ya now?"

"If you have a second," I said, "we'd like to talk to you about something we found at Hollow Hill."

The chief's gaze flicked back to Ryder before settling on me again. "I've got five minutes."

"It won't take three," Ryder muttered.

"Even better." McCord turned and strode across the lobby, our cue to follow.

You could have heard a pin drop as we were led through the bullpen, heads peeking up from tiny gray cubicles. Not even a single phone rang. I assumed Ellen had already spread the word.

I glared at each pair of eyes as we passed. Ryder didn't deserve this.

We were led into the corner office at the end of the hallway.

McCord pulled the papers from one chair and haphazardly pulled another from the corner, this one with some sort of sticky substance dried to the armrest. The office was a pigsty, and I wondered how someone who fancied himself a leader would allow such chaos around him.

His oak desk was covered in folders, coffee mugs, napkins, wrappers. A file cabinet sat next to an overpacked bookcase. An American flag hung on the wall behind his power chair, the only decoration on the bleak gray walls. No pictures, no plants.

McCord tossed a greasy paper bag into the trash can and sank into his chair. I sat in the seat across from him. Ryder remained standing. He pulled a small plastic bag from his pocket.

"Inside this bag is a pendant Louise and I found at the Hollow Hill estate yesterday. I believe it belongs to Maci Jones."

A moment passed as McCord slowly squinted. "You sure?"

"I gave her a necklace with a pendant that looked exactly like this a few months before Leon Ortiz killed her. She wore it every day. It wasn't on her when I found her, or in the house."

McCord leaned back in his chair, expelling air from his lungs. "Do you know how many teenagers have been in and out of that place over that last twelve years?"

"No, I wouldn't," Ryder deadpanned.

"No, I guess you wouldn't. Many. We patrolled it frequently for a while, and because of that, no one goes out there anymore. But before we kicked up patrols, countless locals and tourists partied and did God knows what out there. No telling what you could find if you searched every corner."

"Didn't you?" I asked. "When you were looking for Kara? Didn't you search every corner?"

"There was no sign of her there, or anyone else. As I told you. Seven times."

"Both Kara and Maci were raped, beaten, and murdered with a string. And it's widely assumed the String Strangler lives in the area. I think there's a connection here that's worth checking into. Have you contacted the FBI about the similarities between Kara's murder and the other girls murdered by the Strangler?"

"I have, and that's all I'm obliged to tell you about that, Miss Sloane." He looked at Ryder. "And regarding the pendant, Maci's killer was already . . . taken care of."

"Right, but it shouldn't be discounted," I said. "I mean, how would Maci's pendant end up there? Maybe there was a second person involved in her murder, and he took the necklace. You could check—"

"I want it scanned for fingerprints," Ryder said impatiently, cutting in. "If nothing turns up, fine. If you get a hit, that gives you a lead to chase in Kara's case that I hear has gone cold."

A solid minute passed as the chief stared at us and we stared back at him.

McCord slapped his palms on his thighs and stood. "I'll see what I can do, kids." He took the baggie from Ryder.

"I expect that back after you're done with it."

McCord nodded and stepped around his desk, knocking a stack of papers onto the floor. He pulled open the door. "Good to see you again, Ryder."

This time, I grabbed Ryder's hand and led him outside.

25

LOUISE

Our next stop was at the location where I'd found Kara's body. We parked next to the same pine tree I'd parked under days earlier, hours before I found her body.

Ryder opened my door and helped me out of the truck. My stomach knotted the moment my boots hit the snow-covered ground. The silence and the stillness of the woods reminded me of that night.

"Can you remember exactly where you found her?"

"I wish I could forget, trust me."

Understanding, he nodded. "Zip up. It's cold."

I zipped my coat and narrowed my sights. "All right. This way."

We took off through the woods, the sunlight shimmering off the snow and ice. The temperature stubbornly hovered at around forty degrees, but between the sun reflecting off the snow, my heavy coat, and our brisk pace, I was toasty warm. I had a feeling it had something to do with the man next to me too.

"You were good in there," I said.

"Where?"

"McCord's office."

"McCord's an ass. Been at that desk too long, and the entire town agrees. He's complacent, sloppy, and bored with his job."

"I can see that. How do you know Ellen?"

Ryder frowned as he looked at me. "She looked like she'd seen a ghost when I walked in, didn't she?"

So he'd noticed.

He sighed, as if resigned to the fact that he'd likely get that reaction for the rest of his life. I disagreed with that.

"You know the saying 'time heals all wounds'?"

He nodded.

"Time also helps fade memories. Not erase completely, but lessen the blow, so to speak."

"Where are you going with this?"

"Everyone has a strong reaction to you now because it's their first time seeing you. What I'm saying is, if you get out more and force yourself back into society, everyone's initial shock will fade. They'll remember the Ryder that I'm assuming ran the town growing up. Don't give them a reason to remember your time in jail. Be happy, polite, kind. They'll forget. You just have to get out there. Out of your damn house."

Ryder snorted. "Easier said than done, especially when I run into people like Ellen. We went to high school together and ran in the same crew. She was a cheerleader. She even decorated my football locker a few times."

"I still can't believe you played football."

He stepped in front of me, held back a branch, and motioned me past. "Well, brace yourself. I was also voted class comedian in high school."

"Is that a joke? Did I just witness your first joke since prison?"

"Nope. Serious."

"No. I don't believe it for two seconds."

"And most athletic. I got both."

"No best-looking?"

"They didn't have that category. Politics."

"Are you being serious?"

"Dead."

"Class clown and most athletic." I shook my head. "Hard to believe. Tell me more. What were you like in high school?"

"I got in trouble a lot."

I feigned surprise. "*No.* I'm shocked."

He laughed. "I guess I was your normal run-of-the-mill, rowdy, ADHD kid. I lived for football. Loved everything about it. The early morning workouts, the strategy, the smell of the grass. The camaraderie."

"Do you keep in touch with any of those guys?"

"No." His gaze dropped to the snow. "When you go away, people tend to forget about you."

"No one visited you while you were in?"

"Aside from my brother and getting a few marriage proposals, no."

"Marriage proposals?"

"Oh yeah. I got a lot of letters from women all over the country who'd seen the story when it went national. A few came to visit. Unsettling, really."

"Women do love a bad boy."

"Do you?"

"I tend to go for underachievers."

"There it is—all that forethought."

I laughed. "Exactly. All crashed and burned, of course."

"When was your last boyfriend?"

I scratched my chin. "When was the last solar eclipse?"

Ryder looked at me, tilting his head. "You undervalue yourself, Louise."

I flicked my hand in the air, dismissing what he said, because in reality, I knew it was true. "How did this turn around on me so quickly? Back to you. Seriously, no one visited you while you were away?"

"Seriously, no one visited me. I get it, though. No hard feelings. I know what I did was . . . vicious. Brutal. I get why people would look at me differently afterward. I understand why they would want to distance themselves from me."

"Do you regret it?"

His face hardened, and then he looked at me with a forced smile. "There you go, asking the hard questions."

"Sorry."

He exhaled. "Honest answer?"

"Yes."

"Can you handle it?"

"Yes."

"No, I don't regret it. I don't regret killing Leon Ortiz."

"I don't blame you, Ryder."

"So you've said."

"I really don't. I want you to know that."

"Thanks." A moment passed. "I don't regret it, but I wish I would have thought it through, maybe. Not been so impulsive."

"First, you're in good company there." I winked. "And second, how so?"

"Maybe if I would have had more self-control, a clearer head, maybe if I would have let a few days pass, things might've been different. Maybe I wouldn't have killed him. In which case . . ."

Ryder breathed out. "*God* . . . I can't imagine having the last twelve years of my life back. I think about that a lot. Where would I be right now? What would I be doing? Would I be married with kids? Coaching football? Who knows? Or, on the other hand, maybe I still would have killed Ortiz, but I would've planned a solid exit strategy. I could've been in Tahiti, sipping tequila and starting a new life as Louis Makatozi."

"Louis Makatozi?"

He winked. "Yep. That's my go-name if I ever need to skip town. You now know my deepest, darkest secret."

"I don't know if I should feel flattered or insulted that the name resembles mine."

"Louise is a classic name. Timeless."

"Okay, tell me about this name."

"Well, my favorite author of all time is Louis L'Amour. Heard of him?"

"He writes old westerns, right? Cowboys, revenge, justice."

"Exactly. No one writes about the good ol' days anymore."

"What about the Maka . . . what?"

"Tozi. Makatozi. Joseph Makatozi was the hero in my favorite book of Louis L'Amour's, *Last of the Breed*. It's about an Air Force pilot who gets shot down by the Soviets and captured. Badass. Anyway, I put both names together—*bada bing, bada boom*—and got my go-name."

"Louis Makatozi," I repeated. "I could see him lounging on the beach . . . or eating his weight in Polish sausages, for some reason."

Ryder tipped his head back and laughed. A loud, boisterous laugh. "Sounds not too bad right about now, doesn't it? I guess my point to all that is I spent ten years in that prison cell realizing how important it is to think through your decisions, especially the big ones, with a clear head. You're mad? Sit it out for a while. Walk away. You're scared? Change tactics. Think before you act. *Think* before you act."

"That's why you're so hard on me for getting my car stuck."

"Yes. Every decision you made that night was dangerous. If you would have turned around when you heard the weather warning, or better yet, stayed home and stayed out of this, you wouldn't have had all the trouble you did. You understand that I legitimately could have killed you when you broke into my house? You were nothing but an intruder to me."

"But you didn't pull the trigger."

"No. Because I took a breath. *Assessed* before I acted."

"Noted."

We walked a moment in silence.

"I don't know," I said with a sigh. "All my life, I've been spontaneous. Never set goals, just took life day by day. Kinda lost, I guess. Always searching for something but not knowing what that thing is."

"Kind of like now."

I didn't respond.

"Have you ever considered the fact that maybe you're taking Kara's case so personally because you're craving something meaningful in your own life? You've dedicated your life to this case because you have nothing else in your life to be passionate about? To fill that space?"

"I'm taking it personally because I want to get Kara justice. I'm the only one who will press the cops."

Ryder gave me an assessing look. "I get that, but you're

going above and beyond, inserting yourself into the investigation, interviewing people, searching her last-known locations. Maybe you're making it your personal mission because you're craving to make a difference. Somehow. And you've sunk your teeth into this."

"So, what you're telling me is that you enjoy self-help books as much as romantic thrillers."

"Calling it like I see it."

"Well, call it somewhere else. You're making me uncomfortable."

"Okay," he said, "answer me this. When you were a kid, what did you want to be when you grew up?"

"Aside from the garbage man?"

"Liked the truck, huh?"

"So much. I'd wait by the window on trash day. Truth? A detective."

"Bingo. You're a born problem-solver. You're a do-gooder. You just haven't found the right avenue to apply that passion."

"You know I never went to college."

"There's nothing wrong with that."

"I guess not."

"Only ten point six percent of the US population own their own business. That's nothing to sneeze at. It's the American dream. How'd you get into photography?"

"Well, simple story, really. After high school, I needed a job, so I applied for the first one I came across, which was a receptionist at the local newspaper. One day, the only journalist on staff called in sick, and my boss asked if I could take a few pictures of the county fair for the weekend story."

Smiling, I indulged in the memory. "I remember that day so vividly. The sun was setting, glittering streaks of fuchsia and gold over brightly colored tents and giggling children. It looked like a postcard. Once the families realized I was taking pictures for the newspaper, I became almost as popular as the miniature ponies . . . I'm avoiding a self-deprecating ass comment here, just so you know."

"Small steps. Good job."

"Anyway, as I clicked away, I remember feeling like something came to life inside me. I was having so much fun. I loved the thought of capturing moments that would last forever. I loved finding the angles, the light, the perfect backgrounds. I stayed for hours, taking pictures, laughing, connecting with strangers. And that was it. I found my calling, my passion. You know the saying a picture is worth a thousand words?"

He nodded, hanging on my every word.

"It's so true. Sometimes when you're talking to someone, you see them, but you don't *see* them, if that makes sense. Photographs are a way to capture our spirit, who we truly are. They give us a tangible way to reflect, to remember, to appreciate. Capturing a family's most intimate moments is an honor. Seeing their smiles when they see the pictures."

"There's that do-gooder in you."

"Guess so."

"What made you stick with it? Make that step to turn it into a business?"

I smiled. "A woman named Magnus Archer."

"Sounds like a firecracker."

I laughed. "She was. Magnus hired me to photograph one of her homes that she intended to sell. She was a widow, very wealthy, who'd spent her life painting. She was an artist. We took a liking to each other, and for reasons I'll never understand—and will always be grateful for— Magnus offered to become my guinea pig while I fine-tuned my craft, allowing me to photograph her land, her house, her horses, pets, and even herself.

"I'd take pictures during the afternoon, then we'd sit down with tea in the evenings, go through each one and talk about what I could have done to make it better. She's the reason I had the confidence to take the next step and start my business. She believed in me. A total stranger believed in me. The day she died, I decided to pay that forward. I signed up to be a sponsor at the Sunshine Club, a local program for underprivileged children."

"And that's how you met Kara."

I nodded. "Eight years later, I found her murdered in the mountains of Berry Springs." I blew out a breath, shaking my head. "Kara reminded me a lot of myself. A drifter, spontaneous, no real direction. I felt a kindred spirit with her. I can, I mean *could* relate to her."

"Louise, this isn't your fault."

"I know, but I feel like maybe if I would have mentored her better—"

"Stop. It's not your fault. No one could have stopped me the night I did what I did. You can't control everyone."

My brows arched. "You need to say that in the mirror."

"Message received. But seriously, you've got to let the authorities handle it. This isn't your job."

"Oh no, no, *no,* you don't get to lecture about *jobs.* Why won't you go back to work at Astor Stone? It's obvious they want you back, and you told me how much you loved it."

"Why don't you fulfill your dream of doing something that matters?"

Nodding, I swallowed. Ryder and I were both in a rut. In a weird state of limbo in this thing called life, trying to figure out our next move, but not knowing how to take the next step. Or perhaps not courageous enough to.

"What was it like?" I asked after a beat.

"Prison?"

"Yeah."

"Hot."

"Hot?" It was the least expected response.

"Yeah. You'd probably think cold, right? Nope. Hundreds of felons packed behind concrete walls, restless, constantly moving. I went to bed every night drenched in sweat."

The epiphany hit me. *"That's* why you keep your house so cold."

He nodded. "It's nothing you'd understand unless you experience it. It truly is hell on earth."

"Was there violence?"

"Every single day. Some days every hour, it seemed."

"Did you get in fights?"

"In the beginning, a lot. My first day, an asshole jumped me. I laid him out. Broke his jaw, a few ribs. Spent three days in solitary confinement. After that, a few more. I won each fight, and eventually I earned some respect."

"Did you make any friends?"

"No."

"In ten years, you didn't make a single friend?"

"No. I'd go days without speaking a single word."

"What did you do to pass the time?"

He looked over, a grin brightening his solemn face. "I read romance novels."

I laughed.

"Seriously, I read. So much. Every kind of book I could get my hands on. Anyway, every new guy who came in had something to prove. You'd have to be on your toes until he kicked someone's ass, or his ass got kicked. Then you'd relax until the next new guy. Ten years of new guys. And you were constantly shuffled around. So as soon as you'd feel like your current cell mate wasn't going to kill you, you'd be moved somewhere else and go through it all again. Every sickness or virus in those places spread like the plague. So gross. The nights were the worst. Most of the guys couldn't sleep, so they'd pace in their cells, screaming the craziest shit you've ever heard. Insane, raging screams, or groans like they were dying. They'd bang on the walls, rattle the bars. It was terrible."

"Didn't they get in trouble for it?"

Ryder's laugh answered the question. "I was in a cell with two other guys once for a few weeks. Overcrowding is a huge problem in prisons, by the way. Anyway, they took a liking to each other. Every night, they fucked while I pretended to sleep three feet away. For hours. I remember the smell. God, it was awful." He looked over. "Sorry."

"It's okay," I lied, resisting putting my hand over my churning stomach. A nightmare. Hell on earth. I couldn't imagine.

He continued to talk, as if it were a release. "Every time I'd be up for parole, the damn prosecuting attorney would show the pictures of what I'd done to Ortiz, and parole was denied, every time. Despite the fact that the son of a bitch murdered my unborn baby."

"What did you do your first day out?"

"My brother picked me up. He had a truck for me. I got in and took off—despite his pleas for me to stay with him— and drove straight to the mountains. I spent the day hiking aimlessly. Swam in the river. Ran in the fields. Slept under the stars that night." He laughed. "Like a wild mountain man. I watched the sun rise on the mountain top where I eventually placed two headstones to honor Maci and my baby. Where you saw me that night?"

I nodded.

"While I was hiking that day, I came across a for sale sign. The next day, I purchased the house—my house now—along with the four hundred surrounding acres. The rest is history."

"Lots of space."

"Exactly."

I walked in silence for a few moments. Drips of melting ice fell from the trees, catching in the sunlight before plopping to the ground.

"I'm sorry." He didn't look at me as he apologized.

"For what?"

"For how I treated you the first couple of days. Especially for making you sleep on the floor the first night."

"You were kind of an asshole."

"I know. I just . . . I'm not used to someone in my space, and that's an understatement. I don't—didn't—*want* people in my space. I also don't trust anyone. And the cherry on top of those psychological issues is that spending a decade in prison made me a bit of a germaphobe."

"You don't say." I winked.

"I really am sorry."

"I accept your apology because now I understand the whys behind it." I stared at him a moment. "I will say, though, that I hope your circumstances won't continue to define your life, Ryder."

Just then, the trees opened up to rocky terrain. Boulders shot up from the ground like spears.

I pointed ahead. "That's it. I found Kara's body right up there."

Nerves tickled my stomach as we walked up to the boulders where Kara's body had been tossed to rot.

Ryder's brows squeezed in concentration as he looked around.

"She was right in the middle of these rocks. Here."

"Someone dragged her out here."

"Agreed."

"Question is," Ryder said thoughtfully, "why here? Why this location?"

"The Strangler drops his victims' bodies in remote areas."

"The county owns this land. It's big for hunting. It has to be someone who knows the location. Hunts, maybe."

Ryder knelt down and sifted through the snow and dirt. I pulled out my camera and took pictures of the rocks, the trees, even the sky. Noticing Ryder had stilled behind me, I turned and found him staring at something on the ground.

I crossed the rocks and squatted beside him, squinting at what appeared to be a blue scrap of fabric.

"What is that? A part of a T-shirt?"

"It's a piece of a tarp. That's how he carried Kara here. Son of a bitch wrapped her in a tarp and dragged her." He glanced at the jagged rock. "Probably snagged it when he unwrapped her."

"How did the cops not find this?"

"Could have been buried under boot prints or under a rock. It's been over a week since she was dumped. No telling what unearthed it."

"Did your brother say that her autopsy showed that she'd been dragged?"

"The body was too decomposed and ravaged by scavengers. Would've been hard to tell. I don't recall him saying anything about polyethylene on her skin or hair either."

"Poly-what?"

"Polyethylene. It's what most tarps are made of. If a body is transported by tarp, occasionally the fibers are found in their hair, or under their fingernails if they tried to scratch their way out."

I shuddered, staring at the blue scrap of fabric, wondering if Kara had been alive when she was dragged through the woods.

26

LOUISE

*M*y phone beeped the moment we stepped out of the woods and into the clearing where Ryder had parked his truck.

Stopping by the truck, I listened to the first voice mail.

"Miss Sloane, this is Frankie up at Frankie's Auto, callin' to let you know your car is ready for pickup."

Then the second.

"Miss Sloane, this is Paula from Shadow Creek Resort, returning your call. We have one room, just opened up. Call me back as soon as possible if you'd still like me to reserve it for you."

"Everything all right?" Ryder asked.

"My car's ready . . . and they've got a room for me at Shadow Creek Resort."

We stared at each other with the weight of a thousand words.

Please ask me to stay, please ask me to stay with you . . .

But when I opened my mouth to speak, Ryder spoke up first.

"Well. Do you need to call them back?"

I snapped. I don't know why it happened at that

moment, but I was so sick of the mixed signals Ryder was giving me.

Did he want me to stay with him? If so, why the hell didn't he ask? Did he hate me? Like me? Want to kiss me again?

"I don't know, Ryder," I said, laying on the attitude. "Do you want me to call him back?"

He lifted a shoulder. Like it was no big deal to him.

I grabbed the door handle. "Take me to my car. I'm going to go home. Maybe you're right. I need to get the hell out of here."

The door was locked.

"Why?" he asked as I yanked aggressively.

I spun around, sliding on a slick rock. Ryder grabbed my arm, but I yanked it away.

"Why? Because I'm so damn sick of your mixed signals. I'm going to just . . . get out of here."

"The roads aren't cleared, Louise. Especially not all the way to Ponco. That's a three-hour drive."

"What the hell do you care, anyway? All of a sudden you're worried for my well-being? All of a sudden you've had a change of heart and like me? Bullshit."

His eyes narrowed.

"You don't think I know why you didn't shoot me the night I broke into your house? Because you're still on parole. You didn't want another dead body on your hands. And why you picked me up at the lake when I had nowhere else to stay? Because if I would have died that night from hypothermia, or from the freaking String Strangler himself, it would be a body linked to you. You would've been the one that left me."

Taking a breath, I said, "You couldn't get me out of your damn house fast enough the next morning. And when you realized my car was broken down, you'd rather ride hours on horseback in a snowstorm to escort me to my hotel, rather than offer me shelter for just one more night in your house of ice."

His eyes narrowed on me. He didn't like that.

But I did. I was a bomb slowly exploding, and it felt damn good.

So I kept going.

"You wanted *nothing* to do with me. That's the only freaking reason you've helped me out. To get me out of your hair." Frustrated but on a roll, I began pacing. "But then you hold my hand, seem protective of me, give me glimpses of someone I want to know so badly. You kissed me, right there in your house, gave me the best goddamn kiss of my life. And you give me a look—that *look*—that sends goose bumps right down to my toes. I want to get to know *that* guy. The *old* you. I meant what I said earlier. You can't allow what happened to you to ruin the rest of your life. It's fucking annoying. You are not a victim in life. You're an asshole. You're selfish. You're a jerk. You're so fucking *gorgeous*—"

His lips were on mine before I could finish my tirade, his hands cupping my face gently, disarming me. My head spinning, I melted into the snow, and my camera slipped from my fingers.

Ryder's hand wrapped around the back of my head, fisting my hair as we kissed in the snow with drips of melting ice falling on our shoulders. He released me and pulled back, taking several steps, his chest rising and falling heavily. He opened his mouth, then closed it again as if searching for the perfect words.

"Do you know why that tile by the front door is busted?" he asked.

I shook my head because forming a complete sentence was an impossibility at that moment.

"Because I had to get rid of you. *All* of you. Because even though you were no longer in my space, I couldn't fucking stop thinking about you. It was like you were suddenly tattooed on my brain. Someone I didn't even know. It didn't make sense. I didn't like it. I didn't like this kind of instant power you had over me."

He took a step closer. "You are, Louise Sloane, the most mesmerizingly beautiful disaster of a woman I've ever met in my life. Your lips, your eyes, those little freaking dimples when you smile. You're so beautiful and don't even realize it, and that only makes you more beautiful. When I saw you wearing my T-shirt that day . . ." He looked down and shook his head, then looked back up. "I liked it. You fit, right there in my room, in my bed, in my shirt. I liked it. Do you know why I asked you to wear the blue sweatpants?"

"No," I whispered.

"Because they were the smallest size you had. I wanted to see you, every gorgeous curve of you."

As color rose in my cheeks, heating them, he looked away, scrubbing his hand over his mouth.

"You said a picture is worth a thousand words. Louise, when I saw that picture you took of me at the lake while I was fishing, I . . . I didn't recognize myself. I looked so . . . depressed. Old. It was shocking. You're right, the picture you took was like a slap in the face. How sad to spend the rest of my life like that guy? Alone, tortured. God, I could see it on my fucking face."

His hands curled to fists at his sides.

"I don't know how to change it," he growled. "The last woman I was with died tragically, and my baby with her. I killed the man who killed them. I don't . . . I don't see myself having a relationship ever again. Like I'm jinxed or some-thing. And more than that, why would someone want me and all my damn baggage? I can't even take someone on a date in this town without being side-eyed out of the room."

Frustrated, I waved my arms emphatically. "That's exactly why you can't allow this to define you. What happened in the past doesn't mean the next woman you allow into your life is going to face the same fate. You—the old Ryder—didn't want to be alone. I see it in your eyes. You want a family. You *are* worthy, like you told me I was. You just have to let the past go. One day at a time, which is the complete opposite of how you operate now."

I closed the inches between us and grabbed his hand. "One day at a time."

Ryder blinked, the tip of his nose turning red. I figured that was the closest the man came to crying.

"Something about you has made me feel again," he whispered. "Alive. *Life.*"

He tucked a strand of hair behind my ear, looking down at me.

"I'm not ready to let you go, Lou. I'd like you to stay with me tonight. Please. I'd like you to come home with me."

Lou.

27

LOUISE

I turned into the long driveway to the castle on the hill with Ryder on my bumper, as he'd been the entire drive.

Ansel had not one but *four* new tires, a new axle, new headliner, an oil change, his radiator flushed, and even one of those pine tree air fresheners hanging from the rearview mirror. I wasn't sure what to make of the last improvement, but it smelled fantastic.

The best part, though? The brand-spanking-new visor that didn't flap in my face.

He drove like a new car. Even the steering felt tighter.

When I went to pay, Frankie told me the bill was already taken care of. I pissed and moaned, fought and kicked, but he wouldn't take my money.

I promised Ryder I'd pay him back, but he cut my words short with a kiss. Damn good way to shut me up, I learned.

I would pay him back, though, every penny. For both the repairs and the clothes. It would take a budget and some planning, which would pretty much be an entire life change. Which was probably long overdue.

As I crested the driveway, I frowned. A shiny black Escalade was parked in front of Ryder's house.

The hermit had company? Ryder didn't even have friends.

I glanced in the rearview mirror as he gunned it around me, cutting me off, noticing the car as I did. He blocked in the SUV and jumped out, his hand sliding to the gun on his belt.

Shit.

Wide-eyed, I hit the brakes.

Ryder held up his hand, clearly meaning *wait there.*

My heart pounded as I gripped the steering wheel, watching Ryder do a three-sixty of the vehicle and then disappear on the other side between the house and the SUV. A minute passed, two, three. When he finally emerged, this time from the garage, he motioned me to drive forward.

"What's going on?" I asked once I'd parked in the garage and gotten out.

"Uninvited guests."

"Who?"

I followed him inside to the kitchen, where Mack and Roman were pouring Scotch into short glasses. They glanced up and dipped their chins in greeting. Their expressions grim, they refocused on the drinks.

Something was off. Wrong.

"Talk." Ryder snatched the glass from Mack and downed the shot it contained.

Mack pulled another glass from the cabinet and filled it. "Still slick as shit out there."

"You didn't come here to talk about the weather."

Roman sipped his drink. "We didn't want to do this over the phone."

"You think someone's tapped my phones?"

"Not necessarily—"

"He's afraid you'll go ape-shit and burn down the town." Mack knocked back the shot. "Damn, that's good."

Ryder practically growled. "Someone better tell me what the hell's going on."

Roman pulled a laptop from his bag and set it on the table. His fingers flew over the keyboard as he logged into several secure screens.

I stayed back, but close enough to hear.

"You asked me to pull Maci's file from BSPD."

"That's right."

Roman turned the laptop around. Ryder yanked it from him and began scrolling.

"I read through it, and something stood out."

"What?" Ryder asked as he scanned the files.

"First, let me make sure I'm clear. As I understand it, the story goes that Ortiz broke into your house, and raped and strangled Maci before slipping out the back door. We know this because the front door lock was busted, verifying that he broke in, his DNA was found on her body, verifying he raped her, and boot prints led out the back door, verifying he left out the back. Correct?"

"Yes. What the hell is your point?"

"Is there anything else you remember? Did the cops tell you anything else at all?"

Ryder straightened, one hand lingering on the laptop keys. With the other, he picked up his drink almost mindlessly, as if he sensed he needed it to prepare himself for whatever Roman was about to tell him. "No. It was pretty cut-and-dried."

"Maybe not. A second set of boot prints was found at the scene."

A moment of silence ticked by, so weighted that goose bumps spread over my arms.

"Mine," Ryder said. "They had to have been my prints. Were they mine?"

Mack shook his head. "Size ten and half. You wear a fourteen, if my memory serves me correctly."

Ryder froze, not even breathing as those words took their time sinking in.

I stepped forward. "Someone else was there? It specifically says that in the report?"

Roman nodded.

"Who?" Ryder demanded, his eyes a little wild.

"According to the official report, the cops never identified the second person. They knew it wasn't Ortiz because the tread on the print was different. The report says they scoured Ortiz's social media accounts, pulling the height and weight of his closest friends to determine shoe size. Interviewed most of them. You were already in jail at this point. One of Ortiz's acquaintances wore a size ten boot but was out of town during the murder. His airline and hotel confirmed this. That was it. That was as far as they got."

"Why the fuck don't I know this?"

"Confidential report of the incident. They had no obligation to tell you. And as I said, you were already convicted and locked up at this point."

Mack set down his Scotch. "And besides, even if they were inclined to tell you or ask you about it, you'd already lost your shit and killed Ortiz. You killed him before they could even shake him on it."

Ryder lunged across the counter. I stumbled backward, my heart jumping into my throat. Roman sprang into action, tackling Ryder to the floor and pinning his hands behind his back before I could even take a breath.

"You fucking son of a bitch," Ryder growled from the tile.

"It's not his fault," I blurted.

Roman murmured something in Ryder's ear. Mack stared down at them, his arms crossed over his chest. A second passed, and when Roman finally released Ryder, he jumped to his feet. I held my breath.

Mack bowed up, then sighed. "Facts are facts. But I should've chosen my words better."

Ryder turned away in what I assumed meant he was accepting an apology that was never quite verbalized, and began pacing. "This makes sense. Whoever was there with Ortiz that day took Maci's necklace. Maybe they were worried it had DNA on it, or maybe they just fucking liked it. Whoever did this disposed of the pendant in Hollow Hill, years ago based on the grime it had all over it. Probably thought no one would find it, or it being there would frame the high school kids who went there."

"What pendant?" Roman asked.

Ryder filled in Mack and Roman on the story of Maci's necklace.

"That Kara girl was strangled, right?" Mack asked, and Ryder nodded.

"Maci was strangled twelve years ago, right around the time the first victim of the String Strangler was reported. Kara was strangled with a thin ligature," Ryder muttered as if thinking out loud. "Maci's pendant was found in the estate that Kara said she was going to visit. But we found no string." He stopped abruptly and stared at me. "The fucking string."

Mack shook his head in disbelief and huffed. "Fucker's been using Maci's necklace to strangle his victims."

"Maybe he took them all to Hollow Hill," I said slowly.

"Maybe that's his little murder den. Maybe that's why the pendant was there."

"Where is this pendant?" Roman asked.

"McCord has it. Said he'll scan it for prints. Can you keep a bead on the reports that come through his desk?"

Roman nodded. "Not a problem." He shifted back to the laptop. "The report's in your email. Hated being the one to tell you this."

"Show me exactly where it is in the report."

As Ryder and Roman hovered over the computer, Mack nodded at me, beckoning me to the corner of the room with him.

"Louise—can I call ya Lou?"

"Sure."

"Lou, I don't know much about you, but I know that my boy here has taken a liking to you."

I frowned. "Your boy has an interesting way of showing it."

"He's out of practice. Jaded." Mack grinned. "But you're still in the house, aren't you? Hell, we've never even been in this house before. He's never invited us. My point is, he's made it clear that me, Justin, and Astor aren't welcome here. He doesn't know Roman, so that one makes sense, at least. But he likes you. He's protective of you. I can see it, and so can Justin. And I need you to make sure he doesn't do anything stupid." A crease formed in his tanned forehead. "I don't know this Ryder. But I still love him. Take care of him, will ya?"

"Ryder's not good at taking orders."

Mack laughed. "Ryder took orders from Astor and the government for years, no questions asked. He's just a bit out of practice. He'll listen to who he respects."

The words hit me like a brick. *He'll listen to who he respects.*

Mack slapped me on the back, sending me stumbling forward. "And keep your head on a swivel, little lady. Nothing good comes from hunting a serial killer. Alone, anyway."

Ryder's hand clamped on Mack's shoulder. "Something I can help with here?"

Mack grinned at me. "Protective, see? Possessive too." He turned to Ryder. "Nope. Not a thing."

Ryder stepped next to me, blocking Mack.

"Guess that's my cue." Mack nodded at Roman. "Let's hit the road."

Our attention was pulled to a chorus of knocks at the front door.

Mack cocked a brow. "Little Mr. Social here having a party we don't know about?"

Frowning, Ryder looked at me. Another knock came, and when I shrugged, he strode across the living room and pulled open the door.

A minute of silence ticked by, and then I heard . . .

"Um, is Lou here?"

28

LOUISE

No. Freaking. Way.

I hurried across the living room. Ryder turned from the door and looked at me, his expression a mix of rage and confusion.

On the porch stood Miles, Margie, and Austin, bags in hand.

I repeat, *bags* in *hand.*

Miles looked confused, and Austin looked wary. Margie, on the other hand, gawked at Ryder like a lovestruck sophomore would look at the quarterback of the football team, and I didn't like it. Not one damn bit.

As usual, she was freshly showered and wearing full makeup, dressed from head to toe in the latest duct-tape-free designer duds. I ignored the pang of jealousy, as well as the possessiveness that settled like coal in my stomach.

Grabbing the door, I stepped in front of Ryder, whose eyes were burning holes through the side of my face.

"Hey, I'm so sorry," Margie whispered, the authenticity of her apology fading with the grin creeping to her face as her attention flicked to Ryder. "We checked out of the

Towering Pines to head home but slid on a patch of black ice a few miles into the trip. My dad said the roads to Ponco were still bad, so we decided to wait it out until tomorrow. Thing is, all the hotels are still booked. We tried to call you, but it kept going to voice mail. I guess you don't have reception here."

"Did you leave a voice mail?" I asked, which was totally irrelevant at that point.

"No. Anyway, I remembered the message you asked Austin to give us a few days ago."

My gaze shifted to Miles, to Austin, then back to Margie, but it was Austin who spoke next.

"And Margie here suggested we should crash at your friend's house at the, quote, castle on the hill down county road 2355."

Ryder released a pained grunt from beside me.

Shit. Damn, damn, damn, fuck.

Mack's laughter echoed from the kitchen.

"Oh. Well, uh . . ." I glanced at Ryder, who turned and walked away without a word. I turned back to the crew. "Um, sure. Okay . . . There's plenty of room. Come on in."

Margie wiggled her brows as she stepped past me. "Oh my God. He's *so* hot."

Mack and Roman muttered something to Ryder, then breezed out the front door chuckling. Teasing him, I'd guess, based on the shit-eating grins on their faces.

After a quick survey of the place, Miles turned to me with a questioning frown.

"He just moved in," I lied.

"Oh. Okay."

"So, uh, yeah, come on in."

Bags were dropped by the doorway. My anxiety hit the roof.

Margie, totally comfortable in a stranger's house, sauntered into the living room and walked right up to Ryder, who was glowering at me with his hands on his hips.

"Beautiful place you got here." She thrust out her hand with its long, delicate fingers. "I'm Margie."

"Ryder," he muttered, ignoring her hand.

Not seeming bothered at all by his rudeness, she dropped her hand and smiled up at him. "All this land yours?"

"Yes, ma'am."

"Ma'am." She giggled.

I rolled my eyes.

"Are you sure you don't mind us staying?" she asked, her Southern drawl suddenly twice as thick.

Ryder's gaze shifted to Miles and Austin.

When Ryder didn't respond, Margie took that as a yes. "Thank you. You know, I used to—"

"Louise, why don't you introduce me to your friends?" Ryder stepped around Margie, his focus fixed on the two other men in the house.

I made introductions and hands were shaken. I swear I heard Miles wince. "This is the crew from Ponco who came over to help with the search for Kara."

A minute of silence passed, feeling more like a year, and I clapped my hands. "So. You guys want a drink? Food?"

"Yes," said three voices in perfect unison.

Ryder walked closely next to me as we headed to the kitchen. "I just moved in, huh?"

I groaned. "I'm sorry. But you do need to get some furniture."

When Ryder didn't offer the crew anything, I stepped in. I couldn't take another second of the brutal awkwardness.

"So, what would you guys—"

"Holy shit. Is that Pappy Van Winkle?" Miles gawked at the bottle on the counter, where Mack and Roman had helped themselves.

Ryder nodded. "Fifteen year."

"Want some?" I asked.

Miles nodded, beaming. "Do I want a glass of two-thou-sand-dollar-a-bottle whiskey? Make it a double."

"Two thousand dollars?" Margie gasped. "I want some."

"Austin," Miles said. "You gotta try some."

Austin reluctantly stopped his visual inspection of the house, stared at Ryder a moment, then nodded. "Sure."

I raised my brows at Ryder. He was watching Austin closely.

And that was about it.

I shook my head, grabbed five highball glasses, and poured us each a shot. After passing them around, Ryder included, we settled into the kitchen, me leaning against the counter, Margie and Miles at the breakfast nook, and Austin pacing a bit, glancing out the window as if scanning his new digs for the evening. The guy reminded me of Ryder, always hyperalert. I wondered why.

"So, how do you two know each other?" Margie asked.

"Ryder hired me to photograph his horses once," I said, quickly coming up with the lie.

Ryder's brow raised slightly as he sipped.

"Oh, I *love* horses. Grew up riding them. My grandma and grampa had an Appaloosa." Margie scanned the walls. "Where are the pictures you took?"

"Storage," Ryder said dryly. "I just moved in, remember?"

I cleared my throat. It was going to be a long night.

~

As expected, I led the small talk as Ryder slowly sipped his drink, only inserting himself into the conversation when addressed. I noticed his gaze raking over everything the crew touched, undoubtedly plotting his cleanup the moment they went to bed.

The liquor had done its trick. Margie's voice had reached a high-pitch range, Miles wouldn't shut up about catfish the size of Volkswagens rumored to be in the local lake, and even Austin said more than a few words.

"Well, guys, you hungry?" I asked.

"Yes!" Margie dramatically slapped her hand over her stomach.

I glanced at Ryder, again giving him the opportunity to play host. When he didn't bite, I took over again and yanked open the fridge.

"Oh my God." Margie pushed up from the chair and gawked as she made her way across the kitchen. "That's the biggest fridge I've ever seen."

"That a subzero?" Miles asked.

Ryder nodded.

Everyone except Ryder gathered around the fridge.

Margie wrinkled her nose at the stacks of Tupperware. "What is this stuff?"

All heads turned to Ryder.

"Food."

"Ryder likes to eat organic," I said.

"Why?"

"Uh . . ."

Ryder pushed past me and grabbed a container from the fridge. "Burgers okay?"

"Sounds great."

"Works for me."

He turned, stumbling into Miles.

"Sorry."

Margie stepped back.

"Ow," Austin grunted as she stepped on his toe.

"Sorry."

I heard Ryder exhale deeply as he set the meat on the counter. When he grabbed a few tomatoes, I grabbed a head of lettuce and set it on the counter next to him.

The chatter picked up, settling into a hot debate about the validity of the supposed benefits of organic food.

Ryder disappeared into the pantry. A few seconds passed, so I began preparing the ground beef that I was sure had been locally raised and butchered.

A minute passed. Then another minute.

I washed my hands, and after ensuring no one was looking, slipped into the pantry. Ryder's back was to me, his palms braced against the shelves, his head bowed in misery.

"Hey." I quietly closed the door behind me.

He looked over his shoulder and dropped his hands from the shelves.

"You okay?" I asked.

"Yeah."

"I'm really sorry."

He shook his head. "No. It's fine."

"I didn't invite them out here. I promise."

"I know you didn't." He raised his palms. "It's okay. And even if you did, it's okay. It has to be okay."

"You don't seem okay."

He sighed, his shoulders sagging. It was the first time I ever saw Ryder appear tired. Legitimately tired. "No. No, it's fine. It's just . . . with everything Roman and Mack told me about the boot print, and now this, the unexpected company. It's just . . . a lot. God, I'm fucked up, Lou. I know I am. I'm so sorry."

"Don't be sorry, and I can handle this, Ryder. The second boot print, maybe not, but this unexpected company, I can handle for both of us."

"Really?"

I smiled, closing the short distance between us. "I can make small talk with the best of them. Don't necessarily like it, but I can do it."

"You don't like small talk?"

"No one likes small talk. But sometimes, Ryder, it's a part of being human."

His expression softened, his hands finding my waist and jerking me to him. Goose bumps popped out on my skin.

"Thank you, Lou."

"I like it when you call me Lou."

"I like you, Lou."

We laughed. He kissed my nose.

"Okay, I've got this," I said. "Go for a walk. Go ride your horses. Or, hell, take a relaxing bubble bath in that glorious copper tub. I have a feeling I'm the only one who's ever used it. It's so nice. Or go lock yourself in the library and read a romantic suspense—"

His lips quirked. "No. I'll stay. Thank you."

He wrapped me in his arms and kissed me. This kiss wasn't as desperate and frantic as the ones before. Instead, it was soft and sensual, melting me from the inside out.

Laughter broke out in the kitchen.

I pulled back and glanced over my shoulder. "Someone's about to come in here."

"Let them." He turned my face back toward his and went in for another kiss.

"No." I laughed, swatting him away. "Come on. Or don't. Like I said, I've got this."

"Do you know how to make burgers?"

"Ryder," I deadpanned. "Have you seen these thighs?"

He grabbed my ass, sending a zing up my spine. "I'd like to get a closer look. Maybe throw on those blue sweatpants, or take them off. Either way."

"How much have you had to drink, young man?"

"Not nearly enough to make it through this night."

"Oh, this horrific night of being *social.* Dear Lord, how are you going to survive?"

"I've got you." He winked.

Smiling big, I said, "Okay, come on. Let me handle everything. You go drink your rich-kid Scotch—"

"It's whiskey."

"What?"

"It's not Scotch. It's whiskey."

"What's the difference?"

"Don't. I can't."

With that, I pulled Mr. Antisocial out of his comfort zone and into the laughter. He followed me, for a change, across the kitchen to the stove.

As promised, I carried the conversation for both of us while Ryder picked up where I left off on the burgers. He didn't leave, as I'd suggested. Instead, we cooked together, side by side, exchanging glances, grins, and a few ass pinches.

Comfortable.

Just him and me.

29

LOUISE

The first bottle of Pappy Van Winkle was emptied before dinner. Ryder brought up another bottle, plus a bottle of red wine, as I plated the cheeseburgers, grilled to perfection on his fancy stove with a grill top.

The house smelled heavenly. Margie had turned on her phone to a dinner-party playlist, because of course, Ryder didn't have more than a small radio. If anyone noticed that he also didn't have a television, they didn't say anything.

Margie's constant attempts to engage Ryder in flirtation fell flat. Each time, he'd look at me and wink. Eventually, she gave up, sending me a glance that suggested she knew he and I were more than just friends. I shrugged, and she turned her attention to Miles for the evening.

To my utter shock, Ryder and Austin had taken a liking to each other, engaging in a full-blown adult conversation about Austin's time in the military. The two were indeed similar, I realized.

It made my heart swell, watching Ryder loosen up, and maybe—just maybe—even have a good time. His hand found my lower back a few times as we cooked, his fingers tangling in my hair as I plated the veggies. I liked it. Loved it. It felt very couple-like, as if we were hosting friends.

I could do it every night.

Ryder insisted on cleaning up while everyone else indulged in homemade vanilla ice cream. Yep, Ryder made his own ice cream. If I weren't after the hush puppies, I was now officially in love.

Because of the no-furniture thing, where to sleep was an issue, so we decided to give Margie the master bedroom, and Miles and Austin separate bedrooms. Luckily, Ryder had an entire closet filled with camping gear, which included blow-up mattresses and sleeping bags.

Based on the amount of whiskey both men had consumed, I guessed they'd have been just as comfortable in the driveway.

It was just after midnight by the time everyone retired to their rooms, with Austin having to practically carry Miles to his. The guy couldn't handle his expensive booze, apparently.

The only question that remained was where Ryder and I were going to sleep. Lights were turned off, and Ryder grabbed my hand and tugged me across the living room.

"Where are we going?"

"You'll see."

The light from the full moon pooled on the floor, bathing the pastures outside in a silvery glow. He pulled me into the library, awash with moonlight.

"This room. It's so beautiful."

I was led to the end of the library, to a small door tucked between two bookcases. Ryder pulled open the door, silent on its hinges, to reveal a steep, narrow staircase.

"How many secret rooms do you have in this place?"

"A few."

The stairs were sturdy and silent beneath us as we climbed them. Ryder turned to me just before we reached the top of the stairs.

"Close your eyes."

"Seriously?"

"Yep."

Grinning, I squeezed my eyes shut. He caught me peeking through the slits.

"Cheater."

"Okay, fine." I slapped my hand over my eyes.

His fingers swept down my arm and wrapped around my free hand. My heartbeat sped up.

"Step," he said, guiding me. "Step. Step. Last one."

My feet landed on solid flooring. The scent of fresh lumber filled my nose.

Two hands rested on my shoulders, turning me to some exact position.

"Okay. Open."

I dropped my hand, along with my jaw.

A million stars twinkled under a domed glass ceiling that enclosed a small round room. A large telescope tripod sat at the front of the room, facing the moon. In the center were piles of blankets and pillows.

"Oh my God, Ryder, it's . . ." I ran out of words as I gazed at the night sky so close, I felt like I could touch it.

"I call it the observation room." Standing next to me, he stared up at the stars. "I had it built about six months ago. The lumber is from my land. I sleep up here a lot."

"I don't blame you. I want pictures."

"There'll be time for that."

He repositioned the blankets and pillows, and we sat together on the floor. A few moments passed, and I could tell he wanted to say something. Finally, he did.

"You know how you said sometimes unexpected blessings can happen in chaos?" His dark eyes twinkled in the moonlight.

"Yeah."

"That was tonight. For me, with you. When Roman told me about the second boot print, I was halfway out the door, planning to barge into McCord's office and demand answers. There was no question. When your friends showed up, my immediate response was to slam the door in their faces. But then there was you. You handled it. You handled everything, including me and my neurotic ass. You kept me from driving to BSPD, losing my shit, and no telling what else would have happened. If your friends wouldn't have shown up, if you hadn't have been here, tonight might have gone differently."

My hand slid over his. "Do you think there's any way you can let it go? It's been twelve years. According to Roman, they tried to find the guy and couldn't. Twelve *years*. Can you let it go?"

"Kind of like how you're letting this whole Kara thing go?"

I sighed. "Maybe I need to let it go too. Not let her go, of course, but leave the investigation to the people who are actually trained to deal with it."

A moment passed, and Ryder exhaled deeply. "Six months."

Knowing what he meant, I said, "Six more months of parole. Then peace, Ryder. *Peace.* Let everything go. Live on your land, make friends, organize a weekly poker night, try to get back to a normal life. It's time to let it all go."

His hand squeezed mine. "My boy would be almost twelve now. Becoming a man."

"You can still have that," I whispered. "There's still hope."

"I want to have hope." He looked away. "I want to believe again."

I pulled his chin toward me. "Then believe."

This time, I kissed him.

We fell to the blankets with hungry kisses, complete with fingers tangled in hair. He rolled on top of me, cupping my head in his hands, stroking, kissing as if it were his last breath of air. Eager, desperate. My stomach swirled, goose bumps spreading under the intensity of his touch.

"You," he whispered between kisses. "You make me crazy, Lou."

"I make you forget," I whispered back.

He pulled away at the words and stared at me for a moment before crushing his lips again to mine. My clothes were ripped from my body and strewn across the room. Next came his.

His touch was frenzied, demanding, with so much energy and ache, there was nothing for me to do but let him take me. He wouldn't have it any other way.

A groan escaped my lips as he took my nipple into his mouth, massaging the other with his hand. I gripped at the blankets to anchor myself as he worked his way down my stomach. His hands cupped my ass and squeezed.

He looked up, a twinkle in his eye, a smirk on his lips.

He likes my ass.

I parted my knees for him, inviting. He lifted my ass from the blanket and slid his mouth over me. Unlike his kisses, he took his time between my legs, melting into me, his tongue exploring my folds. He groaned, throaty, and licked some more.

Fisting the blankets, I pulled at them, yanking, a feeble

attempt to release the electricity spiking through me. His tongue circled my clit, his movements soft, slow, and steady as if he had all the time in the world. Tingles spread across the delicate skin, and a warmth pooled between my legs. Just as I was about to lose control, he lifted and positioned himself over me.

Our chests heaving, we stared at each other.

My heart skittered in my chest.

The wild lust was gone from his eyes, replaced by an awareness, as if he'd just realized something for the first time. He searched my face, his gaze lingering on my lips. My heart pounded.

He lowered himself, his tip pressing against my opening. My heart in my throat, I nodded.

And with his eyes locked on mine, he speared into me. Our lips parted together, and a gasp escaped me.

I breathed out heavily. He sucked in.

We wrapped our arms around each other, desperately, saying everything with our bodies, our touch. Slow and steady, we moved together, gripping onto each other for dear life. Gripping onto whatever was happening between us.

He stroked my hair, kissing my lips as we rode the wave. I squeezed around him with each thrust, craving more, more, more, knowing there was no going back after this. Sweat beaded on his back and on my forehead.

Staring into each other's souls, we came undone together, right there beneath the stars.

*I*t had been twelve years since I'd had sex.

Twelve years. No joke.

Despite my better judgment, I confessed that little fun tidbit to Louise after the fact. Her reaction was the opposite of what I expected—she seemed pleased by this. I was glad it pleased someone.

The one thing I didn't confess was that in all the times before, never once—not a single time—did I feel a connection with anyone like I did with her. A deep, visceral familiarity as if I'd known her all my life. Every line of her face, every curve of that damn body, I suddenly realized I'd seen in my dreams. Louise was in my head before I'd even met her.

The fact that I didn't feel this way with the woman I'd proposed to so long ago was jarring. I wondered if *this* was what the beginnings of real love felt like. And that thought scared the shit out of me.

We had sex twice more that night, each time longer than the one before. I couldn't get enough. Having her wrapped around me, submissive, taking me as I came, was like getting hooked on a new drug. I *needed* that intimacy. I needed to be inside her, to feel that connection to another human being. I'd forgotten that feeling, the part of me that allowed emotions, the part of me that I'd let dissolve to dust.

I need *her*.

I needed her to be mine, if only for that moment.

Louise had fallen asleep on my chest with my arms wrapped around her tightly, as if holding her captive. She was mine.

As she slept, I stared at the stars, wondering what the next day would bring. What the future would bring.

Would she leave? Would she stay? If she stayed, could she ever truly accept my past? I was a convicted felon. A murderer. A monster. The former fiancé of a woman who'd died a tragic death.

Did that scare Louise? Did it scare me? Did I believe in chronic bad luck?

On top of all that, I wondered if Louise could handle all the looks and whispers from the small-minded rednecks every time we went into town. Or would it get old, and she'd leave me.

Hell, I wouldn't touch me with a ten-foot pole.

I want to make one thing clear here. I knew I was fucked up. Knew I had problems. There was no disillusionment there. But the fact is, until you've spent a decade in the deepest depths of hell, you have no idea the effect the experience can have on the human psyche.

Looking back at the lives I'd taken while working for Astor Stone—my targets—and at the life I took as revenge for my unborn baby, I realized those events weren't what short-circuited my brain. Weren't what broke me. It was having my freedom stripped away. Living in an eight-by-eight cell, locked in a cage like an animal with no privacy.

No freedom. No escape. Claustrophobia had nothing on those ten years.

I hope your circumstances won't continue to define your life. Louise's words echoed in my head as I lay next to her.

My circumstances had undoubtedly shaped me into the man I was. I knew that. And for the first time, I wondered if that made me weak. Was I acting like a victim? Allowing my past to take over my life?

When I got out of jail, I continued building walls around me in the form of my house, my land, my space. By restricting human interaction as little as possible. Why? Because I didn't trust anyone.

Because I didn't trust myself.

And that was it, I realized. I didn't know who the hell I was anymore. All I knew was that I was capable of cold-blooded murder, and that the man who went into prison wasn't the neurotic asshole who came out.

Who the fuck am I?

Why would anyone want me?

I'd seen glimpses of who Louise referred to as the "old me" since she'd come into my life. I had moments—fleeting, but moments nonetheless—where I'd forget my past. And *holy fuck*, it felt good. But then, like an incurable virus, the past would slap me in the face again, and like a switch, I'd flip back.

Weak.

Louise and I were incompatible on every level. While she lived from day to day, taking life as it came, I planned every minute detail in order to ensure life never threw me something that I didn't expect again. To ensure that I never lost control again.

Minimize.

Isolate.

Control.

Coast.

That was my plan.

Not Louise's. She still had that sparkle in her eye. That hope. That *life* I'd lost so long ago. I loved that about her.

But how could two opposite personalities make it work? Or would we be perfect for each other?

Was Louise the only person to bring back the old Ryder?

Was she the type of woman to stick with a man through good times and bad? Through the nightmares, the sleepless nights, the days planned minute to minute so I wouldn't have to think about the past?

Would Louise stay with me until I found that part of me again, or would she run when the going got tough?

I was about to find out.

LOUISE

J awoke in the trees. That's what it felt like, anyway. Like I was floating in the air, secure in Ryder's arms.

"Good morning," his husky voice whispered in my ear.

I snuggled into his chest, one eye gazing up at the muted orange beginning to push into a star-speckled indigo. Beautiful. Peaceful.

I inhaled deeply, smelling that scent that was Ryder. God, I loved the way he smelled. "What time is it?"

"I'd say six."

I wrapped my arms around his waist, nestling. He squeezed me tighter and kissed the top of my head.

What would this day bring? The roads would be clear enough for me to leave, but I didn't want to.

Does he want me to leave? Will I ever see Ryder again?

The thoughts made my stomach sink.

"Ready for a jog?"

My worry faded into a smile. "Shockingly, yes."

"That's my girl."

My girl.

After dressing, we crept downstairs, my hand in his. About halfway through the living room, I realized I had a stupid grin plastered on my face. Languid bliss from the night before. Ryder must have caught it, because grinning too, he halted, pulled me back into his arms, and kissed me again.

Whatever I was feeling at that moment, I knew it was love. I knew it in my heart, my soul.

We tiptoed into the master bedroom where Margie was still passed out cold, her messy hair fanned out over the pillow, a puddle of drool under her mouth.

"I'm burning those sheets," Ryder murmured softly, and I stifled a laugh.

We stepped into the closet, quickly changed clothes—a few kisses, grabs, and nips along the way—and then made our way outside.

The cold air was exhilarating. My energy level rivaled what I'd normally experience with a triple shot of espresso. I made a mental note to have orgasms on a regular basis going forward, Ryder or not.

We started out at a brisk pace. In our normal routine, we would remain mostly quiet for the first mile or so, until our minds and bodies awoke fully enough to have a conversation. That day, though, Ryder talked my ear off.

He told me about his plans for the land, what he wanted to do to the house. He pointed out things in nature as we passed. He told me stories about how he and his brother grew up in the woods and all the animals they'd seen, including black bears and mountain lions.

Ryder talked and talked and talked, and I listened, my heart doubling in size. It was as if the intimacy, the bond, the surrender between us, that experience had unlocked his armor. He was suddenly a man who couldn't shut up, or perhaps he wanted to talk about anything that didn't involve murder or me leaving.

He was relaxed. *Happy.*

I listened with a smile on my face, nodding and interjecting when I could, but careful not to say too much for fear he'd clam up again. This went on for miles. When we breached the mountain and passed the tombstone that honored his unborn baby, he didn't even look over.

My body felt good, as well as my muscles and my head. Funny how quickly you can crave a good workout, a release of all those endorphins. I swear I'd even lost a little weight. It felt good. Everything about that morning felt good—and right. As if everything was exactly how it should be.

Honestly, I could have jogged in those woods listening to Ryder talk for the rest of my life. But forty-five minutes later, the trail brought us back around, and we were back at the house.

To our surprise, everyone was still sleeping.

"What should we do?" I asked.

"Let them sleep. I've got to go into town for a bit. I'm assuming you can entertain?" He winked.

"Where are you going?"

"Find out what I can about that pendant."

"I thought you were going to drop it."

"I am. The boot print, my past. But I know you're not going to drop Kara's case, and I'm not letting you go it alone."

"I want to go."

He looked toward the master suite, considering, and then he shrugged. "I guess there's nothing here they can steal. I've got my guns and computer locked in the safe."

"What about your secret room and all that money?"

"Added three locks the day you found it."

I laughed. "Of course you did."

"Get dressed. I'll get the coffee."

We turned onto Main Street a few minutes before eight thirty. The roads were still streaked with fingers of ice but would clear by midmorning. The ghost town was crawling with activity, the citizens of Berry Springs eager to shovel their way out of the snow and back into civilization. Donny's Diner had a line out the door.

Still, not a word was said about my leaving.

I'd left a note for the crew on the kitchen island, next to the coffee condiments and a bottle of ibuprofen, telling them to help themselves before setting out, and to give me a call when they arrived back in Ponco safely.

We pulled up to a long brick building with a single window in the front, its shades drawn. Leafless bushes lined the brick, and bare tree branches reached for the roof. A few fallen branches littered the parking lot. A small wooden sign read carroll county medical examiner. A rundown black Tahoe with a Rosie the Riveter sticker on the back was parked to the right of the sign.

Ryder pulled the keys from the ignition. "Ready?"

"To hang out with a bunch of dead people at eight in the morning? You bet."

"You can go kick the cook's ass at Donny's, if you'd rather."

I thoughtfully tilted my head. "Tempting, but no. I'm coming with you, Detective Magoo."

After Ryder opened my door—a new habit that I could easily get used to—we crossed the asphalt. The front door was locked, so we rang the doorbell, but there was no answer. Again, and one more time.

"Just a frickin' minute!" a gruff, husky female voice called out from the speaker.

Yikes.

Two minutes later, the door flung open. I recognized her immediately from the night I found Kara's body. Jessica Heathrow was a short, stocky woman with flaming red curls and tattoos peeking out from beneath her lab coat.

She looked at me, then at Ryder. Recognition flickered, and those green eyes rounded. "Ryder Jagger. Holy shit."

"Good to see you too, Jess."

By the use of a nickname, I assumed the two were friendly.

Jessica opened the door wide, giving Ryder the once-over. "Jesus, Mary, and Joseph, prison did you well."

I grinned.

"Jess, this is Louise Sloane. Lou, this is Jessica Heathrow, the county medical examiner, and the only woman this side of the Mississippi to beat me at arm wrestling."

Jessica laughed. "To be fair, he'd had a pint of moonshine and had two women on his lap."

Ryder grinned.

"Dammit, man, it's good to see you. Welcome back to civilization. How does it feel?"

"Quiet."

She smiled, nodding. "Good. You deserve quiet." Her curious gaze shifted back to me. "What can I help y'all with?"

"Chief McCord was supposed to drop off a pendant from a necklace yesterday to be scanned for prints or DNA. Did he?"

She thought for a moment. "Ah, yes. Yep, sure did."

"Have you found anything yet?"

"I'm busy with a heroin overdose at the moment, which may or may not have been a homicide. And besides, you know I'm not at liberty to share what I find with you, regardless."

Ryder pulled a stack of cash from his pocket, and she raised a brow.

"You bribing me, Mr. Jagger?"

"Consider it a friend helping another friend with that new house payment you've got."

Her other brow lifted. A moment passed as they stared at each other.

Ryder rolled his eyes and pulled another stack from his other pocket.

Jessica smiled and dipped her chin. "Knew you had it in ya." She grabbed the stacks and stuffed them in her lab coat.

"Now that that's out of the way," Ryder said, "I'd like you to look at the pendant as soon as possible."

"Well, McCord told me no rush, so . . . I hadn't planned on rushing." Not one to miss much, Jessica tilted her head to the side. "What's going on? What didn't he tell me? Does this have to do with Kara Meyers?"

"It has to do with more than that. I think the pendant might link to the String Strangler."

"What?"

Ryder nodded.

A darkness clouded Jessica's face, her shoulders tensing. "You know, I've done the autopsies of three of his victims. The first three before the FBI got involved." Her voice lowered. "It's every woman's worst nightmare. The women were alive during the rapes and beatings. Noses broken, cheekbones shattered. He'd focus on their faces. A disdain for women, no doubt about it. Probably wronged in the past, or a messy divorce under his belt. Maybe a few. After he's had his fun, he strangles them to death." She shook her head. "Not proud to say I've lost a few nights' sleep over the Strangler."

"We think Maci might have been the first one."

Jessica's mouth dropped open. She blinked, connecting the dots. "How? Why do you think this?"

"Maci was raped and strangled to death with a thin ligature—"

"I know. I did her autopsy."

Ryder nodded. "The pendant you have back there is the one that I gave to her. Somehow, it ended up at Hollow Hill, where it's presumed Kara visited before she was murdered."

"You don't say. No, McCord definitely didn't tell me this." Pity washed over Jessica's face as she looked at Ryder. "Over a decade, and it's all getting resurfaced again. I'm sorry, Ryder."

"Me too. Can you get to it today?"

Jessica blew out a breath. "I'm gonna be honest with you. I haven't even looked at it yet." She hesitated, glancing over her shoulder. "Come on back."

After keying in a passcode, Jessica led us through a thick metal door that led to the laboratory.

The first thing that hit me was the smell. Bleach and putrid rot.

The second thing was the dead body on the center table, its gray skin illuminated by a single fluorescent light that dangled from the ceiling. Based on the gray hair, the corpse belonged to an older man, despite the fact that his body resembled a prepubescent boy. From lifelong drug use and extreme malnourishment, I assumed. A Y-incision separated the man's chest, exposing his rib cage under puffs of skin.

Bile rose in my throat.

Ryder glanced back at me with a nod, his expression clearly saying, *You okay?*

I shook my head, feeling saliva pool in my mouth.

"Oh. Sorry," Jessica said, catching the look. "So sorry. I forget." She rushed over and covered the body, then handed me a small vial. "Here, sniff this. It will help."

"Can I stuff this directly into my nostrils?" My voice was as shaky as my hand.

Jessica grinned, as did Ryder.

I unscrewed the cap and inhaled a strong eucalyptus/peppermint scent. After I took a deep breath, and another, and another, my stomach slowly began to settle. "Sorry," I muttered.

"No worries. I barfed my way through my first ten autopsies. No joke. Totally numb to it now. Okay, come on in here."

We followed her to a small side room. Stacks of boxes, folders, and clear containers littered the counters. Reminded me of home.

"Let's see . . ." Jessica's fingers danced over the boxes. "Ah, here it is."

She cleared a spot on the counter, then pulled on a pair of blue latex gloves. Next, she retrieved a sterile silver plate. The pendant was placed carefully in the center.

"It's glass." She straightened, frowning.

"Is that an issue?"

"Well, maybe." Chewing her lower lip, Jessica clicked on the lights and slid the pendant under a magnifying glass. "What environment was it in when you found it?"

"Indoors. In a fireplace, to be exact. Like it had been tossed to the side and meant to be burned, then forgotten."

"Indoors is good. Do you have an idea of when the prints would have been transferred?"

"No. We don't know how long it had been in the house. But Maci's incident happened twelve years ago, so . . ."

A minute passed as Jessica leaned over to examine the pendant. She stood up, fisting her hands on her hips. "I'll have to superglue it."

"Superglue it?"

"Cyanoacrylate fuming. It's a technique that uses vapors of superglue to develop latent fingerprints. Works great on glass." She looked at the pendant. "Fingerprints are left from sweat, which is made up of amino acids, fatty acids, and proteins. The vapors adhere to these components, making the prints visible. Then I dust over it and use tape to pull the print."

"How long does that process take?"

"A while. There are multiple steps involved, including time in a developing chamber." She nodded over her shoulder to a small white box with a window.

"Sounds easy."

"Not quite. There's always a risk of overdeveloping the evidence by allowing the glue to seep into the ridges and distort the print. What I'm saying is, it's laborious and requires a lot of attention. And I've got a backlog the size of my ass."

"Can you get it done today?"

"Yeah, Ryder, I'll get it done. For you. But you owe me."

"Your lab coat weighs triple what it did before I walked in. I'd say we're even."

"Feels good too." She winked, patting her pockets. "But I want something else from you."

"What's that?"

"A drink. You look like you could use some time with a friend at Frank's Bar."

He nodded. "Done."

I smiled. *Baby steps.*

"Good. Now remember, I might not get a print, or I

might get a partial, which won't tell us shit. Or even if I do get a full print, if the guy isn't in the system, you still won't have a name."

"But if you do get a full print, and the print is in the system, then we've potentially nailed the String Strangler. And women in this town can sleep easier."

Jessica nodded. "I'd like to go the rest of my career without seeing another one of his victims come through my doors."

"Get it done then."

"Yes, sir." Jessica winked, then slid me another glance. "All right, scat, you two. Hopefully, I'll have something for you by the end of the day."

My heart skipped a beat. *By the end of the day.*

By the end of the day, maybe this whole nightmare would be over.

32

LOUISE

The sharp sound of gunshots made Ryder veer off course as we pulled up his driveway.

Brows furrowed, he pulled the gun from his hip and placed it on his lap as he drove around to the back of the house. "Someone's at the range."

"Who? You said you locked up your guns."

"'I did." His steely eyes narrowed.

We drove down a gravel road that skirted the fields until a dark figure, gun in hand and aiming at targets in the distance, came into view.

"That's Austin." I could tell by the tall, lean frame and dark leather jacket.

Hearing the truck, Austin lowered his gun and turned. Ryder rolled to a stop, sliding his weapon back into the holster. We jumped out.

"Mornin'." Austin glanced at Ryder's hip. "I saw the targets from the road yesterday when we drove up. Hope you don't mind."

"Not at all." Ryder nodded to the gun in Austin's hand.

Austin handed it over. "Sig P938."

Ryder stepped to the range, set his sights, and fired off three rounds. "Very nice. Have two myself."

"It goes with me everywhere."

"Where's everyone else?" I asked.

"Miles is still passed out, and Margie went to, quote, 'go pet your pretty horses.' I told her to wake Miles up, but she said she wanted to wait a bit to get on the road. Make sure the ice melts off." He glanced up at the heavy cloud cover, which was doing little to melt anything. "Don't worry, we'll leave as soon as Miles gets his hungover ass up. I'll drive if I have to. No offense, your place is great. Just ready to get back home."

"Feel free to stay down here as long as you'd like," Ryder said, although his offer didn't have much sincerity to it.

"Thanks. I think I will for a bit longer. Hell of a place you've got out here."

We were almost back to the house when Ryder hit the brakes.

I followed his gaze to see Liberty, saddled, walking along the tree line. "Guess Margie took him for a ride."

"And abandoned him in the woods? He's not in a pasture."

A chill snaked up my spine, a little warning bell. We exchanged a glance that confirmed Ryder felt it too. He hit the gas.

"Check the house," he said tersely, "see if she's in there. I'll check the barn."

"Okay."

My heart raced as I jogged inside and Ryder disappeared down the hill. I searched every room in the house, even the observation room. As Austin had said, Miles was still passed out.

No Margie.

I jogged back outside. When I didn't see Ryder, I took off down the hill. As I slipped through the gate, he emerged from the barn and shook his head.

"She's not in there. But she was. She saddled Liberty and took him out."

Stomach churning, I looked into the woods that surrounded Ryder's land. Miles and miles of dense underbrush and rock terrain. No telling where she went, or why the horse came back without her.

I pulled my cell phone from my pocket. "I'll call her."

"No reception, remember?"

"Dammit."

"Let's get on horseback. We'll start searching where Liberty is. That gives us a starting point."

"What about Austin?"

"Ask him if he's seen her. If not, tell him to put up his damn gun so he doesn't shoot one of us, and to saddle up and help search."

33

LOUISE

ustin, Ryder, and I sat on horseback at the bottom of the mountain. Ryder was on Liberty, I was on Prudence, and Austin was on a chocolate-brown quarter horse named Bullet. We agreed to split up, search for an hour, then meet back at the base of the mountain to regroup.

Ryder took off to the right. I went forward, up the mountain, and Austin to the left. Ryder gave each of us a compass. In the event we got lost, he instructed us to head southeast, which would take us back to the fields.

I saw glimpses of the man who used to run black ops for Astor Stone. Cool, calm, collected, and laser focused. Ryder was in his element. He was a born leader, there was no question about that.

I, on the other hand, was a total mess.

Flashbacks of finding Kara's body sent renewed anxiety through me as I guided Prudence through the brush. I was right back to where I'd been days earlier, searching the woods for a missing girl.

The clouds had thickened, blocking the sun and darkening the woods that seemed to close in around me. It was cold and still. Ice clung desperately to the branches, and snow was mounded on rocks and boulders. Everything was dead—brown, gray, and dirty. And so freaking quiet. I'd heard Ryder's and Austin's shouts for the first little bit, but the comfort of their voices was soon replaced by the wind through the trees.

I wrapped my scarf tighter around my neck as I scanned the terrain from my saddle. Cupping my hand to my mouth, I called out for what seemed like the hundredth time. "Margie!"

God, it was cold.

God, I was uneasy. And nervous.

I checked the time on my phone again. Forty more minutes before I needed to head back.

"Maaargie!"

This time, my voice echoed. I slowed Prudence as a ravine came into view. I guided her to the edge, stood up in the stirrups, and peered over her head.

The ravine was steep, with jagged rocks spearing up from the bottom. I guessed it was a thirty-foot drop. From my vantage point, I couldn't see the entire bottom, so I slid off of Prudence. My heart beat like a drum as I carefully stepped to the edge and looked down.

Margie stared up at me, lifeless. Like Kara, her broken body was contorted around the jagged rocks, her pants around her ankles.

34

LOUISE

I don't remember screaming, but Ryder said I did. What I do remember is turning around and falling into his arms.

"Shhh," Ryder whispered, stroking my head until my ragged breaths began to slow.

When he was sure I was okay, he pulled away and gripped my shoulders. "Lou, I need to check to see if she's alive. I don't think she is, but I need to get down there and check. Is that okay?"

"Yes, yes." I nodded frantically. "Go."

"Stay right here, okay? Are you sure you're okay?"

"I'm okay. Go check on her."

He pulled the gun from his belt. "You know how to use this?"

"Aim and pull the trigger."

"Yes. Assess, aim, and pull. If anyone you don't know comes up to you, I want you to yell for me first, then aim the gun and tell them to stop. If they don't stop, you shoot. Do you understand me?"

I nodded, my heart racing.

He kissed my forehead. "I'll be right back."

Holding the gun in my shaky grip, I watched Ryder make his way down the ravine with a speed and agility that suggested he'd done it a million times. When he reached Margie, I began pacing, uncontrollable tears flowing down my cheeks. Finally, he looked up and shook his head. My heart squeezed in pain and panic.

"Ryder," I called out, my voice cracking as he climbed back up. "Oh my God, she's on your land. You have a dead woman on your land. You're on parole. Oh my God, what if—"

His jaw clenched as he climbed over the edge and stepped close to me. Apparently, the thought had already crossed his mind. "It's fine. Everything's going to be—"

"No, it isn't!" I threw my hands into the air, waving the gun like a maniac until he gently took it from me. "What if you go back to prison? For the rest of your life?" My voice squeaked. I was losing it.

"I didn't do it, Lou."

"Yeah, but everything is tied to you. The pendant, another body. You're a convicted murderer, Ryder. You said it yourself, you'll be the first person they'll look at. They'll try to pin it on you. You'll be taken to the station and interviewed. What if they put you in jail again until—"

"Lou, *stop*. Stop. You're spinning."

"What if we hide the body?" I couldn't believe the words coming out of my mouth. "Or dump it just off your land? I can carry the feet. That way it won't be as obviously tied to you."

What *the fuck* was I saying? And exactly how crazy in love was I with this man to consider tampering with a crime scene to ensure he remained safe?

Mack's warning echoed in my head. *Keep him out of trouble.*

I'd failed miserably.

Margie was dead because of me. If I wouldn't have organized the search for Kara and guilted them into helping, Margie would still be alive. If I would have let the damn authorities handle it, as Ryder had suggested so many times, she would still be alive.

And Ryder, his life just got turned upside down, *again,* because of me. I'd dragged him into the case, kicking and screaming. He would have never gone to Hollow Hill and found the pendant if I wouldn't have chosen to drive through an ice storm that first night, pushed my way into his life, and guilted him into helping. He also would have never known about the second boot print.

Everything was my fault.

Ryder was right, I was impulsive and tunnel-visioned, never looking at the bigger picture. Trademark bad judgment on my part.

One person was dead because of me. Another person might go back to prison because of me, and if not, would spend the rest of his life wondering about the unsolved mystery of his unborn baby's murder.

Ryder grabbed my shoulders, yanking me from my sickening thoughts.

"*Stop,* Lou. You're not thinking straight. We need to get back to the house and call the cops. We're not moving the body. I'm innocent, and I'll remain that way. We have one thing to do right now, and that's to call this in." He wiped the tears from my cheeks. I was trembling. "Don't do this to yourself. Take a deep breath. You didn't do this."

I swatted his hands away, sobbing as I pulled myself onto

Prudence. He tried to help, but I slapped him away. I was a complete, total mess. A train wreck.

Instead of following me, Ryder mounted his horse, grabbed Prudence's reins, and guided me back down the mountain. I cried the entire way.

Austin was waiting in the driveway. Miles was sitting on the front porch, coffee in hand, his hair standing on end. He shot to his feet the moment he saw us. Both men's eyes locked on my teary, swollen face as we dismounted.

"We found Margie." Ryder's tone remained controlled as he delivered the facts unemotionally. "She's been murdered, and was left at the bottom of a ravine about a half mile from here. Based on the marks around her neck, she was strangled."

Miles's jaw dropped. Austin's gaze shifted to the woods.

"I need to call the cops. Everyone, get inside and stay put. They'll want to interview all of us."

Twenty minutes later, the castle on the hill's serenity was shattered by wailing sirens as two patrol cars raced up the driveway. Chaos ensued.

Waiting my turn to be interviewed, I looked around Ryder's home, his land, everything he'd built to protect himself from the outside world. Everything he'd built to put the past behind him.

I'd shattered it all.

I kept it together during the interview, keeping my eye on Ryder the entire time. Not surprisingly, he was interviewed away from the group by Chief McCord and another officer. Ryder had stood strong and stoic as he told his story.

I loved him so damn much.

The officers broke off, a plan in place.

Ryder walked over to me, his expression so intense, my stomach flipped.

"They've asked me to take them to the body." *The body.* "How did everything go? Are you okay?"

"Are you okay?"

"Always." He forced a smile.

Tears filled my eyes again. "Ryder, I'm leaving," I blurted.

"What?"

"I'm leaving. They said we could go—that we should go. I think they want us to talk to the FBI too. I'm going to leave with Miles and Austin. I need to get home. I need to get out of here. I'm so sorry, Ryder."

He closed the inches between us, a flash of desperation crossing his face. "Lou, no, stay. Please. You can't leave me right now. You can't leave just because things got tough. Don't do this."

He clamped his mouth shut as if disgusted with the words coming out of him. Then he sucked in a breath and squared his shoulders. "Why?"

"All of this is because of me, don't you see that?" I snapped, angry that he wasn't holding me accountable. "This is all my fault. Everything. You would have never been in this situation if I would have had better judgment, like you've said. I'm a fucking shitshow, and you're . . . you're perfect. I'm not good for you." My lip quivered. "I'm so *sorry* for all the hurt I caused you."

He grabbed my arm, but I jerked it away.

"I love you, Ryder. I do. I'm so sorry."

I turned on my heel and stumbled inside to gather my things.

35

LOUISE

Two more officers had arrived while Miles, Austin, and I were packing up our things.

We were told not to touch Margie's belongings, that they would be taken care of. Searching for evidence or clues, I assumed. We were also asked to go down to the station to make formal, recorded statements, and also to meet with the FBI agent who'd arrived that morning to investigate the connection between the String Strangler and Kara's homicide.

And now Margie's.

Ryder, the chief, and Detective Darby were still at the ravine with Margie's body when we left, Austin in his truck, and Miles and me in Ansel.

Three grueling hours later, we were given the okay to leave town. Side by side, we pushed out the doors of the police station and staggered across the parking lot like zombies.

"Well, guys, I'd like to say it's been fun, but . . ." Austin unlocked his truck as Miles and I stepped up to Ansel.

Miles snorted.

"Call me if you guys need anything."

"Will do." Miles shook his hand.

Austin turned to me. "I don't usually do this, but . . ." He opened his arms for a hug, and I stepped into his embrace. "They'll find the guy, Lou. They'll find him."

I nodded, looking down as I stepped back, feeling that damn sting of tears again.

With that final good-bye, Austin fired up his old Chevy and disappeared down the highway.

"Keys." Miles turned to me and held out his palm.

I tossed the ring to him, noticing the weight as I released it. My key ring had over two dozen keys, and five or six pointless keychain collectibles that I'd had forever—one, a faded plastic taco, and another a bejeweled kitten with one eye missing. Even my keys were a disorganized mess.

I have to change my life.

"Thanks for driving and for riding back with me," I said as I climbed into the passenger seat.

"Are you kidding? You're a mess. No way was I letting you drive three hours alone."

I sighed, then looked out the window. "I can't believe all of this."

"They'll find him."

Ansel roared to life. As we pulled onto the highway, I looked over my shoulder at the mountain in the distance where Ryder was busy convincing the cops he had nothing to do with Margie's death. I wondered if I would ever see him again.

Tears stung again. I turned away from Miles so he wouldn't see me cry and stared out the passenger window, watching the small town of Berry Springs fade to woods.

I zoned out for a while, both physically and emotionally exhausted.

~

Sometime later, a bump in the road shook me from my daze. I frowned, sitting up straight as I looked around.

The road had narrowed, the trees closing in above us. The sky was dark and brooding. We were on wooded back roads, not the interstate as we should have been.

"Where are we?"

"Headed home."

"I'm no MapQuest, but I'm pretty sure we should be on asphalt right now."

"I figured you'd want to make one last stop at Hollow Hill before we totally close the book on this."

My frown deepened, a little tickle of nerves in my stomach.

Warning bell number one.

"I was there yesterday," I said. "I've been twice now. Took plenty of pictures. I don't know what else we can look for. And believe me, at this point I want out of it. The FBI is investigating now. Kara's case is in capable hands."

Miles glanced at me. "We came all this way, Lou. I feel like the least we can do is take one more look at the last place Kara was known to be."

The SUV hit a pothole, bouncing me out of my seat.

"What way is this?" I asked.

"I told you. To Hollow Hill."

"I swear I went a different way."

Warning bell number two.

Miles shrugged, then turned onto another dirt road. Hollow Hill loomed in the distance. We were coming up on the back side of the estate, a route I hadn't taken before. A route MapQuest didn't know about.

He rolled to a stop and cut the engine. "Ready for one last look?"

I couldn't justify the unease I felt. So, true to Louise Sloane form, I pushed common sense aside. For one last time.

Slamming the door shut behind me, I glanced up at the darkening sky. "We need to get back soon."

Miles nodded, sliding the keys into his pocket. I grabbed my camera and followed him up the uneven path that led to the back of the house.

Wind rustled through the trees, and a crow called out somewhere in the distance.

We walked up the creaky steps, littered with twigs, leaves, and old beer cans. Miles pushed open the back door, which creaked on its hinges.

"You go right," he said, "and I'll go left?"

"Okay."

I turned on my camera and took the same path through the house I'd taken when Ryder and I had visited earlier. Miles's footsteps faded behind me. I took a few pictures of the windows from different angles than before, and other shots of the doorways, old cans left behind. Nothing that piqued my curiosity. I took the side staircase up to the second floor, the steps groaning beneath my weight.

The hall was dark and quiet as I slowly made my way along it, keeping my head on a swivel. I came to the master bedroom, the room where Ryder had found the pendant.

Nerves knotted in my stomach as I stepped inside. I scanned the room, walked over to the fireplace, and took a few more pictures. I made my way to the dirty, cracked window and looked outside. A gust of wind spun dead leaves from the ground, sending them spiraling.

I suddenly felt a presence behind me. I wasn't alone.

Wrapping my fingers around the camera like a weapon, I shifted my weight to my toes.

As I started to turn, a hand came from behind and clamped over my nose and mouth.

I screamed, clawing at the arm pinning me. Fingertips pinched my nose as a forearm locked my head in place. I couldn't move, couldn't breathe.

The spicy Cool Water fragrance wafting from him made me freeze.

Miles.

"Don't scream, don't fight," he snarled in my ear. "It will only make it worse for you. Jesus *Christ,* Lou, why couldn't you leave well enough alone?"

I wanted to say so many things to him—questions, pleas —but I didn't have the breath.

Miles dragged me backward, and I stumbled, dropping my weight. He let me go and shoved me to the floor, where shards of broken glass cut into my hands and knees.

"You son of a bitch!"

I flipped onto my back, fighting like a rabid animal. He grabbed my head, sending his knee into my nose. Seeing stars, I went limp from the shock of it, the pain. Warm blood rushed down my face, and bile rose in my throat.

He flipped me onto my stomach, and even though I fought, he managed to secure my arms behind my back with a zip tie. Terrified, I screamed again. A boot slammed into my kidney, making me vomit on impact. My ankles were bound, and duct tape secured over my mouth. I was hog-tied and silenced, then flipped onto my back to face the horror I was about to experience.

Miles stared down at me, his chest heaving and eyes wild, his face distorted with bloodlust. He looked like a completely different person.

Adrenaline shot through me and I started bucking again, the will to survive overcoming all else.

He aimed a kick at me again, this time at my face. That's when everything got fuzzy as my mind and body retreated to a place of self-preservation, not self-defense.

Blood trickled down the back of my throat. Blinking, I tried not to gag as the room spun around me—until a single object came into focus.

A long, thin black string dangling from Miles's hand.

Maci's necklace.

Miles was the String Strangler.

It wasn't until he unzipped my pants that I began to cry.

36

RYDER

I paced the living room, my fists clenching and unclenching with each turn. The cops were gone. The house was empty and silent again, exactly the way I'd intended.

Except now everything was fucking different.

I wanted Lou—in my space, in my arms, her voice breaking the silence. But she was gone.

I ground my teeth, my gaze darting frantically around the house, not sure what to do, where to go. What the hell to do with the tornado of emotions raging inside me.

Jessica had bagged up Margie's body to take it to the morgue, where it would rest until its autopsy. When I asked if she'd seen Lou when she pulled up, Jessica told me that Austin left alone in his truck while Miles and Lou left together. I didn't like that. Jessica also told me that she didn't have the fingerprint results from the pendant, but she would soon.

McCord told me not to leave town—*shocker*—and to expect at least one more visit from the cops, and another from the FBI. I was advised to stay home and not go anywhere.

My hands were fucking tied. The chief had made sure of that.

I'd picked up the phone to call Lou ten times, but never pushed the button. She'd said herself we were no good for each other. Or was it that she was no good for me?

I looked at the kitchen, where Lou had stood by my side, holding me together while we made dinner for our unexpected guests not twenty-four hours earlier. I looked at the library where we'd read together after I'd confessed the deepest, darkest secrets of my soul. I looked down the hall toward the observation room, where we'd made love under the stars.

There's still hope.

Jesus Christ, the woman had me. From the moment she turned around in that library, she had me. I just didn't know what the hell to do about it. I was spinning, crazy, my carefully planned environment suddenly tossed on its head. My future up in the air.

I closed my eyes and took a deep breath.

What would Old Ryder do?

Old Ryder wouldn't accept wallowing in uncertainty. Old Ryder would make a plan and act on it.

My gaze shifted to my laptop. If I couldn't actively help in the investigation to prove my innocence, I would help behind the scenes. And I was damn good at slinking behind the scenes.

I jogged across the room and powered up my computer.

First, I reread every document Roman had pulled from BSPD regarding Maci's homicide. There was no mistaking a second person had participated in her death. I leaned back, scratching my chin. Leon Ortiz was nineteen at the time he killed Maci and my unborn baby. Assuming his accomplice was close in age, this would put him at around thirty years old now.

Around Louise's age.

Squinting, I leaned forward and clicked into a folder I'd labeled stills. Inside were dozens of images I'd copied from Lou's laptop from her investigation here in Berry Springs, without her knowing. I wanted to know everything she did, in case she bulldozed her way down a rabbit hole she couldn't get out of.

I clicked through the photos of Hollow Hill, the master bedroom where I'd found the pendant. Pictures of the upstairs, the downstairs. She'd been so thorough, capturing every angle, using the best lighting possible. She was a talented photographer, no doubt about it.

I scrubbed my hand over my mouth. I couldn't explain why, but I felt like I was on to something. Something was in these pictures that I was missing.

I scrolled through the thumbnails until a few caught my eye. They were pictures of the inside of Lou's 4Runner, crooked angles as if taken by accident.

Frowning, I leaned forward. I recognized the rundown gas station in the background as being a few miles from the last search location for Kara. I wondered if Lou had pulled over to take pictures of it. Probably so.

These pictures, though, were of stacks of bags in what I was guessing was the back seat. Squinting, I zoomed in. I recognized the stone-washed denim wonder as Lou's duffel bag and grinned. The other bag, black leather, was unzipped. It must belong to Miles because Lou told me they'd driven to Berry Springs together.

My head tilted as I zoomed in, examining the contents. Folded clothes, a bottle of cologne, a condom, an open wallet. Stuffed partway inside the wallet was a receipt from Tad's Tool Shop, dated four weeks earlier. Among the items purchased were a fishing pole, fishing lures, camping tent, thermos, lighters . . .

My heart froze as I stared at the last item.

Poly Tarp Blue Item 57392 $12.99

My brain kickstarted, scrambling to put the pieces of a puzzle together that I knew were right in front of me.

Kara was killed four days after this receipt was printed, telling her friends she was meeting someone to go camping.

Lou and I had found scraps of a blue tarp where Kara's body was found.

Miles was around thirty years old.

Miles killed Kara.

Miles was the fucking String Strangler.

And Miles has Lou.

As I surged to my feet, the front door was flung open. Mack, Justin, and Roman strode into the house. I didn't blink, didn't break my stride as I pulled my cell from my pocket. *One bar of reception.* I dialed Louise's number. *No answer.*

Mack held up a hand. "Whoa, dude. Stop."

"He has her." I dialed again. "Miles, a guy from Ponco. He's the fucking String Strangler, and Lou left with him hours ago."

I grabbed my keys and jogged past them through the front door.

"Wait," Mack called out after me. "Does this have

anything to do with the body that was just found on your land?"

I shoved the phone in my pocket after I got her voice mail again. "And how the fuck do you know about that already?"

I kept moving, and they hurried after me.

"We know about everything already," Mack said. "You know that. Thought you could use a helping hand. Or maybe a one-way ticket somewhere."

"No ticket." I pulled my gun from my belt holster. "Could use plenty of hands, though."

"Where to?" Justin pulled his own weapon and gave it a quick check.

"Hollow Hill," I said quickly. "I think that's where he takes his victims."

I jumped in my truck as Roman and Justin headed to the black Escalade that was blocking me in, but Mack stopped me before I could shut my door.

"Hey, Ryder, keep a cool head. No matter what happens, don't pull that trigger. Not for six more months, man."

I slammed the truck into drive and maneuvered past the Escalade by barreling over a stack of firewood I'd chopped earlier that week. Instead of taking a left out of the driveway, I hung a right, taking a gamble on a shortcut to Hollow Hill, but the Escalade turned left. I knew these mountains better than Astor's boys, and I only hoped my internal compass was guiding me correctly now.

Picturing the back roads in my head, I created a mental map while I sped down narrow dirt roads barely wide enough to pass through. Branches scraped down the side of my truck, but I didn't notice.

I tried Lou's cell three more times with no luck, and desperation forced me to make the next call. Though the reception was spotty, Ellen at BSPD dispatch repeated the words, "String Strangler" and "Hollow Hill." I could only hope she got the message.

Rocks and ice spun up from my tires as I fishtailed around a corner. Hollow Hill came into view, dark menacing clouds looming overhead.

My heart hammered as I pressed the gas, sliding to a stop next to Lou's 4Runner.

Double-fisting my gun, I crept along the side of the house, adrenaline pumping through my veins. I knew how to do this . . . how to track a predator.

The thing was, time was of the essence. I knew it in my gut.

Staying low, I breached the house, sweeping my gun from dark corner to dark corner. And that's when I heard it. Sobs and whispers from upstairs.

Lou.

I took the stairs two at a time, my pulse a steady pounding in my ears.

The next sound was a scream that would haunt me for the rest of my life.

"Stop!" I yelled, sprinting down the hall, gun up. I kicked through the door to the master bedroom as Miles was lowering himself onto her.

My woman.

My Lou.

Rage exploded through my veins.

I leaped through the air, tackling the motherfucker at full speed. We tumbled, our bodies slamming into the wall. Miles lay facedown, not moving, so I spun around and lunged for Lou. Her hands and ankles were bound, her mouth duct-taped and one eye swollen shut, the other wild and red as she processed what was happening.

I frantically checked her over, looking for open wounds or anything that needed immediate attention. My focus was on her, only her.

"Baby, it's gonna hurt," I said before I peeled the tape from her lips.

"Ryder . . ." Tears streaming down her cheeks, she wept.

"Are you okay? Are you hurt?"

She shook her head. I knew she was hurt, in so many different ways, but nothing that appeared to be life-threatening.

My attention was pulled to the sound of shuffling behind me.

Miles.

That rage ignited like a match to gasoline.

I bolted to my feet and spun around as Miles was climbing out through the window. Raising my gun, I sighted on him and slid my finger around the trigger—

Three men burst through the door.

Roman tackled me while Justin leaped onto Miles's back, sending them both through the window.

37

LOUISE

*S*ix months later...

I drained the last of the coffee I'd picked up at the gas station on the way into town. I took a deep breath, my stomach churning, my body pumping with adrenaline that I knew from experience would stay until sleep would finally take me.

Grabbing my backpack, I zipped up my coat and glanced at the clock glowing from Ansel's dashboard, which read *2:17 a.m.*

Here we go.

I pushed out the door.

"Well, well, well. Mornin', sunshine." Detective Tommy Darby emerged from the woods behind a line of squad cars, a few trucks, and an ambulance.

I recognized Jessica Heathrow's Tahoe immediately. It was never a good sign to see her vehicle anywhere at two in the morning.

Darby slapped a hand on my back. "Is this your earliest call yet?"

"Yep. Lucked out, I guess," I said as my boots sank into the dirt, soggy from days of rain.

"This is our third case, right?"

"Fourth." *But who's counting?*

"Well, I hope you skipped breakfast for this one. It's a doozy. This way."

Darby led me down the driveway, weaving around the vehicles. He lifted the yellow do not cross tape as we stepped onto the lawn. A rusted trailer sat a few yards away under a flickering streetlight. Inside, the trailer was lit up as bright as day. I scribbled my name on the sign-in log as Darby began the update.

"Around one thirty, dispatch got a call from the neighbor about gunshots. Three, to be exact. Lieutenant Colson responded—he was on call and closest. Appears to be a home invasion gone bad. The homeowners engaged the intruder, and intruder shot them both. Husband and wife, around seventy years old."

"Any trace of the intruder?"

"Not yet."

We stopped at the concrete blocks that led to the front door.

"Hey, guys, Lou's here. Everyone out so she can photograph." He turned to me. "Don't forget your booties and gloves . . . and you're definitely gonna want a mask."

I patted my bag. "All set."

He smiled. "You're damn alert for it being two in the morning."

"Always am." *Now, anyway,* I thought with a smile.

The uniformed officers moved out, nodding at me as they passed, and one said, "She's all yours."

I slipped into my booties and pulled on my gloves and mask, getting that weird tingle of excitement as I stepped inside the house.

I still couldn't believe I was Berry Springs' new forensic photographer. Some days were tough, but every day I felt like I was doing something that mattered. Something that changed lives, helped people during their lowest lows.

And I loved every second of it.

The woods were beginning to lighten as I pulled up the driveway at home. I was tired and fatigued, but wired.

The smell of fresh coffee tickled my nose as I pushed through the front door. The sight of Ryder, his shirt off and mug in hand, tickled my stomach. His smile lit the room as he crossed it. As had become habit, he kissed my nose, then fell to his knees, lifted my shirt, and kissed my belly. Growing belly, I should say.

Still smiling, he stood and handed me the coffee. "Decaf."

"I'll take it."

"I added sprinkles."

"I love you."

"Love you too." His smile fell. "How'd it go?"

"I didn't throw up."

"Hey, all right! Good job. Our little baby and I are proud of you."

Ryder took off my coat, hung it on the rack, and helped me into the living room. I didn't need the help, but he insisted, as he'd insisted on doing everything for me while I wasn't working. He'd also insisted that I move in with him, marry him, and make a football team of babies with him.

Two of three, done. We're still working on the football team.

After Ryder saved my life on Hollow Hill, Miles was

arrested and taken into custody, where it was confirmed his fingerprints were on the pendant Ryder had given to Maci twelve years earlier. With that solid evidence damning him, Miles's confession followed soon after.

Maci was Miles's first murder, with his friend Leon. Miles went on to lure eight—*eight*—unsuspecting high-risk teens into meeting him, where he would then rape, torture, and kill them. Most he met online, stalking them for months before befriending them, offering help and gaining their trust. He'd met Kara at the Sunshine Club where he'd worked, alongside me, while he hunted.

His deep-seated disdain for women stemmed from life-long issues and embarrassment caused by his mother, Back-seat Betty.

After he was arrested, Miles admitted to following Margie through the woods that day after Austin left for the shooting range—thinking Miles was still asleep—then having his way with her before strangling her to death.

Miles was locked in jail, where monsters like him should be, waiting for a conviction that would hopefully send him away for life.

From that day forward, Ryder never left my side. We'd packed up my apartment together and I'd moved in with him the next week—and immediately began renovations and decorating with his full blessing. He was a completely different man, each day a chink of armor falling off. The old Ryder was finding his way back.

I was treated like his queen, and he, my king. Not a day went by that Ryder didn't tell me how much he loved me, and how grateful he was that I'd pushed my damn way into his life.

He'd asked me to marry him in the observation room

not long after I moved in. Two weeks later, we found out I was pregnant.

Ryder lowered me onto the couch in the living room, now decorated with dark leather furniture, hand-crafted tables, candles, and plants. Warm and homey.

He took the seat next to me and asked for all the details about the crime scene I'd photographed, as he always did when I got home. He knew it helped me to relax, to recap everything, talk it out, cry if I needed to. After that, we switched topics.

"When do you leave?" I asked, grabbing his hand.

"Tomorrow. Max will be by every day to check on you."

"I don't need your brother to check on me."

"I know." Ryder leaned down and kissed my knuckles.

I combed my fingers through his hair. I loved his hair. "Where to this time?"

"Mexico. That's all I know. It'll be my last job until after the baby comes."

"Astor's cool with that?"

"He didn't have a choice. I had it written into my contract when I signed back on. All future babies give me eight months off. In lawyer terms, of course."

I smiled. "You love being back, don't you."

He nodded. "Feel like I'm doing what I'm supposed to do. Just like you feel."

"What's in Mexico?"

Ryder frowned. "Not Roman, that's all I know."

"What do you mean? Did something happen to him?"

Ryder shrugged. "Guy took an op and fell off the grid a week later. No one knows why or where he went." He waved a hand in the air, dismissing the subject. "Anyway, I'll find him. Are you hungry?"

"Starving."

He pushed to his feet. "Organic peanut butter and jelly sandwiches coming up. Grape or strawberry this time?"

"Apricot."

"Ooh, feeling saucy. All right. Be right back."

As I watched Ryder stride into our kitchen, my gaze shifted to the framed picture on the wall of our first kiss, captured when I dropped the camera in the snow.

Home.

Home with my husband.

Home with our baby boy in my belly.

STEELE BROTHERS?

Want to read more about the badass, swoon-worthy Steele brothers? If you haven't read STEELE SHADOWS SECURITY, the complete series is available now!

CABIN 1
CABIN 2
CABIN 3

★ RATTLESNAKE ROAD ★

I am beyond excited to unveil the cover for a top secret project I've been plotting and working on for almost a year. **Rattlesnake Road**, the first book in a series of **standalone** Romantic Mysteries, is scheduled to be released in the spring of 2021. It will be my most evocative, sexy, thrilling ride yet. I CANNOT wait to give it to you.

Rattlesnake Road is up for pre-order now, so you can reserve your copy today!

From bestselling and award-winning author Amanda McKinney comes an emotional and twisted new small-town Mystery Romance...

Everyone hits rock bottom, only the brave escape.

Welcome to 1314 Rattlesnake Road.

A quaint two-bedroom log cabin nestled deep in the woods outside the small, southern town of Berry Springs—the perfect hideaway to escape your past.

Tucked inside thick, mahogany walls lay mysterious letters, untouched, unearthed for decades. Floor-to-ceiling windows frame breathtaking views of mountains, soaring cliffs, deep valleys, and endless lies. Mature oak and pine trees speckle a rolling back yard, tall enough to carry the whispers of the haunted, of stories untold.

Inside sits Grey Dalton, emotionally battered and bruised, her only wish to pick up the broken pieces of her life. But outside, await two men, one a tattooed cowboy, the other a dashing businessman.
One will steal her heart, the other, her soul.

Rattlesnake Road is a standalone mystery romance about love, loss, hitting rock bottom, and clawing your way to the other side.

Your escape awaits...

Pre-order Today

♥ *And don't forget to sign up for my exclusive reader group and blogging team!* ♥

STEALS AND DEALS

★LIMITED TIME STEALS AND DEALS★

1. The Creek (A Berry Springs Novel), only **$0.99**
2. Bestselling and award-nominated Cabin 1 (Steele Shadows Security), **FREE**
3. Devil's Gold (A Black Rose Mystery), only **$0.99**

(1) The Creek (A Berry Springs Novel)

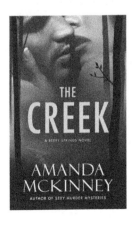

When DNA evidence links Lieutenant Quinn Colson's brother to the scene of a grisly murder, Quinn realizes he'll do anything to keep his brother from returning to prison, even if it costs him his job… and the woman who's stolen his heart.

Get The Creek today for only $0.99

(2) Cabin 1 (Steele Shadows Security)

★ 2020 National Readers' Choice Award Finalist, 2020 HOLT Medallion Finalist ★

Hidden deep in the remote mountains of Berry Springs is a private security firm where some go to escape, and others find exactly what they've been looking for.

Welcome to Cabin 1, Cabin 2, Cabin 3…

Get Cabin 1 for ★FREE★ today

(3) Devil's Gold

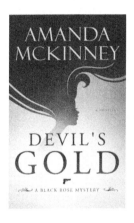

"With fast-paced action, steamy romance, and a good dose of mystery, Devil's Gold is a solid whodunit that will keep you surprised at every turn." -Siobhan Novelties

"...smart, full of energetic thrills and chills, it's one of the best novellas I've read in a very long time." -Booked J

Get Devil's Gold today for only $0.99

Sign up for my Newsletter so you don't miss out on more Steals and Deals! https://www.amandamckinneyauthor.com/contact

ABOUT THE AUTHOR

Amanda McKinney is the bestselling and multi-award-winning author of more than fifteen romantic suspense and mystery novels. She wrote her debut novel, LETHAL LEGACY, after walking away from her career to become a writer and stay-at-home mom. Her books include the BERRY SPRINGS SERIES, STEELE SHADOWS SERIES, and the BLACK ROSE MYSTERY SERIES, with many more to come. Amanda lives in Arkansas with her handsome husband, two beautiful boys, and three obnoxious dogs.

Text **AMANDABOOKS to 66866** to sign up for Amanda's Newsletter and get the latest on new releases, promos, and freebies!

If you enjoyed Ryder, please write a review!

THE AWARD-WINNING BERRY SPRINGS SERIES
The Woods (A Berry Springs Novel)
The Lake (A Berry Springs Novel)
The Storm (A Berry Springs Novel)
The Fog (A Berry Springs Novel)
The Creek (A Berry Springs Novel)
The Shadow (A Berry Springs Novel)
The Cave (A Berry Springs Novel)

#1 BESTSELLING STEELE SHADOWS
Cabin 1 (Steele Shadows Security)
Cabin 2 (Steele Shadows Security)
Cabin 3 (Steele Shadows Security)
Phoenix (Steele Shadows Rising)
Jagger (Steele Shadows Investigations)
Ryder (Steele Shadows Investigations)

★*Rattlesnake Road, coming spring 2021* ★

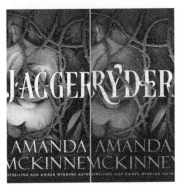

Like your sexy murder mysteries with a side of evil witch?
Check out THE BLACK ROSE MYSTERY SERIES about three
super-rich, independent, badass sisters who run a private
investigation company in a creepy, southern town...

Devil's Gold (A Black Rose Mystery, Book 1)
Hatchet Hollow (A Black Rose Mystery, Book 2)
Tomb's Tale (A Black Rose Mystery Book 3)
Evil Eye (A Black Rose Mystery Book 4)
Sinister Secrets (A Black Rose Mystery Book 5)

Made in the USA
Coppell, TX
02 November 2021

65055289R00198